Winter's Tales

NEW SERIES: 7

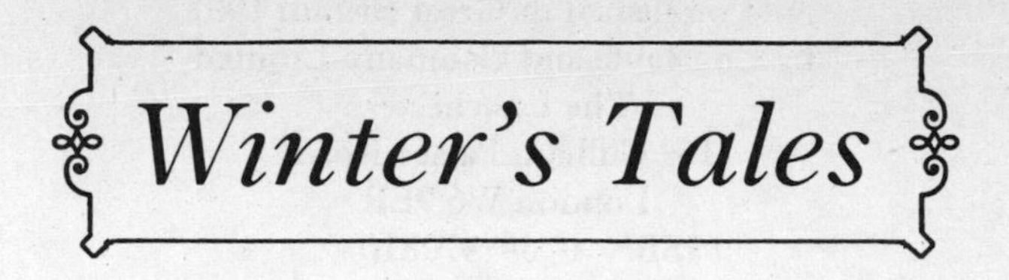

Winter's Tales

NEW SERIES: 7

*

EDITED BY

Robin Baird-Smith

Constable · London

First published in Great Britain 1991
by Constable and Company Limited
3 The Lanchesters
162 Fulham Palace Road
London W6 9ER
ISBN 0 09 470810 X
Photoset in Linotron 12pt Imprint
and printed in Great Britain by
Redwood Press Limited, Melksham, Wiltshire

A CIP catalogue record for this book
is available from the British Library

CONTENTS

ACKNOWLEDGEMENTS

The story by Piers Read was first published in the *Telegraph Magazine*. All the other stories in this collection are original to *Winter's Tales*

EDITOR'S NOTE

The annual *Winter's Tales* collection has become well known to a wide circle of readers. It is designed, first of all, to provide thought-provoking entertainment, and in this I feel certain the new volume will succeed.

But it has other purposes, almost as important. *Winter's Tales* provides a showcase for new short fiction – increasingly important as the outlets for this type of writing decrease, and as the market pressure for the hype-able blockbuster with a magic name on the title page becomes ever more intense. The distinctive form of the short story, with its necessary establishment of characters, atmosphere, plot within a small space, is an art all of its own. It is very different from that of the miniature painter or the cultivator of the bonsai tree, for a story even a few pages long can present the human situation, human failings and feelings, with a power that is unmatched at greater length. This alone makes it essential to keep the art of short-story writing alive.

Many fine short stories are written by authors who later, their talents all the more highly developed for the discipline this form has imposed, have gone on to write at greater length. For this reason we welcome new talent, exemplified by Tony Peake's intriguing tale of sexual ambivalence. Other writers include those who have already established a reputation – Clare Colvin, for instance, who demonstrates yet again her sure handling of the unusual theme, and Laura Kalpakian, writing with certainty and a vigour which is all her own. While some names will be unfamiliar, it is also a delight to find the rightly celebrated novelists Piers Paul Read and Tom Wakefield excelling in this very different form.

But the stories in these pages have been chosen above all to interest, to delight, to stimulate, and to cover as wide a human spectrum – social, emotional, geographical, historical – as possible.

Robin Baird-Smith

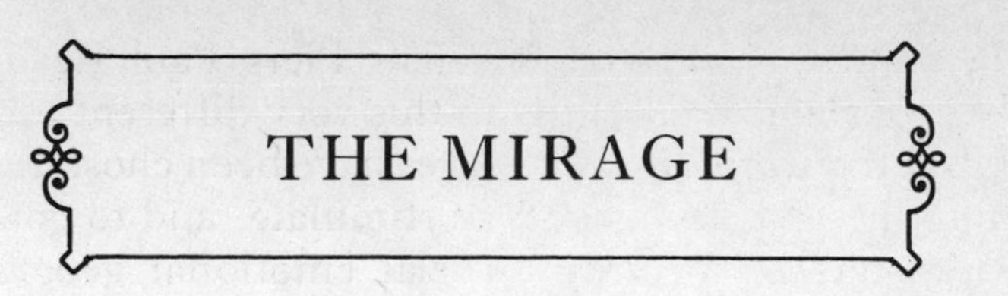

THE MIRAGE

Helen Harris

She married him for children. She married a fountain. And as the years went by and there were no children, she imagined him still as a fountain, spurting continuously in a city square; clear jets playing to no purpose in the noon sun. She imagined herself as a tourist, throwing coins hopefully into the fountain, making wishes, looking down sentimentally at her small change in the blue chlorinated water. For a time, before the doctors told her that it was her deficiency, she imagined him as a dry fountain, its jets switched off, its copper piping exposed on the flaking painted bottom. She imagined that she dived into it drunkenly one night after a party and was smashed to smithereens in the empty basin.

Everything else in their married life, she had foreseen and she had accepted: the importance of acquiring and maintaining their joint possessions, which replaced a more profound communication; their politeness to one another in moments when good manners ought to have been forgotten. She had foreseen and accepted Richard's benign and abstracted expression every morning as he looked forward to leaving for his laboratory, his library spreading, Richard ageing. But the house had been inhabited by wheaten-haired children – Richard's receding blondness – and, as well as jawbones and fossils, there had been gym-shoes and short wet raincoats hanging from low pegs.

They married modestly. Neither of them was of an age any more when an extravagant wedding was called for. Besides, they agreed that there was greater dignity in the simplicity of their ceremony. They went to the Register Office in the morning, she in peach and he in cream; it was summer, and they were back well in time for the small lunch party which was their only celebration. They spent a week's honeymoon in Florence, chosen for its artistic riches, and on the eighth morning of their married life, they embarked on what was to be their regular routine.

Because they had each run an independent household for several years, there had been some brief discussion over whose home should become their joint centre or, indeed, if they should sell both properties out of equity and purchase somewhere brand-new. It was only a brief discussion; Richard's home was, for a start, much bigger. It was a house, rather than Sarah's more modest although pretty mews cottage. And, for all her emancipated principles, Sarah could not help finding something pleasingly traditional about leaving her girlhood nest and moving into her husband's household. Besides, there was Richard's library, and his 'bones' as she jokily called them and what an appalling to-do it would have been to move all of them.

She only took one sideways look at Richard during the wedding ceremony, because her dominant emotion was shame. She looked firmly ahead at the registrar, straight-faced, and hoped that her distance, which was really guilt and evasion, would be interpreted by everyone as solemnity. In the middle of her wedding, she suddenly thought of the Siamese cat, Primadonna, which she had had to give away to a friend because of Richard's asthma, with wistful affection. Richard stood beside her, also very rigid, with a serious expression on his pale, bespectacled face. He didn't respond at all when she turned to look at him and she hoped that he was immersed in his own justification. But she guessed he wasn't. For the awkward part of it was, she suspected that Richard loved her.

He had lived alone for so long; she had hoped, yes, honestly hoped that he had asked her to marry him for company, to have his meals cooked and his clothes washed and his fossils dusted. Then the private crime she was committing would not have seemed nearly as serious; it would have been a straight exchange. But Richard had pursued her in such a way, so doggedly and so desperately, there could be very little doubt; he had set his heart on her. They met at a party given by some distant friends of hers, and in the hall as people were leaving, Richard had cornered her and asked urgently for her address. She had been amused and only a little flattered; it was hard to take seriously the admiration of a man who in the mid-1980s still wore flared trousers and who, into the bargain, had had a small fragment of bone in his pocket which had fallen out when he fished for a scrap of paper. But he was a scientist, and she respected his science; it seemed worthy and serious, in contrast to her own light-weight world of fine arts publishing, and she agreed to have dinner with him when he telephoned her two days later. He became one of her regular dinner-companions – there were three or four of them – and through a combination of stubborn persistence and some genuine scholarly charm, he succeeded in elbowing out the others. She let him, although she could easily have repulsed his advances, had she seriously wanted to. She contemplated the imminent fruition of her idea. For a long time now, she had viewed the men she met as, first and foremost, baby donors. They didn't suspect it, or at least she fervently hoped that they didn't, but as she sat beside them in the theatre (good seats) or at the opera, or listened to their dinner-table conversation with a look of polite appreciation on her face, she was usually assessing the possible child they could enable her to produce and whether the partner that she would have to accept in payment would be anything approaching tolerable. So far, much as she wanted that child, he hadn't been. A small Gerald, fussing and throwing tantrums and picking at his school dinner, or a small, and for the sake of chance, female William, coquettishly brushing her ginger curls was one thing, but the prospect of a lifetime of William or Gerald devastated her. But she thought she could put up with Richard.

He courted her, that was the only word, for a little over a year before he brought himself to propose to her. His feelings were not in doubt but he remained a careful man and he doubtless wanted to be quite sure Sarah was the gentle, well-bred woman he thought she was before committing himself.

He proposed to her at Aldeburgh where they had gone for a day's excursion on a blowy Sunday. Walking delicately along the beach among the fish heads, he had stopped and taken her hand, and she wondered afterwards how he had selected that particular spot; if he had been looking out for it carefully all day or if he had chosen that particular piece of beach quite arbitrarily, suddenly forcing himself to face acceptance or rejection. She had stood for a moment, motionless, since that seemed to her what was expected of her. Then she had looked up at him with a serene and fulfilled expression, which came to her quite easily, and answered, 'Oh darling, I thought you were never going to ask me.' She kept her serene, fulfilled expression for the rest of the day and, in fact, it was only when it came to telling her numerous friends of the engagement in the days that followed that she reflected ruefully that the love of a palaeontologist was perhaps a dubious compliment.

She knew that she had been on the verge of becoming an old maid and she supposed that Richard alone must have loved the fusty, dusty quality which accompanied this. He must have been enchanted by the regulated tidiness of her spinster's cottage, the glass-fronted bookcases full of neatly organized books and bibelots, and, in the kitchen cupboards, all the tidily printed labels. Richard alone must have been seduced by her cautious, considered movements: the way she carefully shook out her pleated skirt before she sat down, her prudence in the way of having an umbrella, a raincoat, a cardigan. And it was just as well, because she did not intend marriage to transform her into something blowsy, if more wifely. The longed-for babies would come, but they were babies which would somehow leave her immaculate, as sprucely dressed and finely poised as she had always been.

Their married life began then under a major misapprehension. This is not to say that their days were in any way spoilt by it; the first period of their marriage was in many ways an extremely happy one. There were all the new-found pleasures of joint living: a welcoming voice when you unlocked the front door at the end of the day; more elaborate, ceremonial suppers; the development of small, shared rituals It was not for several months and, even then, only accidentally, that they discovered the disparity in their hopes.

Although she had never spoken to Richard about their having children – she was worried that her real motives might have been revealed – Sarah assumed that he must realize she was using no contraception. But he was astonished when she became concerned some months after their marriage because nothing had yet happened. In fact, he misunderstood her concern at first and thought precisely the opposite: that something unintentional had happened.

They were having their Sunday breakfast, which they had both until then found one of their cosiest shared rituals. On the table there were the tea things and the old silver toast-rack, the butter curls and the home-made gooseberry jam. The rain spitting at the window only made it cosier. But, suddenly, it all became a dismal pretence; a make-believe meal for two people who were only playing at being a couple.

Richard stammered, 'I had no idea . . .'

Sarah wanted to punish him, not for his short-sightedness, but because he had unwittingly made her crime even worse. Not only had she married him solely for the wheaten-haired children she would extract from him; he didn't even want them.

'What d'you mean, you had no idea?' she snapped. 'What do you suppose most people get married *for*?'

Richard looked at her, bewildered, shaken, and replied with the worst thing he possibly could have, 'But not us, Sarah, surely?'

She exclaimed bitterly, 'Why ever not?'

The breakfast table lost its cosy character, the toast and the tea things went untouched. Richard argued that he had thought theirs was a marriage of mature, self-sufficient people who would seek their happiness in each other, and in their work, and not in rearing young. But in the course of a thoroughly miserable morning, Sarah convinced him that, since nothing at all had been said about his objections beforehand, within marriage, babies were her right.

Richard took it well. After an initial period of shock and resentment, because the shock distracted him from his work, he accepted this new aspect of his life bravely. He told himself that, in fact, he should have foreseen it and the failure to foresee it was simply unscientific on his part, and therefore inexcusable. He had failed to study the data with sufficient care and this essentially unwelcome development was therefore his own responsibility. He shouldered it, even seeing it on braver days as a heady risk he ran every time he made love to Sarah. He thought that he might in the end have nothing against children if they turned out to be rather nice little girls with plaits. He compared the risk, privately, to the thrill he had sometimes experienced as a boy when he let his bicycle career out of control down a steep hill near his home in Hastings and waited for the disastrous crash that might or might not occur.

But, for an extraordinarily long time, it didn't, and meeting Sarah's despair was a challenge which surpassed him. Why on earth should she want a baby? Why on earth should she want a baby so much?

Sarah said that without one her life was not complete, and this baffled Richard since it seemed to him that it so copiously was. It also insulted him, just a little, for surely it implied that he alone was not enough for her? But this was hardly a sentiment which could be voiced, without sounding grossly conceited. So he kept what he termed his 'ruffled feathers' to himself and tried to give more weight to her other reasons, which seemed to him no less implausible. She said that unless you were completely arid, which sounded to Richard unpleasantly close to a reproach, having children was a biological imperative. You ignored it only to the detriment of the rest of your existence. Richard wanted to say to her that surely one of the supreme achievements of human evolution was that people were now free, if they chose, to devote themselves to the analysis of ancient animal bones or seventeenth-century delft china instead of to suckling and nappy-changing. But he hesitated to contradict her too vehemently on anything for, as the months passed, her mood seemed to slowly spoil and she became more and more susceptible to little outbursts of peevish bad temper.

Eighteen months after they were married, they embarked on exploratory tests, against Richard's wishes. He was privately worried that the tests would – naturally, that was their purpose – expedite matters. But at the same time, he was beginning to hope, secretly, guiltily, that it was simply too late for the pair of them, and he even planned to buy Sarah a small dog or cat as a consolation, should the tests prove negative. Somewhere very deep down, unacknowledged, he was offended though by the suggestion that the failure to conceive might stem from him and he hoped, by his attendance at the infertility clinic, to dispel this.

That was a grim period for both of them. It was naturally easier for Richard, since he had less emotion invested in it and since he was more attuned to scientific procedures. But the fact that he found it easier made Sarah more resentful of him, so he had to put up with frequent sharp reproaches, which he felt were all too often perfectly unjustified: taps left dripping, water sprayed excessively around the bathroom when he had his shower.

Two years after they were married, he went to a conference in Oslo. It was the first time he had had to himself since his marriage and he was dismayed to discover how much he enjoyed it. He enjoyed coming back alone to his empty hotel room after a late-night brain-storming session in the bar. He enjoyed the immersion in his beloved subject and the rich prolonged contact with those of like mind. But he also enjoyed his long solitary walks around the grey city in the early morning, the ease and congeniality of his own company.

He felt so concerned and guilty, he telephoned Sarah

on the third or fourth night from his hotel room. Her voice shook as she spoke to him and for a few foolish seconds, his spirits lifted because he thought it was emotion at hearing his voice. But her tears broke through as she explained to him, 'My period's come.' He felt utterly dejected then for he realized that he had become totally secondary to Sarah's real concerns.

In the third year of their marriage, the decline became irreversible. Sarah's entire life seemed to consist of temperature-taking, mucus-checking and trips to the hospital for cyclical hormone tests followed by what amounted to instructions to Richard to perform his conjugal duty at such and such a time on such and such a day. What joy there had been in their sex life, never in truth the most rampant and unbridled, disappeared entirely as it became a regimented obedience to all-powerful outside authorities, whom Richard imagined as stern white-coated monitoring figures, standing around their bed as he laboured dutifully. Not surprisingly, his performance suffered, and with increasing frequency these unhappy sessions ended in Sarah berating him bitterly for his failure to fulfil what had become the sole purpose of these exercises.

He was offered, and happily accepted, a Professorship at a London college, one of the youngest in his field to be so honoured. Sarah seemed to take little interest in his professional progress or, for that matter, in her own. While he had once been charmed by how studiously she read up all the fine arts periodicals in the evening and assiduously attended lectures, she had long dropped any pretence of pursuing that interest now. All she cared about was her wretched baby.

In a forlorn attempt to right matters, Richard suggested a holiday. Limply, Sarah consented. And because Richard thought it needed a very major trip to shake her out of her ridiculous condition, and there were some excavations there that he wanted to visit, he organized a huge and expensive expedition to the Middle East. In Egypt, the crowds of little boys constantly running after them put a new idea into his head and, one evening on their hotel balcony, when Sarah appeared mellowed by the fabulous sights of the day and by the heat, he asked her, warily, why they didn't adopt a child, maybe from a Third World country, and give it a better chance in life?

She didn't get angry, but she said flatly no, it wouldn't be the same thing at all; she wanted *their* child. It was then that Richard, usually mild and forbearing beyond all reasonable expectations, for the first time said something harsh to her. 'Ours?' he asked coldly. 'Or just *yours*?'

Perhaps out of remorse, or perhaps because the holiday really had refreshed her, Sarah seemed to improve for a time after that. She came to the party held to welcome Richard to his new chair, looking so elegant and gracious, he felt quite proud of her. She even patted him on one cheek and teasingly called him 'Professor' as they got ready for bed afterwards.

But his hopes, which had doubtless risen unreasonably, were soon dashed. He came home one night to find her reading a thick tome on new techniques of *in vitro* fertilization, with a most uncomfortable picture of a baby squashed into a test tube on the front. Inwardly, he groaned; was there to be no end to it?

Apparently not. Sarah, whose brief revival of interest in her husband seemed to have been largely prompted by duty, rather than any real feeling, joined a group for people who were experiencing difficulty in 'starting a family' and this group, which met weekly on a Monday, became the main preoccupation of her life. From them, she brought home information on the latest advances in infertility research. From them, Richard felt furiously, she gained a further justification for her obsession, since they all shared it.

Few of their friends had children, such was the nature of their friends. But part of the group's policy was to encourage members by promoting its success stories and, most weeks, Sarah would come home burbling about some rosy baby produced by ex-members, which had been handed round after the talk like a refreshment. As Richard listened to her gushing about 'the dear little thing', he thought that this was what it would be like if she were ever successful in her quest. He stopped dead, for what he had shocked himself by thinking was: if, God forbid, she were ever successful in her quest. He went to work and sat in his office with an 'In Conference' sign on the door. It had hit him that if that was the way he felt, then he should surely put an end to it. Shouldn't he? Time would of course eventually do that for him. But Sarah was still only thirty-nine; this miserable fiasco might continue for several years more. And if it didn't, if against all the odds her recalcitrant ovaries and fallopian tubes and follicle-stimulating hormones did finally yield up the child of her dreams, would their life be any better?

It occurred to him that he was perhaps unjust, selfish and unkind. He had read a fair amount about the idiosyncrasies of the female reproductive system himself over the past few years and it sometimes seemed to him remarkable that women were capable of any rational behaviour at all with so many pernicious hormones rampaging about their bodies. Was it so surprising that Sarah, to all appearances a cool and rational person, should have been seized in her late thirties by this, this mania? On the other hand, did he want to stay saddled indefinitely with someone so distressingly different from the calm collected lady in peach whom he had married? Divorce had until then never occurred to him; it was something rather racy and ruthless which only other more brazen people could bring themselves to. Now he considered the possibility for the first time.

Sarah was so wrapped up in the workings of her reproductive system, she appeared not to notice the change that had taken place in Richard. This convinced him more than ever that there was right on his side. For could he really be said to be married to her any more if she failed to notice such a profound alteration?

He walked around with the idea of divorce sticking in his throat like a monstrous gobbet of indigestible pudding for about three months before he broached it. He had feared a terrible outburst of tears and recriminations and was almost disappointed that Sarah should take it as calmly as she did. She agreed that it was, regrettably, the very best thing and they both made appointments to see their solicitors. Grimly, Richard supposed that, for the purpose for which she wanted a partner, more or less anybody would do. And from the near disdain with which she had lately taken to treating him, he guessed that she had never accepted the doctors' verdict and still suspected him secretly of some shortcoming or thought there was maybe some undetected chemical incompatibility between them.

Once they had agreed on their course of action, funnily, relations between them seemed to improve enormously. They were more united in planning their divorce than they had ever been in their attempt at marriage. When everything was settled, and they were meticulously business-like about settling it, when all they were waiting for was Sarah to find a flat, they experienced a brief period of total contentment with one another. Neither of them any longer had any expectations of the other which he or she could not fulfil, and they lived in quiet agreement. They lived in such ideal agreement, in fact, that they both thought, for an infinitesimally brief moment, of cancelling the divorce. One especially warm and sunny evening, they went for a walk together on Wimbledon Common. If it hadn't been for the unspoken but shared feeling that, with a divorce pending, such a thing was inappropriate, they would almost certainly have held hands.

Because of the years of suppressed resentment, and the enduring conviction that she had cheated him, Richard made no effort to keep in contact with Sarah. They drifted far apart, as is possible even when separated by only a few miles of London streets, and Richard lived, for a long time, the life of an embittered recluse, whom fate has unfairly cheated of his rightful happy ending. He became everything which Sarah had unspokenly accused him of being: a dry obsessive, a man of bones and book dust, whose principal source of pleasure lay in the sight of a small rib cage or a tail that had not wagged for millennia emerging from the desert sand. Until one day, in autumn, without warning, he caught sight of Sarah in the street. His legs seemed to liquefy and he thought for a nauseating moment that he would have his long-awaited heart attack. For Sarah, walking towards him on the opposite pavement, so that he could not see its contents, was pushing a push-chair, and he did not know whether she had miraculously become pregnant after all in the dying days of their marriage but, having extracted what she wanted, failed to let him know, or whether she had through some less strict agency adopted a baby, or whether she had in the end lost her reason completely and the push-chair was empty.

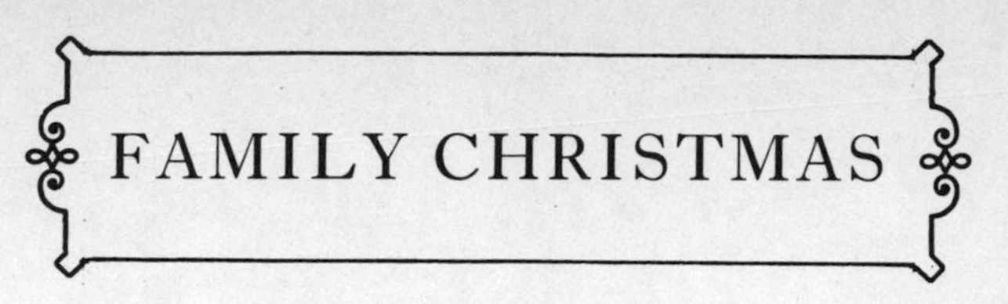

Piers Paul Read

Outside a tall terrace-house in Kensington, on Christmas Eve, the back of a blue Mercedes estate gaped open as a middle-aged man, wearing corduroy trousers and a green jersey, loaded it with suitcases, holdalls and bulging black dustbin bags. The dustbin bags were filled with delicately wrapped gifts, some round, some rectangular, some square, and were difficult to fit in. In due course it was done. The middle-aged man turned to his grown-up son with a smile of satisfaction as if he had just solved a particularly complicated Chinese puzzle.

The slim young man, in his early twenties, inclined his head as if to give praise where praise was due. The father then went to the front of the car, ready to get in and drive off; whereupon his plump, ebullient daughter, a little younger than the son, tumbled out of the house clutching a battered Globetrotter suitcase in one hand, and a bunch of plastic supermarket bags in the other. Behind her came the mother carrying a sheepskin coat and a wicker basket filled with delicacies from Marks and Spencer and thc contents of the fridge.

With a sigh, the husband reopened the back of the car, and dismantled what he had so carefully constructed to fit in the new pieces. The others got into the car – the mother in the front, the children in the back – and at ten-past-ten they set off for the country. Twenty minutes later, when thcy were half-way out of London, the wife remembered that they had forgotten to switch on the burglar alarm and mortice-lock the front door. With a curse, her husband turned left and left again, and then got lost in a maze of culs-de-sac and one-way streets designed to protect the residents from through-traffic.

The middle-aged man, at the wheel of the Mercedes, was Oswald Benson, a Circuit Court judge. No one who attended his courts – the clerks, the barristers, the jurors or the accused – could have imagined that without his wig he would turn into just another irritable paterfamilias; nor that someone who had pronounced so frequently upon the sanctity of marriage and the importance of the home should find Christmas with his family so difficult to endure.

It did not surprise his wife, Alexandra. The tantrums over loading the luggage, setting the burglar alarm, getting lost in side-streets, arguing with the children about what music to play on the stereo, had been the prelude to Christmas over the past twenty-five years. Although nine years younger than her husband, and looking young for her years, a touch of melancholy had settled gracefully upon Alexandra as she had passed from youth to middle-age. It enhanced the grave beauty of her features, and suited her mood that Christmas which was to be her first since her father had died.

Her daughter Sissy seemed to read her thoughts. 'It will be odd without Grandpa,' she said in a short space of silence between two thunderous tracks of UB40.

'Yes, we shall miss him,' said the judge in an ingratiating tone, as if hoping to make up for his earlier tantrum by saying something that would please his wife.

'And he won't even be there for the wedding,' said Sissy.

'Of course he won't,' sneered Sam, her brother. 'He hasn't gone abroad. He's dead.'

'I know that, you idiot,' said Sissy. 'It's just sad, that's all.'

A new track started, curtailing the quarrel. What had they done, Alexandra wondered, before there was pop music *en route* to numb the mind? Had she and her brother bickered in the same way? The only journeys she could remember were those going back and forth from boarding-school, and those had been by train.

Her thoughts returned to her father. She remembered how she had revered him as a child, but as an adolescent had rebelled venomously against his ex-Indian Army idea of how a teenage girl should behave. Then she had married and had children, and finally had found his old-fashioned values endearing. Words like decency, honour and duty had meant something when he had used them: coming from Oswald they always seemed hollow.

The saying that no man is a hero to his valet should, she considered, be applied to wives now that wives performed the services of the valets. Certainly, Oswald was no hero to her. If she had grown melancholy, he had grown pompous, expecting the kind of respectful attention in his home as he received in court, and delivering the kind of moral homilies to his family as he gave, before sentencing, from the bench.

It was this habit of his of giving everything a moral colouring which most irritated Alexandra – particularly his complaints about her extravagance. Certainly, she did not work but that was partly because he disapproved of women pursuing a career. Their standard and style of living seemed similar to that of most of their friends. Some of those might be merchant bankers, like her brother Hugh, but it was well known that judges were paid enormous salaries so that they need never feel tempted to take a bribe. And if his did not stretch to giving her daughter a decent wedding, and providing a roof over her head, then he could hardly object if she realized an asset of her own.

These were her thoughts as they reached the village of Sittrington on the edge of the Lincolnshire Wolds, and drove through the rusty gates of the manor-house which was the home of her family, the Eliot–Johnstones.

The main house had been built in the reign of Queen Anne, with two wings and a pretentious portico added early in the nineteenth century. It had been a weakness of her father to let it be thought that it had always been the seat of the Eliots who had fought for the King during the Civil War, when it had been bought by the brewing Johnstones in 1874.

Alexandra's first task upon arriving was to mollify her mother who, though warned by telephone that they would not get there for lunch, had already defrosted a large lasagne which could neither be refrozen nor eaten instead of the turkey on Christmas Day. Then, since her mother, now aged seventy-six, was both a little vague and short-sighted, Alexandra had quickly to whisk through the fridge and the larder, looking for mould on the crumpets and pork pies, and checking the sell-by dates on the cartons of cream.

When the luggage had been unloaded, they had tea in the kitchen and talked about the wedding which was uppermost in Sissy's mind.

'Can I have it here,' she asked her grandmother, 'like Anne?'

'Of course you can, darling. Anything you like.'

'I'll pay you £10,000 to elope,' said Oswald, his mood improved by three crumpets with butter and honey.

'You're so stingy, Dad,' said Sissy.

'Why don't *his* parents pay?' asked Sam.

'It's always the parents of the bride,' said Alexandra.

'An outmoded convention,' said Oswald.

'You didn't think so when we married,' said Alexandra. 'Did he, Mother?' she added in a louder voice; her mother was slightly deaf.

'Did what, darling?'

'Father paid for my wedding.'

'Did he?'

'And for half our house in Fulham.' She said this to her mother but the words were meant for Oswald, so selective in what he remembered.

'Goodness,' said Sissy. 'Will you do the same for me, Dad?'

'Things were different in those days,' said Oswald. 'Property wasn't so expensive, and there's been inflation . . .' Then, to escape the awkward turn in the conversation, he finished his tea and went upstairs.

They always slept in Alexandra's old bedroom, and as Oswald unpacked his suitcase he thought nostalgically of the days when a judge would have a valet, or even a wife who looked after her husband's clothes. He put his shirts in the chest-of-drawers, and his jackets and a suit into one half of the wardrobe which faced the four-poster bed. The other half contained all Alexandra's old clothes – coats, jodhpurs and the dresses she had worn as a débutante or bridesmaid. Oswald never opened that half of the wardrobe, partly because he knew there was no room to hang his clothes, and partly because he also knew that behind the old clothes was hidden the painting that Alexandra wanted to sell to pay for their daughter's wedding.

The thought of the painting – and the knowledge that it was there – stirred up feelings in Oswald which he had hoped were extinct. Having emptied his suitcase and hung up his tweed suit and smoking-jacket in the innocent half of the wardrobe, he lay back on the bed and stared at the canopy above him. The wardrobe. The painting. Money. Where had it all gone? On mortgages, school fees and Alexandra's extravagance – her insistence upon having two of everything: two houses; two cars; two holidays abroad; two sets of school fees; double the parental assessment for the children at university; and even (he had noticed in the dustbin bags) two gifts for everyone at Christmas.

Of course there had been expenses for which, he acknowledged, he himself was partly to blame – a Mercedes rather than a Volvo, and the second mortgage to pay for the mill in the Dordogne and the further loan to rebuild it when they realized it was slipping into the river. It had been a folly; they could only resell it at a dreadful loss; and now a large part of his salary went in paying interest on his debts.

He could have kept his head above water if Sissy had not chosen this moment to get married. It seemed unfair that in an age when the young either lived in sin or had children out of wedlock, his daughter should decide not just to marry but in a church and from Sittrington like her cousin Anne, the daughter of Alexandra's brother, Hugh.

As Hugh had proudly told him, this had cost more than £15,000; and it had been made clear to Oswald, by his wife and daughter, that neither would countenance fewer guests, a smaller tent, a less lavish lunch, a simpler dress or sparkling Saumur instead of genuine champagne. He had seen the glint in Sissy's eye as she had watched Anne walk up the aisle; he also had some idea of his future son-in-law's expectations. His father was another of those damned merchant bankers.

There was also the question of contributing to a roof over their heads. Covertly, Oswald had calculated that if he was to do the same for his children as his parents had done for him, it would mean giving each of them, in today's money, more than £150,000. How could he possibly find sums of that kind? Paltry amounts could be saved by resigning from the Garrick, or be raised by selling the house in France. More substantial assets could be realized by moving from the house in Kensington to a mansion-flat but, since so much of that was mortgaged, it would hardly raise the requisite amount.

By far the best solution seemed to be that either his mother or Alexandra's should die. Neither had much money but both lived in valuable houses. Hugh had told him Sittrington was now worth over half a million pounds and, with no primogeniture in the Eliot–Johnstone family, Alexandra was due for a half-share. Unfortunately, in the context of their immediate needs, her mother, like his, was physically healthy. It was becoming increasingly possible that they might die before she did.

He remembered the custom among the Hindus by which widows were burned on their husbands' funeral pyres; and old Eskimos, he seemed to remember, lightened the burden of the next generation by leaving the igloo to die in the cold. In England, it seemed, the contrary custom prevailed: widows inhabited many of the largest houses.

For the second time since entering the legal profession, Oswald thought about murder. As a rule, he avoided envisaging a crime, not just because he thought it wrong but because it might lead him to feel some sympathy for the criminals he was paid to punish. Nor would he wish to lose either Alexandra's mother or his own. He was fond of both old ladies. He liked spending Christmas at Sittrington, and going to Sunday lunch on Primrose Hill; but the natural death of either seemed preferable to the alternative Alexandra had proposed for raising some money – the sale of the painting hidden behind the old dresses in the wardrobe.

The artist who had painted the picture was to have been the victim on the one occasion he had contemplated murder before. Then, it had not been for money, or even for love, although love had entered into it; but from a pure, red-hot loathing, the embers of which were still warm to this day.

It made it no easier to forget that period of his life when the work of the painter, David Cutler, was constantly reproduced in colour magazines as he won yet another prize, or as his paintings set records in the sale-rooms for the work of a living artist – particularly those from what was humorously called his 'blue period', not because they were tinged with that colour, like the paintings of Picasso, but because they were graphically and colourfully obscene.

It was during this period that Alexandra, in revolt against her parents, had been the favourite of the four or five mistresses that Cutler had had at the time; so favoured, indeed, that he gave her a major painting for which she had posed entitled 'Nude with Legs Akimbo'. It was this which had remained hidden in the back of the wardrobe at Sittrington, and which until that moment Alexandra had refused to show to the importunate dealers who knew of its existence, or even the art historian working on a Cutler *catalogue raisonné*. But at every approach its value increased until the sort of sum now mentioned would not only pay for the wedding but for a house or a flat for the children – if not in Fulham, then in Wandsworth or Shepherd's Bush.

What would humiliate Oswald, if the painting were to be sold, was not just to be bailed out by this gift from Alexandra's former lover but that the model for this obscene painting was so clearly his wife. If she had not aged so well, or if Cutler's style had been less realistic – it had been described as 'by Schiele out of Ingres' – then it might not have mattered; but it was quite out of the question, so far as he was concerned, that the wife of a judge should be shown in such a pose on the walls of a gallery or in the pages of a magazine.

As he reached this point in his rumination, Alexandra came into the room. Seeing her husband lying gloomily on the bed, she glanced nervously at the wardrobe and said, 'Have you had a look at it?'

'No. I remember it only too well.'

She sniffed and started to unpack her suitcase, avoiding as always the left-hand side of the wardrobe. 'People aren't so easily shocked these days,' she said.

'On the contrary. They're more prudish now than they were in the 'Sixties.'

'That's because of AIDS.'

'They no longer relish the obscene. Even *his* paintings are more respectable.'

'He still paints nudes . . .'

'But not in such a posture, or with such a look.'

She blushed and frowned at the same time, not at what he said but at the distaste with which he said it. 'It might not be shown in a London gallery,' she said, 'and even if it was, it wouldn't necessarily be known that it was me.'

'Of course it would. The dealers know. Cutler knows, and with his passion for self-advertisement, he'd tip off *Private Eye* or *The Londoner's Diary*.'

'And then?'

'There's nothing they like better than to ridicule a judge, particularly one like me . . .'

He did not finish his sentence. She did, silently, for him: '. . . who holds forth about sexual morality.'

'It would ruin my career,' he said. 'I'd never make the High Court.'

'Nonsense.'

'And the children? How would they feel to see their mother like a model on a pornographic postcard?'

'That's unfair,' she said.

'To whom?'

'To David's talent.'

'A talented pornographer is still a pornographer.'

'There was a time when you weren't so averse to that kind of thing,' she said quietly.

'It was different then,' he said, thinking that the principle in law that a wife could not give evidence against her husband should be extended to life as well.

'Why?'

'It was the 'Sixties. We were all infected by the spirit of the time.'

'Quite. And now we're older.' She had a way of making a truism mean more than it said.

'It isn't just that,' he said, getting up off the bed and going to the dressing-table to brush his hair. 'We've seen the consequences of kicking off the traces . . .'

'What consequences?'

'Promiscuity, illegitimacy, an epidemic of divorce.'

'Our children are just as moral as we were.'

'Our children, perhaps.'

'And anyway, those are just statistics.'

'The statistics reveal suffering.'

'People suffered in the old days, from repression, hypocrisy and miserable marriages.'

'It's worse today.'

'That's a matter of opinion.'

When Oswald went down, Alexandra remained in the bedroom to finish her unpacking and then sort out the presents from the black plastic bags. She was annoyed with herself for having argued with Oswald, both because she was bored by the repetition of their entrenched positions and because she was afraid of inadvertently revealing some of the thoughts that were passing through her mind.

Luckily, she could count on her husband's blinkered vision – his blindness to the things he did not wish to see. It was obvious, for example, that Sam slept with his girl-friend and Sissy with the young man she meant to marry. It was likely, also, that neither was their first lover. She could not be sure. Oswald's moral posturing made it impossible for the children to confide in her without asking her to keep things from him. This, they would never do: that was what she meant by their morality.

She could never quite decide whether it was the law which had made Oswald so self-righteous, or whether his self-righteousness had drawn him to the law. Perhaps it was inevitable that a man who was deferred to throughout the day should come to believe in his own superior wisdom: the same sort of thing happened to headmasters and consultants. The only misfortune was that she could not believe in it too.

Yet she knew that she was inconsistent because she had come to respect her father who had held similar views. Was it because he came from an older generation that his values had seemed genuine and Oswald's sham?

Or was it because Oswald was her husband, and she knew him too well?

She had met him at the time she had been posing for the picture and had married him at David's suggestion. She frowned as she thought back: had it been as bad as that? No. She had certainly been drawn to Oswald from the moment she had met him at a débutante dance and had even believed at the time that she loved him because she had accepted from David that it was possible to love more than one person at a time. She knew she could never marry David, and Oswald was eminently eligible – intelligent, responsible, ambitious, just the kind of young man of whom her parents would approve.

She had also sensed that he possessed that quality which she now found annoying – the ability to see only what he wanted to see – and had calculated, with the painter, that he might not notice if she continued to pose on odd afternoons. The mistake had been to accept the painting as a wedding present or, at any rate, to bring it home and hang it on the wall. It had ignited a keg of jealousy in Oswald she had not thought he possessed. He had made her promise not to pose for, visit or even speak to the painter and then had watched the house and followed her on days she had thought he was in court. One terrible afternoon, he had burst into the studio to find her half-dressed – preparing to pose, she had insisted, which had been only half the truth.

The anguish, the rage, the lies, the protestations – and David detached, half-contemptuous, half-amused. Then suddenly she was pregnant and everything changed. The loyalty she had not felt towards a husband suddenly welled up in her for the father of her baby – and Oswald *was* the father of her baby, she was sure of that, since David had had a vasectomy after fathering nine illegitimate children, and anyway no one was *that* immoral in the 'Sixties, not, at any rate, with the first child.

She had stopped posing for David Cutler and had settled down in Fulham as the model wife of the young barrister and mother first of Sam and then of Sissy. The painting had been removed from the wall and then from its frame – the canvas rolled up, taken to Sittrington and hidden in the wardrobe behind her jodhpurs and old dresses.

Over the years, she had never forgotten it was there, and had sometimes worried that her parents would find it and be shocked by what they saw. But such was the pace of life at Sittrington, that nothing was ever moved or changed. Only rarely – usually after reading something about David in the papers and never when Oswald was there – did she take the canvas out of the wardrobe, unroll it on the carpet and consider what she saw – as a memory, as a work of art and, finally, as an asset.

Never, since she had become pregnant, had she been unfaithful to Oswald or even considered it until two months ago when, playing tennis, she had caught a carnal glint in the eye of a man over the net. He was the partner of a friend and she had found she reacted to his look in an unexpected way. He was not her type at all – a hairy, sunburned man in his middle thirties who was said to write film-scripts although no one had ever seen or even heard of any of his films. He had once been married to an Australian and seemed to do very little; he was always available to make up a four. He smiled as if confident that he was attractive – indeed he was altogether vulgar and she felt ashamed at responding to someone so banal.

She had seen him since – not alone but at the tennis club – and she could tell quite well what he was after. So could her female friend – there were several winks and nudges. What she had not done was treat him with anything more than common civility; but nor, she had to concede, had she made it immediately apparent that his flirtatious looks were a waste of time. Indeed his attentions improved her morale. Only a man, she thought, could have advanced the proposition 'I think therefore I am'. 'I am desired therefore I am' was nearer the mark, which was why Alexandra paid attention to how she looked and what she wore. Fortunately, like her mother, she had no tendency to run to fat; her figure was the envy of her dieting friends and in shorts on the tennis court could, as she had seen, draw the eye of a younger man.

The question she would have to answer in the New Year was whether or not she was to draw more than his eye. At times she thought she would because Oswald was so pompous and life so dull. It had depressed her over the past few years – adding that shadow of melancholy to her expression – that Sam and Sissy had all the fun and that she was reduced to living vicariously through them – trying not to trespass upon their privacy but longing to know more about their lives.

Oswald had the distraction of his professional life – he was always working on a summing-up; but whatever role she had ever had seemed to have gone when the children had left for university. The tennis club, the hairdresser and raising money for Save the Children left both the space and the time for a lover. If she was reasonably discreet, what harm would it do? There might be some gossip but it was unlikely to reach Oswald, aloof on the bench, or her mother, here at Sittrington.

She stopped, wondering why she had coupled her mother with her husband. Was it because she was holding a present for her in her hand – a minor gift, rectangular, wrapped in gold paper, a box containing three bars of Floris soap? Why was she not anxious about how the children would react if they were told that their mother had a lover? They would be incredulous, of course; the horizon for the cessation of sexual activity is always around five years beyond one's age. Sam thought that it should be forbidden by law after the age of thirty. Perhaps she wanted them to know . . . To know what? That she was more than she seemed? That she was not just a judge's wife? That she was still as capable of passion and sensation as she had been when she was the nude with legs akimbo?

But her mother . . . It was not that Alexandra feared rejection. Her mother's love had never depended upon her good behaviour. Even when Alexandra had been at her worst, flaunting her liaison with David Cutler and bringing Bohemian friends to stay who smoked hashish in the garden and, worse still in her father's eyes, took the port decanter into the drawing-room after her parents had gone to bed, her mother had never said a harsh word but had made sure that her clothes were washed over the weekend and that she had eggs and apples to take back to London.

It was not, then, that her mother would disown her if she happened to hear the gossip or see the painting, but rather that the behaviour which led to the gossip might prevent her becoming like her mother. It had always reconciled Alexandra to the idea of growing old to see her so serene. Would an affair with the tennis player, she wondered, mean that her face would lose its melancholy beauty and become lined with the raddled sensuality which so disgusted her in some of her friends?

What she would dearly like to know was whether or not her mother had ever had a lover – whether, to be exact, she had had an affair with Alan Chichester who had been around so much when they were young. At the time, of course, they had suspected nothing; and their father had always treated this neighbour with the same courtesy he had extended to all. Yet Alan, who was a widower, had always been their mother's friend – sharing her interest in gardening, taking her to country-house concerts and even meeting her in London to go to the opera which Alexandra's father had loathed.

Alexandra had once discussed this with Hugh. They agreed that, because their father had not just disliked opera but skiing too, it had seemed natural to them at the age of thirteen and fifteen, that Alan, with his son Pete, should accompany them, two or three years running, on skiing holidays in France. But what convinced them, looking back, that their mother had almost certainly had a full-blown affair, was the suddenness with which this intimacy had ended.

Si jeunesse savait, si vieillesse pouvait: there must be a moment in life, thought Alexandra, when the lines of declining vitality and increasing experience cross. Was it possible that a last savour, a final fling, was an accepted but unacknowledged convention? Surely, if her mother had got away with it, then she would too?

She went downstairs. Like many large houses with ill-fitting sash windows and antiquated central heating, there were only two rooms which were warm in winter – the kitchen, with its Aga, and a little room called the 'office' which had once been the sitting-room for the housekeeper or cook. The library, with its bound volumes of *Punch* and *Horse and Hound*, and shelves of novels from the 1930s, was never used; and the drawing-room and dining-room only on formal occasions – a lunch party, a dinner party, or by the family at Easter or on Christmas Day.

She went to the drawing-room to put presents under the tree and found Oswald sitting stoically in an armchair beside the newly lit fire.

'Why don't you sit in the office?' she asked, annoyed because now someone would have to relay the fire on Christmas Day.

'It's been commandeered by the children.'

'It'll be warmer.'

'They're watching television.'

'Send them up to Mother's bedroom.'

'They're smoking.'

Alexandra put the gifts she had brought down in their appropriate places. She saw a bulging parcel on hers, ineptly wrapped: another Shetland jersey from Oswald.

'You'll help yourself to a drink, won't you?' On previous Christmases, he would have been given a glass of gin by her father. She now went along the passage to the office, intending to turn the children out, but saw Sam and Sissy lolling so comfortably on the sofa, that she had not the heart to disturb them.

She went on to the kitchen where her mother sat by the Aga with the cat on her knee.

'Shall we go to church at midnight,' her mother asked, 'or to Communion in the morning?'

'I don't mind.'

'It's rather pretty at midnight. Your father always preferred it, although I'm not sure he would have gone with the new vicar.'

'What's wrong with him?'

'He was rather too Catholic for your father's taste –

you know, lots of incense and dressing up in fancy vestments. Your father thought he was queer.'

'Perhaps he is.'

'He is married. I had a long talk with his wife. She says she intends to become a vicar too.'

'Father can't have liked that.'

'No, poor man. And the way they minced around at his funeral. He must have been turning in his coffin before it even got into the ground.'

Alexandra opened the oven to take out the Irish stew.

'I do miss him,' said her mother.

'So do I.'

'He rather liked Christmas, although he pretended he didn't.'

'I know.'

After supper, because the grown-ups were tired and the children were watching a film, they decided not to go to church that night but to go to Communion in the morning. 'Anyway,' said Alexandra's mother, 'it always seems wrong not to go on Christmas morning, and it is rather too much to go twice.'

While Oswald remained watching television with Sam and Sissy, Alexandra went up to fill their stockings. When they were small, she had enjoyed stuffing a pair of Oswald's huge socks with toys, puzzles and bars of chocolate – thinking of their delight and excitement when they awoke the next morning. Now she was only irritated that they still insisted upon having stockings when they went to bed later than she did and no longer believed in Santa Claus. It was a shameless device to increase the total number of presents, and with a certain relish she bulked out the stockings with some old apples she had brought up from the kitchen.

She was half-asleep when Oswald came to bed and awoke before him the next morning. Her mother had a part-time gardener called Jack and there was a woman from the village who had come in to clean the house for the past twenty years called Mrs Hunmanby but neither turned up on Christmas Day to make breakfast, lay the fires or put the turkey in the oven. She worked hard to get everything ready and was irritated that Sam expected a cooked breakfast on Christmas morning as well as a gargantuan feast at lunch. This meant frying bacon and eggs on the hotplate of the Aga as she tried to boil potatoes and make the bread sauce.

Oswald, too, ate a cooked breakfast and was disconsolate without a morning paper, while Sissy was grumpy at being woken up in time to go to church. Both children went to please their grandmother. They were not so sensitive to their father's feelings: they never went in London.

The church at Sittrington was at the other end of the village, and it was the custom that they always went on foot. That morning the three women walked together, discussing how to arrange things for the wedding. 'The white Mercedes that Anne had was rather vulgar,' said Sissy. 'I'd rather get hold of a Rolls.'

'Couldn't you walk?' asked Oswald who followed with Sam, a few paces behind his daughter.

'Oh *Dad* . . .' she said. 'Think of the dress . . . and all the bridesmaids . . .'

'It seems absurd to hire a Rolls-Royce to take you less than half-a-mile.'

'But the dress would get dirty,' said Sissy, 'and it's going to cost hundreds and hundreds of pounds.'

'It doesn't matter if it gets dirty,' said Sam. 'You're only going to wear it once.'

'It might rain,' said Alexandra.

'Umbrellas,' said the judge.

Sissy sighed, as if in despair at her father's obtuseness.

'I'm sure it won't rain,' said the grandmother looking up as if the wedding was later that day. The sky was clear. A pale sun shone through the ground mist to reflect off the frost on the fields. It was cold and crisp, appropriate weather for a Christmas morning, and on the path leading to the church the breath of the congregation vaporized in the air.

There was the usual cannonade of greetings, and half-embarrassed exchanges between Sam and Sissy and their contemporaries in the village whom they had played with when small. Then they were seated, the judge next to his mother-in-law in the front pew.

To Alexandra, the vicar was indeed bizarre, mincing around the altar in multicoloured vestments she had not seen before. His wife, who served as an acolyte, wore a white polo-necked jersey beneath her black robe, turned down to look like a clerical collar. Alexandra glanced nervously at Oswald, to see how he would react to these antics at the altar, but he had already assumed his 'Church-as-the-pillar-of-society' expression and was enjoying, as he sang 'Away in a manger', the sound of his own voice. Unwisely, she then looked at Sam and Sissy who, when they caught her eye, started giggling and drew disapproving looks from a farmer on the other side of the aisle.

Yet despite the incense and the prancing acolytes and the vicar's lisping sermon, the story was still the story of Christ born in a manger; and Alexandra, who considered herself a Christian in only a nominal way, was none the less moved by hearing the story once again – particularly of how Joseph, when he thought that Mary was pregnant by another man, offered to separate discreetly rather than denounce her as an adulteress and have her stoned to death as the law prescribed. How unlike Oswald; how like, perhaps, her father if he had known about Alan.

When the service was over, the congregation dispersed and Oswald walked briskly towards the house with his children. Alexandra, however, arm-in-arm with her mother, went round to the side of the church to look at her father's grave.

'I miss him terribly,' she said.

'Yes,' said Alexandra. 'It must be lonely without him.'

'Especially here, at Sittrington. It was so much his house.'

'Do you want to move?'

'No. At least, not from the village but what I thought, if you agreed, was that I might move into the cottage when Mrs Williams gets her council flat.'

'And what would happen to the house?'

'I think Hugh and Jane want to take it on.'

Alexandra was silent as she took in what her mother had said.

'You and Oswald would never want to live here, would you?'

'He wouldn't, no.'

'What Hugh suggested, if you agreed, was that he should buy you out, as it were.'

'Can he afford it?'

'Apparently, yes. He not only earns a great deal but Jane's parents have given her some money.'

They turned and walked back towards the entrance to the churchyard. 'You could still come here, of course,' her mother went on. 'That would have to be a condition.'

'It wouldn't be the same,' said Alexandra.

'I know, darling, but life must go on. You can use the money to buy a house in the country of your own.'

'Or flats for Sam and Sissy.'

'Exactly. It's always sad but one must be brave about things like death and age and change.'

'I know.'

They went out of the churchyard into the village. 'You know,' the mother told her daughter, 'at first, when your father died, I just couldn't bear it. Everywhere I looked, there were his things. His clothes were the worst. Hugh took some of his suits but that tatty old jacket and those baggy trousers he liked to wear were still there in his wardrobe. Then, suddenly, one day, I pulled myself together. I went up with Mrs Hunmanby and took everything out of his wardrobe. We made a pile of wearable things to give to Oxfam and a pile of things to be thrown away. It was all quite invigorating and when we'd finished in his dressing-room, we went on around the house, clearing things out of the cupboards that had been there for years. Your old jodhpurs, for example, were perfect for little Sally Sexton who's just got a pony, and your old bridesmaid's dress went to the school for their dressing-up chest. We turned out everything and got Jack to remove all the rubbish from the cupboards – broken suitcases, cardboard boxes, an old roll of canvas, that kind of thing – and put them all on a bonfire on Guy Fawkes Day. It was a pity you weren't there. It really was one of the best we have ever had at the village; but emptying the cupboards made me realize that it was absurd for me to go on living in such a large house alone, and I said so to Hugh when he came for a weekend, and he said that he'd like to take it on.'

They reached the gate to the manor. 'I know that Father wanted Hugh to live here,' said Alexandra. 'He would be happy.'

'Yes. And if I hadn't decided to move out, he might have bought himself something else with that money of Jane's.'

Alexandra stopped, turned and looked at her mother. 'You were happy with him, weren't you, Mother?'

'With your father? Yes. More than I had a right to be.'

'You had *every* right to be . . .'

'No. There are some things that I regret . . .'

She waited.

'Once . . . Do you remember Alan?'

'Yes.'

'I was very fond of him and once – once or twice – when I was lying in bed beside your father, I would wonder what it would be like to be married to Alan.'

'Just wonder?'

'Yes. It was very disloyal.'

'Were you in love with Alan?'

'I suppose I was, yes.'

'And he was in love with you?'

'Perhaps but he never said so.'

'Why not?'

'He was very fond of your father and I was his wife. And when he couldn't bear it, he went away.'

'Did Father know why?'

She nodded. 'I think so, yes, but we never talked about it.'

They went into the house. In the kitchen, Oswald was basting the turkey which he had taken out of the oven. 'Is this right?' he asked Alexandra. 'It was getting burnt.'

'Fowl with legs akimbo,' she said. 'Burnt, like the nude.'

He looked puzzled. 'I don't understand.'

'Come upstairs and I'll explain.' She covered the turkey with foil and put it back in the oven.

Later that morning, for the first time in their lives, Sam and Sissy saw that their father had been crying. He did not look unhappy and said that he had been chopping onions for the stuffing. Since Sissy had helped her mother make the stuffing in London, they knew that they had caught him lying – this too for the first time in their lives.

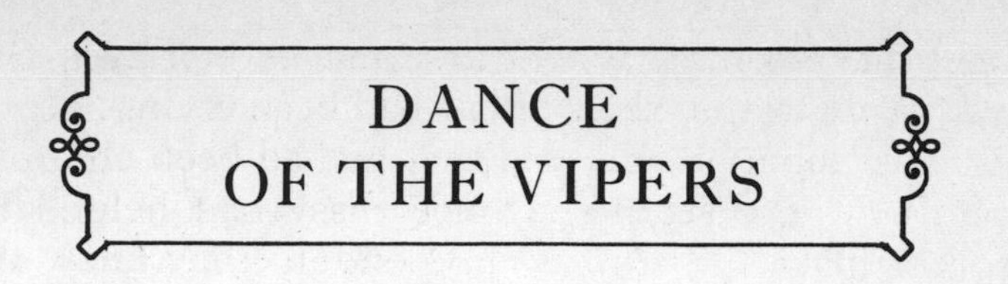

Tom Wakefield

Vera Rushton decided that she would wear the green and yellow chiffon scarf. She was tired of things matching. Her daughter Barbara had said that it was possible to dress sensibly and still look attractive. Ignoring this observation Vera decorated her throat with the exotic material. She smiled with satisfaction as the flimsy, almost ethereal garment floated over the beige shoulders and frontage of her twin set. April was a changeable month – why not reflect it in one's dress.

Outside the sun shone and there was the merest hint of a breeze. Perfect weather for the dazzling chiffon scarf which came to life as soon as Vera stepped on the pavement. In spite of the brightness of the day, Vera was filled with a quiet sense of foreboding. This was Thursday. And every Thursday since the death of her husband, Vera had visited her daughter Barbara, her only child. The visits had been regularized at Barbara's insistence. 'So like her father – but without the kindness,' Vera thought as she made her way to the bus-stop. Neighbours would often tell Vera how lucky she was in having such a dutiful daughter.

After eighteen months of this weekly visiting Vera felt anything but lucky. Indeed, she felt as though she was being programmed for old age. And at sixty-one she did not feel old, although Barbara tried to make her feel so. The only way that Vera could get through the time was to be smiling and subservient. It was as though Vera had to pay for her lunch by agreeing with all that

Barbara said and by accepting all the veiled criticism that her daughter delivered. But was it veiled?

'I'll just give you a little pasta, Mother. We don't want you getting any bigger than you already are – do we?'

'Our home-made parsnip wine has turned out beautiful this year – you could take a bottle home with you – but, better not. Women shouldn't drink alone – and at your time in life there are other things to consider – like – er – like – er – blood pressure.' She felt she might well suffer from it – or that it might well rise – if she were subjected to more than the prescribed weekly portion of her daughter's dulcet-toned personal remarks. Visiting her daughter was like going to the dentist. The anticipation was the worst part. Throughout the visit one remained compliant and servile. When it was over, there was a sense of relief – but this was followed by a slight ache.

Vera would have long since stopped the visits had it not been for her grandson. As it was, she only saw him for little more than a quarter of an hour. Barbara had this strictly time-tabled. 'Michael, it's time you settled to your homework – you know your father will want to see it when he gets home. Mother, if you are catching the twenty-to-five bus, you had better be getting ready. I know you hate rushing and it can't be good . . .'

Vera sighed as she pressed Barbara's doorbell. Orders flew from Barbara with such ease and fluency.

'Oh, Mother, it's you,' Barbara exclaimed as she opened the door.

Vera wanted to say, 'Were you expecting anybody else?' but instead smiled gently and muttered, 'Hello, dear.'

Barbara did not exchange the greeting but cooed, 'I'm making a macaroni cheese. I know you like it.' Vera felt that if she were offered much more pasta she might well explode. Pasta with tuna, pasta with beans, pasta with a trace of corned beef, pasta with peas . . . pasta, pasta, pasta. Vera longed for a pork chop and, as she entered the kitchen, her stomach rumbled with disgruntlement.

Barbara followed on behind her. 'I do like that suit, Mother.'

Vera cast all trepidation from her and said, 'And the scarf? The scarf? Do you like the scarf?'

Barbara emitted a weak titter. 'Well – well – well – er – it is cheerful, Mother. It is cheerful. I'll say that for it.'

Vera was about to lower herself into the chair like a deflated air-balloon when . . . 'Hello, Gran. We've been sent home early from school. Our teacher's off sick. Nobody to replace her, so they've sent us home.' Vera's grandson looked older than his eleven years; he had faint furrows on his brow and his large brown eyes gave him an expression of permanent surprise. Grandmother and grandson talked to one another as if they were both the same age – somewhere around twenty-two.

'Eh, Gran, what d'y'know? We've got snakes at the bottom of the garden.'

'Will you stop that, Michael,' Barbara shrieked. 'Putting such rubbish about. You know we want to put this house on the market soon. Why not tell everyone we have rats too. I'll have your pocket-money stopped. I hate lies. Even silly lies. Please don't encourage him, Mother.' Barbara began to grate the slab of cheese with more vigour than was necessary.

From the kitchen doorway Michael beckoned to Vera and she followed her Pied Piper into the garden. He placed his forefinger on his top lip. Vera nodded understanding. Silence was the order of the day. She tiptoed after him in follow-the-leader fashion. At the point where the crazy-paving ended they crossed the lawn and skirted the currant bushes which screened the compost heap and cucumber frame from view. The smell of rotting vegetables and mulch caused Vera's nostrils to twitch. This was a very private part of the garden. Again Michael placed his forefinger on his top lip. Again Vera nodded obedience and complicity. She watched as he slowly moved his forefinger from his lip, unstretched his elbow and extended his arm. Her eyes travelled down his shoulder, over his forearm, wrist, hand – along the line of his finger.

Vera could see the three snakes very clearly. They were less than three yards away. One lay coiled, fat and satisfied, basking in the year's early sunshine. But it was the other two serpents which caused Vera to stand as immobile as a block of stone. Their dramatic zig-zag patterning dazzled her eyes as the sunlight cast its glow and warmth upon them. These two seemed to be involved in some strange kind of dance. Most of their bodies were lifted from the ground, they swayed to and fro, from time to time they intertwined with one another – and then they would separate. 'Was this a courtship?' Vera wondered.

If it was the beginnings of a reptilian romance, the rest of the garden did not seem to want to witness or celebrate it; there were no sounds from busy insects, no birdsong, and the breeze had faltered and finally stopped. The pair of snakes were now intent on some kind of unworldly hypnotism; their heads not an inch apart, each looked into the eyes of the other. They hovered like this – eyeball to eyeball.

Vera detected no enticement, no attraction, no passion, no love in this confrontation. Forked tongues began to quiver – not with anticipation but cold rage. 'They are competing for the favours of the quiet, fat one,' thought Vera. She felt saddened that it was not possible for both of them to win. The weird swaying movements commenced again and Vera marvelled that a battle could be so wondrous and . . .

'The macaroni! Michael! Mother! Macaroni! Macaroni's on the table.' Barbara's voice not only pierced the air but also Vera's body; she flinched as the sound seemed to strike her between the shoulder blades. There was a faint rustle of leaves and debris – and in a fraction of a second the vipers had vanished.

'Thank you for showing me the snakes, Michael. Thank you so much,' Vera whispered to her grandson and gently stroked his hair as they made their way back to the house.

As they entered, Michael spoke out in firm, deliberate adult tones. 'Mum, we did see the snakes. We saw three of them. Gran saw them as well. Didn't you, Gran?' Vera nodded affirmingly and smiled.

Barbara reacted swiftly, almost violently. She banged the cutlery on the table. 'I'll hear no more of snakes. No more, I tell you. I warned you, Michael. Now enough is enough. Up to your room. Off you go. Don't answer me back. Up you go. No lunch. Nothing until after your Gran has gone. Upstairs! Now!'

Vera watched her grandson leave her presence regretfully. If she remonstrated with her daughter it might make matters worse for him. The horrible unfairness of Barbara's treatment of him made her feel sick and fatigued – and yes – even old. She sat opposite her daughter at the dining-table and looked down disconsolately at the platc of macaroni cheese. The steam drifted into her nostrils and added flavour to her general state of nausea and repugnance. She wanted to speak – to say something in defence of her grandson but the fear of her own oncoming tears checked her tongue.

Barbara spoke just as Vera picked up her fork. 'Did you buy your scarf locally, Mother? Or have you been going around all those church jumble sales again?'

Vera did not answer her daughter. For a reply she replaced her fork on the table; she no longer felt the need for tears. Rebellion began to course through her being; she felt both angry and elated.

'I hate to say this, Mother – but it just doesn't go – it doesn't suit you at all. You know I've never been one to mince words, Mother – well – it's – it's just cheap and vulgar.'

Vera wondered if Barbara's blatant cruelty would ever end. She chose not to answer her daughter. Instead, she got up from her chair and removed the gaudy chiffon scarf from her throat. She did not do this quickly – but slowly, with great care – almost as though she were nursing the material into life. Now she held the scarf between her fingertips. She brought it to life by gently waving it to and fro in the air, letting it bend and glide. She watched it hover, making balletic, magical patterns as it floated this way and that. (Vipers are beautiful and ought to be revered.)

'Mother! Mother! Do sit down,' Barbara commanded.

Vera obeyed, releasing the chiffon from her tenuous grasp and watching it float and coil and finally settle itself near her daughter's feet.

'Eat up, Mother. It'll be getting cold.'

Vera sat quite still, her hands folded in her lap.

'Mother, eat up.'

Vera did not answer, nor did she move. Her face, void of any expression, she gazed into her daughter's eyes. Barbara could not detect any semblance of contrition in her mother's stare. She glared back. They sat and stared – eyeball to eyeball. Barbara knew that her mother would soon tire of this childish behaviour; Vera had never been able to cope with a challenge. This was what came of spoiling one's mother – just like children – no thanks for anything. Indignation gave Barbara more energy, yet Vera did not cede. The two women continued to glare at one another. Green eyes met blue eyes and neither colour blinked.

Slowly, Vera brought her right hand away from her lap; she rested it on the edge of the table. Now her hand touched the edge of her plate. In one swift movement she struck.

She seized a handful of the yellow edible slime and hurled it from her. It made a choking, splattering sound as it hit the wall behind her daughter. Barbara glanced over her shoulder and recoiled at the unsightly mess of macaroni cheese trickling down to the floor – it seemed to be defiling the whole house. Somehow she managed to suppress her revulsion and turn her attention back towards her mother. A gentle clicking noise seemed to be coming from Vera's throat – then Barbara's revulsion turned to horror as her mother began to hiss-ss-ss-ss.

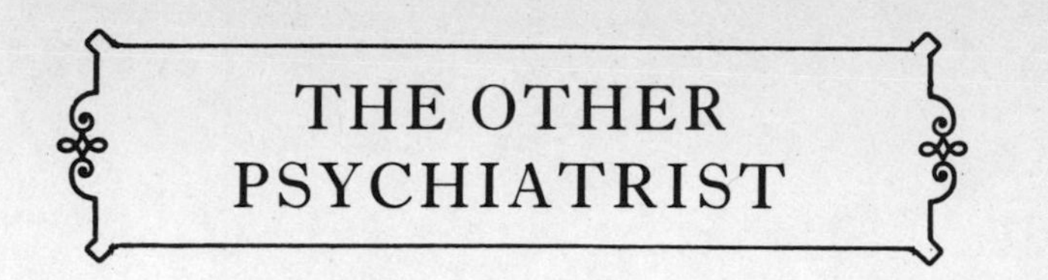

Patrick McGrath

I remember Otto Spiegel as a lanky, twitchy sort of a man, a man clearly uncomfortable in his own body, constantly fiddling with his spectacles and brushing imaginary specks of dust from his clothing. In all the time I knew him he wore the same suit every day, a shabby grey affair with threadbare cuffs and baggy trousers that flapped about his long legs like slack sail-cloth. He was not a particularly gifted psychiatrist; an orthodox Freudian, he was deeply resistant, almost pathologically so in my opinion, to new ideas. He had been working for more than a decade on a paper concerning the neurotic fear of fluids in women; when it appeared, if it ever did, and I harboured grave doubts about that, it would of course be out-of-date at once; but to Otto Spiegel this was not apparent. He saw himself, I believe, as one engaged upon the painstaking composition of a seminal work. Such labours cannot be hurried.

We were both employed at a private mental home in upstate New York called Green Briars. The house itself was built by a banker in the late nineteenth century and was a classic instance of the architectural fashion of the period. A formidable façade in grey stone, with steeply gabled slate roofs, towers, courtyards, mullioned windows and gargoyled drainpipes, it sprawled across a broad and elevated shelf of land amid rolling hills and thick woods, and was a nightmare to heat. Fortunately there was no shortage of patients, drawn exclusively from wealthy Manhattan families, and the place was thus able not only to maintain itself but to flourish.

The medical superintendent was a bluff and genial man called Bill Franklin, who behaved rather like a country squire, tending to his tenantry with a sort of benign neglect, and getting away to fish as often as he possibly could. Benign neglect in fact formed the corner-stone of his psychiatric outlook; a relaxed atmosphere, he believed, pleasant, rural surroundings, fresh air, good food, and a fixed routine – such conditions alone did much to soothe the troubled breast, and Bill was fairly content to leave it at that. When pressed, he dignified this country club regimen as 'milieu therapy'. For a man like Otto Spiegel, with a seminal paper to write, Green Briars was the perfect retreat. In fact, because the man was in both his thinking and his character so clearly inadequate, it was only in a place like Green Briars that he could have survived. He'd been there more than a dozen years when I arrived, almost as long as Bill Franklin himself. He was a fixture.

How well I remember our first encounter in the senior staff common-room. Bill Franklin had shown me round the facilities and introduced me to a number of the patients and staff. Not much of a fisherman myself, I did my best to respond intelligently to his conversation which, in marked contrast to the flat, professional monotone he adopted in describing case histories, trcatment methods and the like, became distinctly animated on the subject of fly-fishing. Anyway, he brought me into the senior common-room and, pulling out his pipe, introduced me in an offhand manner to the four or five psychiatrists present. There was some polite interest shown in where I'd just come from, who I'd trained with, that sort of thing, then one by one they drifted back to their crossword puzzles, their chess games, their novels. Only Otto Spiegel paid me a more than formal and cursory attention. 'Dr Wilson,' he said, in that very dry, rather high-pitched voice of his, 'would it be impertinent to inquire about your, ah, theoretical affiliation? You mentioned Professor Pitz; am I to take it that you adhere to his' – here the man paused, and, in that precious manner I grew so to loathe, began to polish his spectacles – 'dogma?'

I determined not to rise to such a clumsily dangled piece of bait. 'No, Dr Spiegel,' I replied. 'Dogma I leave to the Freudians. I'm fairly eclectic in my approach. What about yourself?'

Now it was his turn to prickle. Bill Franklin, you see, had mentioned to me already that Spiegel was a Freudian; I watched his reaction with interest. First, he blinked very rapidly for several seconds, as though struggling to assimilate what had been said to him; then, turning away, he murmured, 'Quite, Dr Wilson,' – and, replacing his spectacles on the bridge of his nose, resumed his newspaper. This was our first skirmish, and I think I emerged from it quite well. Bill Franklin, with a twinkle of amusement, reminded me that dinner would be served in ten minutes, and left me to my own devices.

I soon settled into the routines of life at Green Briars, and this being the fall of the year, I was daily treated to the glories of New England foliage on the turn. My caseload was not heavy, and the general atmosphere of the place remained, as I'd predicted it would, largely a reflection of Bill Franklin's personality – relaxed, affable, moderate – and not even Otto Spiegel's dusty obsessiveness could do much to upset it. Until, of course, Margaret Edgar arrived; but that wasn't until just before Christmas, and at that time Spiegel's efforts to discredit my professional reputation, and undermine the therapeutic work I was trying to do at Green Briars, were still in their infancy, and had not yet begun seriously to disturb me.

We were to have one more contretemps in the weeks following my arrival, after which, by tacit and mutual consent, we avoided each other entirely. It occurred during one of Spiegel's so-called study groups. These occurred once a month; their purpose, as Spiegel declared on a paper pinned prominently to the common-room notice board, was to 'enable the professional staff to engage in meaningful discussion of developments in psychotherapeutic thinking relevant to treatment procedures in this setting.' Apparently he got an average attendance of two – Dr Fox, a bearded young sycophant whose bedroom was next to mine; and Dr Hooper, who was very old and very deaf. On the evening in question I found myself with nothing pressing to do, and decided on a whim to see what Spiegel had to offer.

The 'study group' took place in the library, a room I was fond of – dark wood panelling, glass-fronted bookcases, leather armchairs into which one could sink to a wickedly luxurious depth, and a good big fire burning in the hearth. The armchairs had been grouped around a low table, and I arrived to find Drs Spiegel, Fox and Hooper already installed. 'Ah, Dr Wilson,' said Spiegel, dryly, 'we are honoured.'

I nodded to Spiegel and the others and sat down. Spiegel then informed me that this particular evening he intended to speak briefly about a facet of his own recent work. He hoped, he said with a patronizing smile, that an eclectic like myself would not be intimidated by what I might construe as jargon, but would feel free to contribute my remarks, when the presentation was over, without inhibition. 'You are', he added, glaring at me with ill-masked hostility, 'among friends.'

Needless to say, this did not dispose me to listen to the man's nonsense with much sympathy. And nonsense it was; I hadn't realized that such thinking still went on within the profession. He had taken for his topic 'The Psychosexual Significance of Rain', and, after citing a number of extremely boring dreams which he claimed to have been told by his female patients, began to develop the predictable and obsolete idea that rain, in the unconscious mind, stands as a symbol of urine and semen. 'The typical dream-dilemma of the obsessional neurotic in whom fear of fluids presents as the dominant symptom', he went on, 'involves, as one might expect, being caught, out in the open, by a shower – and having no umbrella, or other means of covering, to hand.'

At this point he had been talking for seven minutes, and my sense of tedium was already profound. How to escape?

'The meaning is clear, I think, gentlemen: the patient, in a fruitless attempt to repress her desire for the discharges of her father's penis, finds herself being quite helplessly drenched.' Spiegel paused to remove his spectacles. 'In this way she is able to fulfil her forbidden desire, but does so in such a manner that she is essentially passive and helpless throughout the experience. She is, in short, *victimized* by the shower of rain' – a perceptible flush crept up his cheeks – 'and will begin to run about in search of shelter.' He paused again. 'Running about is of course well established as an unconscious representation of the sexual act, and thus it is that the patient is able to enjoy sexual intercourse with her father, while simultaneously doing everything in her power to avoid it. Honour is, as it were, satisfied, while being at the same time besmirched.'

Can you credit it? Spiegel drew forth a rather grubby

handkerchief and dabbed at his brow. A log fell in the hearth and sent a shower of sparks up the chimney. Quite ostentatiously, and quite loudly, I yawned. I then watched with amusement as Spiegel blinked at me for several moments. He was quite incredulous. He had never, I think, in the course of his reclusive, mousey life, been so insulted.

I stood up. 'Excuse me, Dr Spiegel,' I said, 'fascinating as all this is, I must retire.' A gibe rose to my lips, but I did not voice it.

As I left the room I heard Fox say, 'Please go on, Dr Spiegel'; and Hooper, the old man, murmured, 'Is it that late already? I had no idea.'

In the weeks that followed, as I say, we avoided each other studiously; how was it then that I came to know just how poisonously my 'insult' was festering in Spiegel's mind? I will tell you. The human being constantly emits tiny messages that signal, more clearly than words ever can, just what is going on inside him, both consciously and, more important, unconsciously. It is to such signals that the psychiatrist is professionally, even temperamentally attuned; his radar, as sensitively calibrated as a bat's, registers these minute psychic tremors with uncanny precision; this in fact is his job. And it was by these means that I began to understand just how implacably hostile were Spiegel's feelings toward me. Something as subtle as the flash of his spectacles, the movement of his eyes over the top of his newspaper, when I entered a room; something as fleeting as his reaction when, on himself entering a room, he registered my presence there. It was enough. I doubt that Bill Franklin knew what was going on, I doubt that any of them did – psychiatrists, like everybody else, must go off duty sometimes if they are not to go mad. But with regard to Otto Spiegel, I was never off duty. I could not afford to be. For he was watching me, and I was watching him watching me; and the grudge clearly continued to fester. It occurred to me in November that if the man did not lance it himself, then someone would have to do it for him. Without doubt that would be me.

But before we reached that point a catalyst presented itself – or rather, herself. This was a new patient, a young woman called Margaret Edgar, and she was referred to Green Briars by her father, John Edgar. About this man I learned a little from Bill Franklin, who was in fact a buddy of his. The family was old New York, apparently, and had for several generations controlled a large brokerage firm on Wall Street. This John Edgar, the current patriarch, was an aggressive, domineering man – not Bill Franklin's words, these, but the inference I drew from the thumb-nail sketch he gave me – who had fathered four sons and steered them all into the business. It was not hard for me to imagine the power he exerted over those four young men. They certainly feared him, and quite possibly hated him – my own father was such a man, and I too have brothers, so I know whereof I speak. But what happens – and this was a question which, as Margaret's intended psychiatrist, I now had to answer – what happens to the daughters?

What happens to the daughters? One of three things. Swaddled in wealth and love, they become pretty little creatures who marry someone who went to school with their brothers, and live happily ever after. Or, running on the same juice that has reliably fuelled the family for many, many years, they become sturdy, independent women who make their own way. Or – and I have observed this sad dynamic more than once – dazzled and terrified by the great thick crush of males into the midst of which they've been thrust, they construct private worlds, and withdraw into them, for it is only there that they find some small measure of control over their existence, illusory though it may be. Margaret Edgar was apparently of this third type; and the private world she had constructed was the familiar one of the obsessive neurotic.

Bill Franklin introduced me to her one wet morning in December. She was sitting on the edge of one of his Queen Anne uprights, while Bill leaned back in the big padded chair behind his desk, hands behind his head and pipe between his teeth. The high, narrow windows of Bill's office overlooked a deep vista of hills and trees, somewhat grey and misted this particular day. It was a warm room, comfortably furnished, a room designed, like the man himself, to put one at one's ease. Yet this little woman on the edge of her chair was coiled like a spring. She was tense, she was wary, she was frightened and hostile. She would not speak.

Bill introduced us, and then put forth the idea that Miss Edgar might care to consider me her doctor, at least for a few weeks, until she'd settled in. She turned her head towards me. Her hair was scraped with some severity from her forehead. Her skin was white and unblemished, and in some odd way was distinctly reminiscent of fine bone china – a complexion delicate and expensive, a skin that bespoke old money and taste – though this impression was no doubt influenced by her clothes, which in their quiet lines suggested to the discerning eye tailoring of the very highest quality. She was a small woman, slender but in no sense boyish, and she held her body, as I say, coiled like a spring – the hands folded demure and unmoving in her lap, her knees and feet pressed together. Only her head moved as Bill Franklin suggested that she consider herself my patient. Those cold blue eyes fixed me with an incurious stare. 'Does he smoke?' she said, and I said to myself, 'She's mad as a broom.'

'If smoking offends you, Miss Edgar,' I replied, pleasantly, 'I shall not smoke in your presence.'

'That's hardly the point, Dr Wilson,' she said. 'There are still emanations. It clings to one's clothing and fouls one's breath.'

I caught Bill Franklin's eye as he quietly set his pipe in an ashtray. An expression of comical self-reproach briefly touched his face. Margaret Edgar saw me catch his eye and turned to him. 'I'm tired, Dr Franklin,' she said. 'I've had a long drive. I should like to go to my room, and I should like luncheon served to me there.'

Bill was on his feet and shuffling round the desk. 'Of course you're tired,' he said. 'Forgive me for keeping you so long.' He put his head out of the door, and a moment later a nurse appeared. Margaret Edgar left without another word. Bill then took a slim buff folder from a drawer and tossed it to me. 'There's not much there,' he said. 'Read it over and tell me what you think. Apparently she believes her father's been trying to poison her. Thinks he's the devil. Mad as a broom.'

I took the buff folder and nodded. My own thoughts precisely.

As Bill Franklin said, there was not much in the folder. Margaret had by all accounts been a happy and well-adjusted child, though quiet and somewhat solitary. The first indication that all was not well with her occurred during her seventeenth year when she ate tainted fish and was quite violently ill with food-poisoning for a day and a half. This trauma appears to have mobilized a powerful residue of latent neurotic energies in the girl, and from that time on she became increasingly distrustful of the food and drink that were put before her. Her family was not unduly concerned;

Margaret, it was thought, had become conscious of her figure, a perfectly normal thing in a girl of her age. How were they to know that an extensive set of paranoid delusions was taking root in the girl's mind? She shared her mental life with none of them, and besides, overshadowed as she was by those four loud and ambitious brothers, who could be expected to notice that, in her quiet and genteel manner, Margaret was going mad?

Margaret was twenty when her disease first announced itself in unequivocal terms. It happened, predictably, at a family meal. John Edgar and his sons had returned from a hunting trip in Canada; they had brought back, strapped to the roof of the station-wagon, a magnificent cow moose, which had promptly been butchered, and a joint of which was this night to be served to the family and a handful of close friends. It was a jovial scene, and John Edgar, relaxed after ten days of purely male company in the woods, was in expansive and garrulous mood. His eye, for once, fell upon his daughter; perhaps – and this is no more than a guess – for the first time in his life he recognized that Margaret was becoming a beautiful woman. His response to that realization – and with it, no doubt, a hastily suppressed stirring of physical attraction – is interesting. He became even more hearty. He became boisterous. He urged his moose meat upon her. He was attempting, I believe, to ignore altogether the fact that Margaret was a woman. He was attempting to treat her as a fifth son.

Margaret stared at the plate of steaming meat before her. This, remember, is more than two years after the tainted fish had first precipitated her illness. In that time it had been slowly dawning on her that her father wished her dead precisely because she was *not* his fifth son, and the means that he was employing to this end was poison in her food. She looked again at the steaming plate of moose he'd served her – and knew that at that moment her very existence hung in the balance. She overturned the plate and fled weeping from the room. The party was ruined, and John Edgar – at the moment when, of all times in his life, he should have called upon some precious stock of inherited wisdom, when he should have exercised a full human understanding, an understanding of necessity comprising to a large extent compassion – failed her. Failed her utterly. And became, instead, angry. The incident demonstrates quite clearly, I think, the spiritual poverty of this captain of finance.

The next six months, for Margaret, must have been sheer hell. For she had lost her protective colouring, she was no longer the invisible daughter, she was now 'difficult'. John Edgar now *saw* her. He watched her as though she were a problematic account, an unpredictable stock. And what he now could not fail to notice – although it had not claimed his attention for two and a half years – was that when Margaret did attend family meals, and this was growing rarer, she ate almost nothing, and what she did eat she very carefully tasted before swallowing even a morsel. He did not take long to discover, now that he'd picked up the scent, that she bought her own food, prepared it and ate it in her bedroom – and this of course infuriated him. He forbade her to eat in her room. He demanded her presence at meals. He insisted shc cat her food. We may well wonder who was the more humiliated by this regressive activity, the father or the daughter. Did he forbid her to leave the table until her plate was clean? The buff folder was, as I say, sparing in its details, and much of this account of Margaret's illness is the product of psychiatric intuition; so whether or not John Edgar actually forbade his now adult daughter to leave the table until her plate was clean, I cannot say. But it would not surprise me.

The antagonism between Margaret and her father did not abate, for both had strongly obstinate personalities; and the atmosphere in the house became increasingly tense, increasingly explosive. When it did explode, the situation was not unlike the moose dinner. This time, though, it was fish, fish, curiously enough, that John Edgar had caught on a trip with Bill Franklin, and when Margaret refused to eat it, he would not permit her to leave the table, but must have her *reasons* for refusing his fish. And then it all came out in a flood of bizarre, hysterical accusations that left the family utterly dumbfounded. Margaret subsequently withdrew into an impenetrable silence, and in his bewilderment John Edgar turned to his old friend Bill Franklin. Within a week Margaret was at Green Briars.

And now she was my patient.

I knew it would not be easy. To begin with, I was a man. I belonged to that vast clan of hunter–dealers that pressed their poisoned meat and fish upon her, and this excluded me completely from her world. I should in any case have been excluded from Margaret Edgar's world, for regional and social reasons; but the simple fact of my maleness was by far the greatest obstacle to the creation of an empathic bond between us. She would sit in my office for an entire hour without uttering a word. Although still only twenty, she was not a girl, she was a woman, and in her withdrawal the effect of her cool beauty was if anything heightened. Oh, in how many ways did I attempt to penetrate that chilly façade, to get to the desperately unhappy, and desperately sick, woman within! How many nights did I lie awake attempting to formulate what in medical school had been termed 'strategies of psychotherapeutic intervention' – I finally had to prescribe myself Nembutal, so preoccupied, and disturbed, did I become at my failure to get through. And still she gave me nothing. I could not get a reaction. I talked to her about her father. I described her situation to her in the terms I have done here. I am your ally, I told her – everything I did and said was designed to communicate that to her – I am your ally and I am here to help you get well! But her mistrust was so pathologically deep that I don't believe I roused even a flicker of a response in her. She saw me as a man, and therefore one who in some manner intended to poison her. I was out to do her harm; of this, I believe, she was totally convinced. And oh, how desperately frustrated I would feel at times! At times I wanted to take her by those stiff, well-tailored shoulders and *shake* her out of her statuesque immobility – sitting there, frozen, in my office in her neat, trim suits, her head still, her eyes staring, unseeing, at the window, her knees and feet pressed firmly together. And then at other times, when I experienced my deepest despair of ever getting through, I would want simply to fall to my knees before her, and nuzzle my face between her knees, until her legs parted; or gently lift her, and carry her to my couch, and lay her down, and undo her blouse and plant soft kisses on her white throat and her breasts. I did not attempt to deny these feelings to myself, though of course I never acted upon them. Perhaps, in retrospect, I should have done. Perhaps that alone might have made a difference.

Six weeks Bill Franklin permitted me to try and get through to Margaret Edgar; and I could not. I was at my wit's end. I will not attempt to hide the fact, then, that when Otto Spiegel suddenly entered the picture, in a state of high indignation, and demanded that *he* treat

Margaret Edgar – that I was not a good deal relieved. Let him, thought I, ignobly, batter his head against this brick wall. Still, there was something terribly pathetic about entrusting a poor sick woman like Margaret to that dusty stick of a creature, that dead wood Spiegel; but the decision was not mine. Bill Franklin was moderately sympathetic; he would have liked, he said, to give me a little more time with Margaret, for he believed that I might eventually break through to her; but when Otto Spiegel had learned the history, he'd been so furious that a woman who so clearly conformed to the type which he had for more than a decade been studying should have been given to *me*, that he demanded, very forcefully, that the patient be transferred to *him*.

I can well imagine the line of the man's argument. Fear of fluids. The father's sperm. All that *shit*. Quite possibly Margaret Edgar did refuse to drink at her father's table; more to the point, though, she refused to eat his moose and fish because she thought it poisoned, and she thought it poisoned because she'd deduced that her father didn't love her, and about *that* she was probably right. Now Spiegel would go poking around in her dreams and construct god knows what grotesque fantasies about her infantile sexuality, her Electra complex, the whole steamy, sticky mess of the Freudian sewer, seething, I have no doubt, with all the carefully projected nastiness and excrement of Spiegel's own mind. For in taking Margaret away from me, he was of course primarily motivated by hatred. It was an act of cloaked aggression, directed at me, and I was unable to prevent it happening. In Green Briars, Otto Spiegel wielded a good deal more power than I did. And thus, in one way, did Margaret Edgar pass out of my life; though in another way we were inextricably bound to the end.

It was late January by this point. Bill Franklin was, as

I say, mildly sympathetic when he took Margaret off my hands, but I could not fail to notice that there was a touch of coolness in his attitude toward me that had not been there in my first weeks at Green Briars. Again, it was one of those things that a psychiatrist is trained to pick up, and doubtless if I listed the myriad of tiny signs, the microscopic bits of unconscious behaviour that led me to this conclusion, you would laugh. Therefore I shall not; suffice that Bill Franklin now accorded me a good deal less of the warmly paternal support than he had once. I knew of course why this was: Otto Spiegel was turning him against me. There was one other sign, though, and about that I could not be mistaken: a number of my other patients had also been transferred, on a variety of pretexts, to other doctors. My caseload, by 1 February, was very light indeed. And this caused me much anxiety; I had not realized how deep, how pervasive, Spiegel's influence was. In other words, because of this irrational grudge of his, he was prepared systematically to undermine my work at Green Briars. It was manifest paranoia; and what was so disturbing was that Spiegel was in a position to act it all out, to make it stick. Hence the steadily lowering cloud of darkness beneath which, in those early days of February, I laboured.

It was a wet and overcast month in our part of the state, and there was a fair bit of depression about, and not only in the doctors. One observed it in the patients and nursing staff as well. Even Bill Franklin was uncharacteristically gruff in the common-room, and to others besides me. I heard him snap quite sharply at Fox one evening, and on another occasion he blew up very melodramatically at a long-time member of the nursing staff who'd left a linen closet unlocked. The patients, unable to stroll in the grounds, moped about the house with expressions of deep gloom, apart from one old madwoman named Elsie Rockefeller who lived in the attic and seemed quite paradoxically to spark up when all other spirits sank, and could be heard wildly cackling to herself day and night until it threatened to drive us all mad, and someone prescribed a hefty dose of Largactil, q.i.d., and that shut her up.

Margaret had been Spiegel's patient for only a week or so when I realized what was happening to her. I encountered her on the corridor outside my room – her own room was on the next landing, and she passed my door on her way to the back stairs – and I was shocked at what I saw. Not that the change in her was in any sense dramatic; it was not a thing that would be apparent to the untrained eye, but the whole bearing and *affect* of the woman immediately communicated a state of profound clinical depression. It was then that I realized that, in just a few days, Spiegel had brought her to the edge of a black and possibly terminal despair. That she was suicidal I had no doubt in my mind, no doubt at all; and I determined that, distasteful though it might be, I must impress this fact upon Spiegel before it was too late.

I found him in his office. Our conversation was, to say the least, acerbic. Perhaps had I tried harder to mask my intense contempt for the man I might have succeeded; but with Otto Spiegel that was impossible. His feelings for me I need not elaborate further; the antagonism was so deep, and so virulent, that I doubt he could have tolerated an exchange about the weather, let alone what he immediately took to be an unwarranted and impertinent intrusion into his professional practice. 'I suggest, Dr Wilson,' he said at one point, 'that you attend to your patients as you see fit, and allow me to attend to mine. You do', he said, and his eyes shone for an instant, 'still have patients?'

I left his office. I left before I said something I knew I should regret. It was not easy to remain in control of myself, but I did. I spent a long, unhappy hour pondering my next step. Margaret Edgar, it was clear to me, must immediately be considered a risk to herself, and assigned a nurse both day and night. Spiegel was blind to this; would Bill Franklin be equally complacent if I brought the matter to his attention? Bill Franklin did not hold me in particularly high regard at this point, a state of affairs engineered, as I've indicated, by Otto Spiegel. What then would be his reaction should I come to him and tell him that one of his senior psychiatric staff, one, moreover, who bore toward me a rabid antipathy, was treating a patient incompetently? It occurred to me that I might possibly do Margaret more harm than good – that *I* would be seen as the one poisoned by acrimony, that my professional judgment would be regarded with even more suspicion than it already was, and Spiegel's claim upon the woman further strengthened. I was caught on the horns of a cruel dilemma; I decided to wait, and in the meanwhile keep as close an eye on Margaret as I possibly could.

Another week passed, a miserably oppressive week, and still the snow did not come. With time on my hands now, I was able to maintain a periodic surveillance of Margaret; she had not, of course, been assigned a nurse, and when not in the grip of Spiegel moved freely about the house. I would wait, after breakfast, in the bathroom on the landing I shared with Fox, and when she passed I would slip out and follow her, and ensure that she reached the sitting-room, where she whiled away her mornings gazing at the rain. For some reason I feared that she would cast herself down the stairs; to prevent this I made certain she was always aware of my presence behind her before she descended. It wasn't much, but it was all I could do in the circumstances.

It was around this time that Bill Franklin sacked me. I was, you see, at Green Briars on a six-month probationary contract, the understanding being that after performing competently for this period I would be taken on full-time. But my contract would not be renewed. I was to leave Green Briars in the spring.

Oh, he was quite nice about it. He talked about the mansion of psychiatry having many rooms, and such; suggested that this type of setting was not one to which I was particularly well-suited. Perhaps the criminally insane were more my line, more appropriate to my 'talents'. I can't say I hadn't been expecting it; but when, finally, I took the bull by the horns and brought up Spiegel's name, he cut me off very sharply indeed.

'Dr Spiegel is no concern of yours,' he said, with a firmness of tone that would brook no contradiction. 'Nor will I discuss my senior staff with someone in your position.'

'Dr Franklin,' I said, 'I'm extremely concerned about Margaret Edgar.'

'Your concern for this patient', he said, 'has been noted, Dr Wilson. I am aware that you follow her about. This must cease.'

'But – '

'*This must cease*. Margaret Edgar is no longer your patient. Do I make myself clear, Dr Wilson?'

Was I to leave it at that? Throw up the sponge, walk away? For a week I did nothing; but the sight of Margaret, and the prospect of her *dying*, convinced me that all other considerations paled to insignificance beside it. I realized that if she did die, then I would bear a large measure of responsibility, that my silence would have played as crucial a role as Otto Spiegel's fumbling incompetence. I knew I had to try Bill Franklin once more, before it was too late.

But I did nothing. The days passed, and I seemed always to find another good reason not to tackle Bill Franklin. Forbidden now to keep a protective eye on Margaret, I resorted to subterfuge. I watched her from places of concealment. In this I was, I knew, taking a big risk, for such behaviour is open to a variety of interpretations. Nevertheless I watched her, through half-opened doors, from behind curtains, from the shadowed alcoves in which a house like Green Briars abounds. And I watched her depression steadily deepen. Her gait grew stiff, her face an ever-hardening mass of blank indifference, as she moved like an automaton about the corridors and stairwells of the house. And as all expression gradually drained from her, my physical response to the woman, which I never attempted to hide from myself, became quite paradoxically, and quite dramatically, intensified. This is something I cannot satisfactorily explain, and yet it was undeniable – as though the utter negation of experience permitted her beauty, which of its nature tended to a sort of cold purity, fully to realize itself. And it became impossible not to associate the idea of her death, with which I was daily confronted, with the *image* of her death, with her *in* death.

On two occasions I visited her room while she was downstairs. Like a hotel room, it gave almost no clue to the identity or inner life of its occupant. In the closet hung a long rack of expensive clothes, chosen, as one would have expected, with quiet and fastidious taste. Beneath them her shoes were lined up neatly, all pointing straight at the wall. I sat down at her dressing-table and examined the few objects she had set there – a glass swan from Tiffany's, a Fabergé egg – and it was then that I realized that the very absence of personality suggested more about Margaret Edgar than would a trunkful of bric-à-brac. It was the same negation, the same withdrawal of self into the obscure regions of the psyche, that produced such blank inscrutability in both her person and her environment. In other words, her investment, in the world, of her own being, was negligible. This alarmed me still further.

I do not fully understand what prompted me to go to Margaret's room the second time. Even to one with extensive training in its structure and functions, the unconscious mind remains to a large extent an enigmatic mechanism. Perhaps, you will say, I simply wished her to find me there, I wished to be alone with her in her bedroom; but this interpretation, so characteristic of the reductive Freudianism Spiegel espoused, is too crude, too clumsy, somehow; intuitively it is all wrong. Anyway, she did find me, she found me sitting at the dressing-table with her egg between my fingers. She stood in the doorway, her image frozen in the glass before me, her eyes upon my mirrored face, and mine upon hers. We both of us seemed unable to move, and a long, an interminable, moment passed.

'Forgive me,' I said at last.

Then, with minute, rapid movements, she began to shake her head. She moved aside, as though to let me pass through the door. I rose, turned, and took a tentative step toward her. Her hands were trembling. 'I only want to help you,' I whispered. The head-shaking grew more agitated, and she shrank against the wall; clearly she was close to hysteria, and I knew I could do no good by staying. I left, and the door immediately closed. I regained my own room, and sank, suddenly exhausted, into an armchair. My own hands were trembling violently and were still, I discovered, clutching the egg.

Margaret Edgar committed suicide five days later. She took a massive overdose of sleeping-pills, and when they discovered her it was too late to do anything. She'd found the pills in an unlocked bathroom. You would not expect, in the light of what I've told you, that this news should shock me; and yet it did, it shocked me profoundly. I will never forget my emotions of that day, nor the hideous atmosphere of discreet urgency that suddenly descended upon the house; anyone who has worked in psychiatric care will recognize that awful bustling *hush* that attends a suicide. Curiously, it was the day that I was to leave Green Briars, and the bleakest irony of what was, probably, the bleakest episode of my life, was that when I came down the front steps for the last time, a suitcase in each hand, two men in white coats were wheeling a loaded gurney across the gravel to an ambulance. It had finally begun to snow, and the melting flakes produced a spatter of dark spots on Margaret's white-sheeted body; and for a moment I was unable to go forward. Turning back toward the house I saw, standing in one of the sharp-arched windows of the senior common-room, the figure of Otto Spiegel, polishing his accursed spectacles.

And this, you might think, would be the last I saw of him, the man who in his blindness and his folly had brought about the death of a tormented and friendless young woman. There was no scandal – John Edgar would have seen to that – and for the next two years, which I spent in Europe, I heard nothing more about the case. Until last week, that is, when I attended a psychiatric convention in New Orleans.

There was a cocktail party the evening before the opening session. I'd noticed a clutch of dusty Freudians in the corner, conversing in the veiled and mutually suspicious way that Freudians do, when suddenly that familiar, lanky figure, in that familiar, threadbare suit, detached itself from the group and bore down upon me across the room. I glanced about for means of escape, but there was none. He greeted me with what, for Spiegel, passed as warmth, which immediately put me on my guard. He was wearing a red bow-tie with polka dots; and after some awkward pleasantries he turned the conversation to Margaret Edgar. 'Desperate business,' he said, his eyes upon me like a hawk's; 'tragic. You knew she was suicidal, of course.'

I nodded. He produced a sort of sigh. 'I should have listened to you,' he said.

'You should have listened to me?' I said warily.

'Oh, indeed I should. We might have avoided the whole terrible business We must both take responsibility; it won't be the first time, I'm afraid, nor the last.'

'I must take responsibility?' I said.

'Oh yes. Dr Wilson, you are young. It would surprise you, I think, if I gave you any idea of just how many of their patients doctors kill. We are not, alas' – he set down his glass, removed his spectacles, and extracted a handkerchief – 'infallible. None of us.'

'But *I* must take responsibility?' I repeated.

He paused in his polishing and glanced at me. He lifted his eyebrows. He frowned. He completed his polishing and replaced his spectacles. 'Dr Wilson,' he said, 'this is not an easy thing to say to you, especially as our relations at Green Briars were not always, ah, cordial. I understand that in the aftermath of an event of this nature, the mind tends to shy away from that which it wishes to avoid seeing. This is perfectly natural, perfectly healthy. But you and I are psychiatrists; we cannot permit ourselves the same . . . leeway . . . that we might accord the man in the street. Dr Wilson, you committed one of the most serious errors a psychiatrist can commit. You are young, as I say, and I have no doubt you will not make the same mistake again. You will make others, oh yes, you will make many others. But you must not attempt to evade your responsibility for Margaret Edgar's death.'

'*My* responsibility?'

His next words chilled me, chilled me to the bone, so vividly did they demonstrate the devious lengths to which the man's paranoia – clearly, now, grown to monstrous and florid proportions – had driven him; and I am still unable to grasp their full implications. 'But good God, man,' he squeaked, 'they were your Nembutal!'

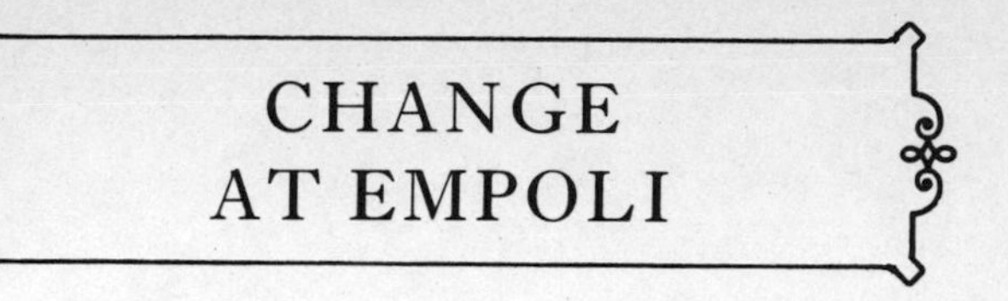

Laura Kalpakian

I

You have no passion, only lust. No spirit, only appetite. Why have you come to Italy as students of art? You do not give a damn for art. Or, perhaps I should point to what one of you has so generously deposited on the hall floor of these offices, point to that and say, That is what you give for art, for Italy, for love, for life. That. You are welcome to that. But I am leaving.

Oh yes, that's what she should have said. Dignified but its underlying tone unmistakable. She pulled her hat down a bit tighter and pressed her coat against her throat with a kind of dramatic savour, as though these words had actually traversed her lips in front of their intended audience. She was a woman best described as handsome: a face dominated by a firm jaw and wide green eyes, pale skin and dark hair. She checked her own wrist-watch against that of the man across from her. He was deeply ensconced behind a newspaper but his watch testified silently with hers – 9.34. The 9.20 should have left fourteen minutes ago. She pushed the train window down and scanned the platform, fearfully scouting for Giorgio. Perhaps Giorgio had called and told them to hold the 9.20 till he could get there. Silly. People like Giorgio could not command trains. Giorgio could not command his own cat, unless he could flatter and court and smarm. That's the way Giorgio dealt with everyone, except his wife, whom he bullied. Disgusting. None the less, Corinne chided herself for having phoned him from the station. She should have waited, called from Empoli.

She would not feel safe until the train pulled out and she kept a careful watch on the platform, prepared to vanish into the women's toilet if she saw Giorgio Carruthers running towards the 9.20, coat flying, terrified at the thought that he was about to cease being her assistant and now would become Director of the university's Institute for Italian Art. Giorgio would be sweating like a pig, would implore her, beg her not to leave the Institute and the filthy students. He would say they were young and thought it a mere harmless prank. Corinne would fix her green-eyed gaze on him, curl her lip in utter contempt and ask: They are adults are they not? Adult American students in a university programme, guests in a foreign country? Giorgio would sputter here and she would continue mercilessly: I am – I was – Director, administrator of an Institute for Italian Art, not the crossing-guard at an elementary school, to shepherd, protect and hold innocent hands. These students are drunken, disrespectful, irresponsible oafs. When I was their age, Giorgio, I had an infant daughter and a husband and I was in graduate school, if you get my drift, Giorgio.

And, realizing he could not cajole her, Giorgio would next threaten, The university will sack you on sight. Your reputation as an administrator will be smashed. A woman as old as you will not be able to find another job.

Giorgio, you are young enough to be my son, though I thank God many times over, I am not your mother. Nevertheless, I am going to offer you this bit of wisdom. It is not my own. I got it from Max who is very wise indeed in these matters. You would do well to heed Max, Giorgio, though I know you haven't enough inner dignity to understand. *There are moments in life when all that is left to you is gesture.* You perform that gesture because without it, you are merely stranded and pathetic. The gesture is all that stands between you and pathos. Do you understand? Of course not. Ah well, *your* response to the students' thoughtful offering is your own affair. I know why you and the other two instructors suck up (no other phrase is possible, Giorgio) to the students. Their presence here allows you to live in this beautiful, medieval Tuscan town. It is, as they say, a very good gig. So if you wish to chuckle and excuse this calculated heap of dung on the floor as a youthful, harmless prank, Giorgio, do so. But I shall not. I shall never. Never.

Her speech had gathered conviction and velocity as the train gathered conviction and velocity and by 10.05, it had rounded a curve that left the city itself behind. But at the time, the moment – yesterday morning – when this speech was best delivered, Corinne had been without words. Words – English or Italian – failed her altogether as she sat in her office (door closed against the offending substance in front of it) and listened to Giorgio and the other two instructors in a classroom down the hall splutter and demand of the students, *Who did this?* Listened to the students giggle and rustle in response. Corinne knew who did it, knew with a kind of absolute imaginative certainty that Adam Black, vulgar, shiftless, shallow Adam Black, had squatted there, defecated, while the rest of them, say a dozen or so of the twenty students, watched, laughed. The picture, unthinkable as it was, did not defy the imagination. That's what was really appalling.

From her office she heard Giorgio's fruitless and finally ridiculous harangue, heard him dismiss the students for the rest of the day with vague and (as they well knew) empty threats. She kept her eyes on the voluptuous Annunication angel painted by a less-than-masterful seventeenth-century hand in the arch of her ceiling and heard the students' footsteps, their giggling, casual obscenities, their overt contempt. *The old witch.* They did not even do her the honour of *bitch*, which at least implies malice aforethought. Witch. Hag. Sexless crone. *Strega nonna* in Italian, but they did not have enough Italian to know this. Their American voices echoed down the thick corridors of the building, the broad stairwell that led to medieval streets. She brought her eyes from the ceiling and rested them on the shelves where her personal collection of slides, Renaissance and medieval art, were neatly catalogued and housed. Shelf after shelf. The students' loutish guffaws melted into the noises and cries from the street below. Corinne rose, picked up the name-plate from her desk: *Corinne Mackenzie, Director*, and dropped it fastidiously in the bin. That, by way of notice.

She had never taken off her coat or gloves and in leaving the office (as she had in entering) she walked over, around, beyond the excremental token at her door, moving on conspiratorial tiptoes, quickly, down the broad staircase. At the huge heavy door, she let her breath escape, then opened the brass bolt, stepped, swept into the currents of the narrow medieval street, thick with shadow at its base, alight with autumn sunshine at the housetops.

Despite the mid-morning cold, people stood about smoking, talking, gesticulating broadly. Old men engaged in heated political quarrels, while women chatted on their way to market. Messengers on motor scooters plied the streets like small noisy skiffs, cutting through a sea of people, mothers pulling hapless children in their wake and workmen brushing masonry dust from their shoulders as they all moved about in the shadow of the Italian national bird: the restoration crane. Overhead clothes-line pulleys squealed and ancient shutters creaked open in the morning air. Cathedral bells tolled, making their august presence felt in the very stones as Corinne hurried to the sunny square. The chestnut vendor there who knew her for a good customer was surprised, even offended when she pushed right by, running for the Number 10 bus chugging at the stop.

It was market-day and well-dressed women laden with parcels, flowers and gossip pushed and shoved to get on the bus. In front of Corinne an aged woman, stooped into a crescent, hoisted herself up the steps. A young man rose to give her a seat near the door. He pushed toward the back with Corinne right behind him. In the lilt and legato, the staccato of Italian all around her, she feared she yet heard thc students, their flat American voices, their coarse contempt, their menacing laughter. She clung to the pole and rocked with the bus, closed her eyes tight and, like a quilt for comfort, a fable to hide under, she told herself ovcr and over Max's story of his family's forced flight from Germany in the 'Thirties.

Not surprisingly, Max came from a mixed marriage: his mother, a Christian, a painter and a cellist; his father a noted historian axed from the university because he was a Jew. They became prisoners in their own country and so, when Max was six, elected instead to become refugees. They bundled up and fled one night in a carefully planned exodus, first to England for fourteen months and then to America. Little Max had clutched an armful of toys to take with him but his father took them away. Little Max cried and his father stroked his cheek and said sadly, *This, your skin, your flesh – this is what you get to take with you. It is all you get to take.*

Do not cry. You are lucky to escape with your skin. None the less, in a gesture of covert rebellion (entirely consistent with Max's adult character), he managed to secrete a single toy beneath his many jackets and when his father found out, he was angry. Max's family's flight, now more than fifty years ago, somehow put her own in comforting historical perspective. Corinne too was a sort of refugee, fleeing obscenity, vulgarity, stupidity and undeserved contempt. She had built this programme, worked day after day, contributed. The same could not be said of the students. And now, they forced her to this cut-throat gesture. But it was all that was left and she would carry it off. Like Max would have. Fitting, that Max should somehow aid her when he was not here to help.

Ordinarily, Corinne Mackenzie was not a woman who did things in haste. She preferred always the slow and voluptuous enjoyment of endeavour. She cared nothing for efficiency, and yet, when she reached the sunny, spacious flat she'd lived in for two years, she tore off her coat and gloves and with frantic, unseemly haste, flew, pulling clothes from the closets, cosmetics from the bathroom shelves. She moved swiftly through the flat, bedroom, bathroom, study, sitting-room with its balcony where potted flowers were already crunchy from the autumn frosts. She flung things into two open-mawed suitcases and when they would not zip shut, she flung things out. She took the phone off the hook and refused to answer the bell when it rang from the street. Giorgio. Of course. That afternoon (before she took sleeping-pills at five) she had successfully ransacked her own flat, at the last jamming her books into shopping-bags and hauling them downstairs to the greengrocer, the ever-obliging, aging, courtly Signor Vitti. She gave him (to his open-mouthed amazement) 150,000 lire and asked him to surface-freight the books and keep the change.

The following morning she phoned Giorgio from the station where she awaited the 9.20 to Empoli. She told him she was about to board, to change at Empoli and go to the Pisa airport. He said she was making a mistake, a silly gesture. It was only a harmless student prank, he said. All in the past. He begged her to reconsider. He said it had been cleaned up.

To be capable of gesture is to be assured that one's imagination is alive and well. For a woman of Corinne's age, it testified as well to vitality of the spirit. Of course she did not look her age. Good health, good habits, good genes and discreet applications of the dye bottle worked in unison to create the artistic impression of a woman on the graceful side of fifty. She felt no compunction about the dye bottle. By profession, temperament and training, Corinne Mackenzie was dedicated to art and so, naturally, though she was an American, she was more at home in Italy than anywhere in the world. Italy shared her values: honour artifice – presentation is everything. Honouring artifice, Corinne's personal presentation was such that you would never have believed her to be the mother of a woman as old as Allegra. Indeed, mother and daughter might have been transposed in the sense that women Corinne's age were supposed to be shrewd, practical, cautionary unto calculating, and utterly without imagination. Such a description better suited Allegra who, despite all Corinne's efforts (beginning with the flamboyant name, ballet lessons, piano lessons and travel in Italy before she reached pubescence), had grown up to be a tremendous disappointment. Married, middle-class, matronly.

Mention art to Allegra and she thinks it's a new caddy at the country club. Disgusting. Allegra, her hideous husband and her ineffectual father always playing revolting bridge. Always looking for a fourth. Well, wait till the boy grew up. The boy was the image of his insurance-mongering father. No doubt he'd play bridge with them. Rubbers.

'Mi scusi, Signora, ma non parlo Inglese.'

The man across from her emerged from behind his newspaper and she realized she'd actually been talking aloud. To him. She laughed. *Non importante*, she said, *niente*.

He was well dressed, well fed and exuded a sturdy sort of well-being, so attractive in a man. His hair was dark, heavily salted with grey and she reckoned him to be on the graceful side of fifty. No matter that he did not speak English, Corinne spoke beautiful Italian and of course he said so. People always said so. From Poggibonsi on, Corinne and her fellow passenger enjoyed a languorous conversation, sitting in the shuttering squares of thin sunlight as the train plunged into the countryside where rags of November tattered the trees. On the hillsides the leafless vineyards lined up, row after row of them, their skinny arms twisted round wire and one another, synchronized as anorexic chorus girls. Corinne and the man leaned forward with intensity and relaxed against their seats, speaking as though they had time and time and time in front of them, none of it bounded by the railway's timetable. She found herself forgetting all about Allegra and Giorgio and the filthy students and basking in this man's attentions. There are some things only a man can do for you.

He was an engineer, returning home after business in Roma. He gave her his card: *Dottore Ing. Paolo Branchi*. Naturally she was impressed. She would have given him her card but she was no longer Director of the Institute for Italian Art. She could not say that she was leaving because of a pile of dung, so she said simply she was an artist, a devotee of Renaissance angels and after two years in Italy, on her way to the Pisa airport to return to America.

Paolo leaned forward. He was clean-shaven except for a manicured goatee framing his voluptuous lips. He smelled of something discreet, yet tangy. His eyes were rich with experience and he had the air of a man who rose from contented beds. He wore a wedding-ring. He said, as an artist, Corinne should never leave Italy. As a woman, he added, she should never leave Tuscany. His voice was low, ripe with respect and innuendo, as though he, Paolo, recognized that Corinne and Italy deserved, were worthy of one another. Then he said he must get off here. The very next stop. The one before Empoli.

He alighted from the carriage, carrying his briefcase and an overnight bag. She watched from the window as the November wind snatched at his coat. Pausing at the station door, he turned and waved and for a single moment – until the train pulled sluggishly forward – she thought he might just

Sad. He might have been an amusing companion, someone to have a coffee with at the bar of the Empoli station while she waited to change trains. She might have had more than a coffee with him. After all, she had no plans. No tickets as yet. No one waiting for her at some foreordained destination. She might have had many things with him. Her sorrow at leaving him deepened into a sorrow at losing him, more intense than if he had been her lover. As lovers they would have had a past to cherish mutually, something like the toy Max secreted under his many coats, to hold that past against all future change and incident. But as it was, they exchanged a wave and bid goodbye as well to all the artful might-have-beens, to possibility spun of tissue so fine, so fragile she could almost hear it shred and tear, catch on the metacarpal branches as the train hurtled over the autumnal landscape. Earth and sky neutralized each other, as though hammered out by some ancient, expert hand into that singular colour you could only think of as Tuscan blond, the very gold of those fat, pale persimmons still clinging to the blue–black trees.

Corinne Mackenzie made it a point of honour never to complain about the trains running late. To do so would have displayed a foreigner's too-tidy sense of values and played (historically speaking) into Mussolini's arms. Of course, it was no accident that the great Italian railway stations had all been built in the Fascist era and why – given that era's values – they all had the ring, the flavour of vast movie-stages, sets decorated in the manner of the Kordas, where anything from battles to bedrooms might have been successfully choreographed, as long as they were false, immense and costly.

The railway station at Empoli, on the other hand, had been entirely overlooked. It still retained its sleepy, intimate, well-tended air. The date on the ornate iron grillwork was 1890. The platforms were flagstone rather than concrete. Under rounded, eye-pleasing arches of peach-coloured stucco, planters full of geraniums pinched in the November cold. Doors leading to the bar, porters' offices and the station itself were neat panes of glass framed in green paint. Corinne pushed the station door open and once inside her heels tapped on a floor of polished marble, an odd, velvety maroon colour. So well maintained was the Empoli station, you might have thought it a myth – and given that it predated Mussolini, perhaps it was.

Yes, the man at the ticket window said, because her train had been late into Empoli, there would be a lengthy wait for the train to Pisa. Two hours. At least.

Corinne gave her two bags to a tiny muscle-bound porter (with a tip; she knew what language was really spoken here) and said she would collect them in time for the Pisa train. The prospect of the wait was not so bad. She had no plans. No ticket as yet. No destination firmly in mind and no one waiting there. She might get to the Pisa airport and say simply, give me a ticket on the first plane to Paris. To London. To Milano. Hang the expense. Isn't that what credit cards are for?

'Signora?' The station *capo* addressed her as though she had been speaking to him. Perhaps she had. He was a burly man of forty or so with that Italian air of lewd gallantry. Italian men left you no choice: if you responded to the gallantry, you also, automatically, responded to the lewdness as well. With characteristic panache, Corinne informed him it was *non importante*, absolutely *niente* and left him nurturing an air of bewilderment unbecoming on a man.

Suddenly famished, she went into the station bar where she ordered a *pannino* and a *dolce*. Make that two. Of each. *Caffe latte*. In the warm, bright bar she loosened her scarf and coat and bolted her coffee in the Italian fashion. Ordered another. She noticed for the first time the bar had two sets of doors. One led to the platform. One led to the street, the town of Empoli. In all the many times she had changed trains at this station, in the twenty-five years she had been coming to Italy, Corinne had never stepped outside those other doors. She wondered fleetingly what the town of Empoli was like. She moved to the doors, peering through the green framed panes of glass. She did not open them, knowing somehow, that would have been an irrevocable step.

Corinne returned to her coffee and watched the reflections of four other people in the mirror behind the bar. The mirror gleamed with colourful bottles of every stripe and hue set on high shelves of thick greenish glass. The young bartender, ruddy, expressive, convivial, washed glassware and carried on a spirited conversation with a woman and an older man. They all seemed to know one another. Under discussion was the woman's worthless son who was breaking his mother's heart. Talk about broken hearts! What about your own daughter? Your only child who spurns all art, all understanding, emotion and possibility and marries a man who plays bridge and sells life insurance. What could be worse? Grubbing money off people's fears. A vile, low profession, insurance – of course, everyone has to have insurance. I have it through the university, or at least I do for the moment. Did. But can you imagine living, *sleeping* with a man who gets people to spend money not on what they can taste or hold or relish or remember, but against the possibility, the *certainty* of death? Death insurance. To barter in *morte*, yes? He's no better than Allegra deserves, really. Not a single ambition, that girl, not beyond tennis and shopping and golf and that insufferable bridge. Just like her father.

Allegra's father had no other name. That was all he was, Allegra's father. In some ways, all he had ever been. How could Corinne have married such a man? Trying to explain was like confessing to a youthful, inexplicable passion for rutabagas. He best resembled a rutabaga. In retrospect anyway. At the time she could only ascribe the marriage to a blinding assault of hormones. She recognized the fatal mistake quickly but there was, equally quickly, Allegra and no way out.

Instead Corinne poured her considerable energies into graduate school, fell in love (though not into bed) with Max. Allegra's father knew this, but the marriage still endured, a puddle of marital inertia. Max, of course, gave her the ticket out with the museum job, because Allegra's father did not want to move to the city. Corinne did. But even with divorce she could not get rid of the man. He pined mercilessly for Allegra. Called her all the time, finally moved to the city to be near his daughter. Visitation every other weekend. And then, *Would you mind, Corinne?* Every weekend. *No, of course not. If that's what Allegra wants.* Corinne was free on the weekends, free to work if need be, to be Max's accomplice, to exult in emotionally extravagant love affairs. Exulting and then – just as surely – despairing. (But you could do that in those days, you see. People did. Fell in and out of love and bed. It was only a question of stamina and imagination then. Not having to ask grim questions or take blood tests. The very term 'safe sex' would have sounded ludicrous. Ludicrous, I tell you! Like something missionaries would do once a month whether they needed it or not. A woman would no more think of carrying a condom in her purse than a man would carry a tampon in his pocket!)

Still, every Sunday evening there would be a bitter metallic taste when Allegra returned holding father's hand. Corinne envied their love, then – more poignantly – resented their camaraderie as Allegra became a young woman: the female version of her father. It was as though, together, father and daughter had played a trick on Corinne, used her body to incubate and, that done, dispensed with her, regarded her thereafter with perpetually innocent perplexity. They seemed to watch Corinne from a great distance, neutrally, expressing neither admiration nor condemnation for her passion, her courage, her imagination. (And Max believed you must have all three, or none at all.) Allegra and her father preferred the neat four-square confines of the tennis court and the bridge-table. Later, after Allegra married, her husband joined them. And no doubt, so would Allegra's son. They tolerated Corinne on family occasions. And, since that's all it was, toleration, they scarcely noticed one Thanksgiving when she (purposely) had too much to drink and said, loudly and for the benefit of the other guests (all card players, naturally), how much she despised bridge, hated it, announced that the shuffle of the cards reminded her always of flatulence. They went right on shuffling shuffling shuffling

'Signora? Signora, Allegra?'

She explained to the bartender that Allegra was her daughter and she was about to turn to the woman whose son had broken her heart, but the woman was gone.

A man came in. A workman, judging from his cap and paint-flecked clothes. He ordered a drink and from one of the high shelves lining the mirror, the bartender took down a bottle of thick metallic-looking liquor, maroon as the marble floor. The man took the drink down in one gulp. Winced, hard. Shivered. Tipped his cap. Smiled and left.

It was not a drink Corinne knew. She had seen the label of course. One does not come to Italy time and time again over the years and – well, of course she'd seen the label. Her eyes swept over the bottles sparkling invitationally in the warm light and the high mirror. Fifty or sixty of them. Maybe more. She could remember having tasted maybe a dozen. Maybe two. The other thirty-odd she had never tasted and there wasn't time now. Not before the train came. There might never be time. The gleaming Unknown inside the bottles seemed to wink and tease her in the light, glisten with the same imputation of lost possibility, like Paolo's sad wave.

The young bartender put a glass of mineral water in front of her while he made exaggerated drinking motions. He picked up a paper napkin and thrust it at her. He wiped his own eyes with it in broad gestures and then handed her a clean one. He put it in her hand. She watched him – as though at a great distance – pinking with exertion and the steam from the dish-water and his arms up high indicating *drink, drink* and she felt suddenly flushed and weakened, terrified at what she'd done. At what she'd done and left undone. The flat unlocked. The hot water heater still on. Forgotten something essential like the laundry still flapping on the balcony lines. Something urgent and important that she was powerless to change or effect. She patted her face with the paper napkin and drank the water, thanked the bartender, but declined his insistent motions that she should sit. She would feel better outside.

Once on the platform she buttoned up her coat and paced in long, quick strides, unsuccessfully willing away thoughts of the unlocked flat and laundry on the balcony lines. Unthinkable that Giorgio Carruthers should find her stockings and slips and panties flapping on the balcony in a sort of brazen, come-hither way. But she certainly couldn't go back and collect them, to turn off the hot water heater. She'd left that on too. Too? Was there something else? The wind rattled and shook her, like an angry parent to get her to confess, like Max's father had shaken him when he found out Max hid the toy in spite of his father's warnings that he was lucky to have escaped with his skin.

Shivering, she pulled leather gloves from her pocket and put them on her fine, long fingers. Artist's fingers.

That's what Max always said. He would turn her hand over in his and say she had artist's fingers and hands. An artist's mind and eye and imagination. And then he would laugh in that peculiar, jagged way and add that for all that, she had a model's body. She rather took offence at this. If he had slept with her, she could have absorbed it as a compliment, but since he never had, the observation smacked of the clinical and faintly obscene. Though you couldn't really take offence. Not with Max. So funny and urbane. The most civilized man in America. Difficult. Of course. But civilized. And like any civilized person, very few things were good enough for Max. Over the years even this paltry number had dwindled until talking with Max was like clinging to a slippery rock in a sea of mediocrity, holding on so that one should not be swept into that vast ocean of what was tacky and vulgar and beneath contempt, as though these things were constantly nibbling at your ankles and if you once slipped, or lost your vigilance, they could suck you in. You could drown in a sea of mediocrity. Max could wear you out.

She had met him in graduate school. She was still married to Allegra's father but the real love of her life she had just discovered: Renaissance angels, so muscular, handsome and ineffably gentle. How then to account for her falling in love with Max who was such an insufferable snob, even then, but so powerful a personality, so blond and beautiful and fastidious and funny and arch? Such a delight. He was two years her senior and after he graduated, the months passed in a grey Max-less fog, framed in the faces of the Renaissance angels and punctuated by his frothy acerbic letters and long-distance telephone calls. So consummate were Max's political skills – even then – that when she graduated, he ushered her right into the enviable position in the European Art Department of the prestigious museum where he worked. She left her husband. Fine. Grand. Wonderful. Corinne was convinced that once relieved of her ineffectual husband, Max would surely

But he didn't. True, he squired her about everywhere and on the arm of the most civilized man in America, Corinne found herself dining in celebrated company: artists, musicians, scholars, curators, actors, authors. She became, in effect, Max's accomplice and went everywhere with him. She remained his accomplice while she fell in love with other men who, one by one, dropped from her life with great crashes, like shingles falling from a steep roof. She remained Max's accomplice even when she fell in love with Dennis, besotted by Dennis, about to die of cirrhosis of the heart for Dennis. And even when she married Dennis (probably the happiest day of her entire life), she could not quite vow off Max. She tried. He always wooed her back. The snob. Flattery. He said (and it was true) Corinne was the only person in the world not frightened of him. Offended, yes. (Wasn't everyone?) But always ready with the quick retort and never frightened. Corinne instinctively knew how to fence, (verbally) thrust and parry, kick and duck. She got occasionally hurt but never really wounded. Not until that night. That night Max seemed to slip, to lose his balance, to tumble, snatch and claw at everything and everyone in his path. Even Corinne. Especially Corinne.

It was the usual gathering of educated, civilized people who of course agreed with Max that America was a grubby place where nothing worked right, commercial, shallow and vulgar. England – England was even worse. Max confessed to having lived in England and to being an Anglophile. (And their hostess, the wife of a well-known artist said she was, too. Always had been an Anglophile because England was so) Not any more, Max went on. He vowed he would never go back to England. The strikes. The breakdowns. The general despair of society and had you ever seen anything more jingoistic and preposterous than that Falklands (so-called) War? What a lot of posturing! Nothing worked in England, the place had gone to pot and now the English were stuck with their narrow, tawdry little country where nothing worked and everything was inefficient. Europeans in general but the English in particular were living off their past – Max continued, having got up a great sail of hyperbole and invention fuelled by twenty-five years of his own uncontested flashing wit – they served up their past like a huge dead bird without having taken the trouble to fully pluck or bleed it, or cook it either for that matter, just putting it, neck wrung and dead eyes staring, on a silver platter, the pale, feathered carcass still sort of oozing

This vivid unfortunate metaphor over dinner made everyone blanch. Dennis looked positively ill. The mouth of their hostess twitched as she tried to daunt the conversation over to gardens or something, but it was no good (Corinne could have told them this, all of them) trying to stop Max once he'd got going, not when he was so funny, even if he was angry, even brutal, that little golden gleam of malice twinkling on the rice paper of Max's brittle wit. Oh, maybe he sometimes went too far. That night, of course, he did and Corinne, vaguely desperate, exerted herself on behalf of the others, interrupted (she was the only one who could) his soliloquy on the great, dead, feathered bird of the past and said, *Ah yes, well with all this decay everywhere else, at least we have Italy, yes? Tuscany. At least we have that.* Closing her eyes and under the spell of the wine and the candlelight she willed herself away from the dreary-yet-another-dinner-party to the golden poplars, dusky cypresses, the yellow light of the Arno.

Max's jagged laughter sliced, ripped right up the middle of that illusion and that's what he said it was: a stupid illusion because you had only to go to Italy nowadays to know the Italians did not deserve their beautiful country, which was going to hell anyway. The Italians did not offer up their past. No. They sold it. They would sell the Sistine Chapel if the price were right. Slavering after tourist dollars, the Italians all posed and simpered and all that nasty greed made it plain that from the Medici, Michelangelo and Leonardo right on down, they were all either peasants or pickpockets. They would kneel at the feet of the Virgin while they picked your pocket in the church.

Corinne's face stung. As though Max had slapped her cheek. Hard.

My roses have the blight this year, their hostess said. At our home in the country, the roses have withered before

Corinne rubbed her cheek, feeling for welts. As Max must have; because she knew, swiftly, absolutely and correctly that Max had lied about his father. His father had not stroked his cheek. His father had slapped him, hard across the face, sent him spinning. His father had flung down the toys, smashed them: *You can take nothing with you. You are lucky to escape with your skin*.

None of them escaped. They're very old rose bushes and I'd hoped it was just the

Corinne peered across the candlelight. Amazing. Max had grown old. You could see it in his still-handsome face. Some crucial change. Max had rounded a curve in time, after which the world lost savour. Beyond that pivotal moment, all change was – and henceforth ever would be – for the worse. Nothing would be the same or as good as it once was. Not men or women or food or sex or wine or music, not books or movies or countries. Nothing. Max had been somehow shipwrecked in the present: sputtering, angry (look at him), beached with his civilized wit while the future sailed off without him and the past vanished golden in the haze. *Max is going to die*.

She and Dennis left almost immediately. Once home, Corinne went into the bathroom, turned on the harsh light and regarded herself in the mirror. Had she too grown old without knowing it? In spite of good sense, good health, good habits and the dye bottle? Had she too

Corinne made love with Dennis that night: rich, slow, voluptuous love, the way Corinne liked to make love, like whales make love, she always thought, like whales' warm-blooded bodies heat up the ocean around them, like whales savour the succulent present.

And then everything happened so fast. After that night, within, say, a month and a half of that night, Dennis left. Gone before she could utter a wordless *what?* Out of her life after a brief chat in front of the fireplace (*what? what?*), followed by the click of the closing door. Dennis's key on the kitchen table and a letter from his lawyer. Odd, clunky, Latinate phrases which, when you finally translated them emotionally, meant that Dennis had got rid of the old wife so as to marry a new one.

And where was Max when she needed him? When she needed his cutting ability to say nasty things about Dennis and how Dennis had never deserved her in the first place? Oh, Max had quit. Within a month or so of that night, Max had quit, without even so much as a nod of farewell. Quit. Not simply the museum but the country! Gone to Europe for an indeterminate ever. Switzerland or Sweden or Scandinavia. Some cold place. *Why* couldn't she remember where Max had gone? Impossible! Anyway, she had it in her address book. If she'd brought it. Maybe she had left it in the centre desk drawer in the flat. Even so, she should have it engraved on her heart and mind where Max went. He had been her friend for twenty-five years. More. (But let us gently round it off there.) Friends, colleagues, accomplices, though never – no they had never

Anyway, she'd long since quit lusting after Max. A little abashed, however, to say how long she had lusted, hungered for him without ever guessing, well guessing, maybe. Yes, guessing. But not *knowing*. And not wanting to know. And anyway, in those days, things were different. You couldn't pop into court because you'd lost your job, haul them up and say you'd been discriminated against (whimper, sniff) because of who you went to bed with. In those days it was different. Well, some things were different. Some things stayed the same, like the way Max could persistently fire her imagination. The sly smile. The half-hooded eyes. The air of intimacy Max spun, as though he pulled thread from his body, like a spider, bound her imagination somehow with that silken, gorgeous cord. *Oh Max, Max!* He drove all night to be at her dissertation defence. 'Renaissance Angels.' And though the huge room was filled with friends and students and colleagues (to say nothing of Allegra's father and the hulking, heavily judgmental faculty), once Max was in the audience, Corinne was speaking to and for and with Max alone. As though they were in bed together and she wanted his approval. And she got it. There are some things only a man can do for you.

He got her the job, didn't he? Those early months at the museum were filled with richness, lustre, wonder. Oh, there was the job itself, the city, its pace and excitement, and of course the pride in going about with Max, in being Max's accomplice. Then too, she'd got rid of Allegra's father and fallen in love with Barry, wonderful, slow, voluptuous love with Barry. Of course it didn't last. The shingles all fell, crashed down from the roof and she was crazy with grief because there are some things only a man can do for you. To you.

Never mind, said Max. Barry never deserved you anyway. Come to Sunday brunch, Corinne.

That Sunday brunch with the snow flurrying thickly at the white window, where all this emerged, for sure, for knowing and never again simply guessing, even if you did not want to know, never guessing how, (oh remember in those days if you were found out, you could be ruined; it was the kind of thing people tolerated only if they did not know and only guessed) how, if it emerged at all, it should be like some tropical flower. Like an anthurium, she thought. Not at the time. At the time she had thought no such poetic thing but later she thought of it – snow and all – like an emerging anthurium, with its hard little yellow tongue wagging out, *I fooled you, I fooled you, I fooled you* (not that it made a damn bit of difference, so passionate and powerful was her attachment to him, was his personality, not one damn bit of difference) that snowy Sunday. She had not brought anthuriums. Hothouse freesias. Common freesias. Yellow.

And rather confused, she stupidly offered them to Max's friend – oh bloody say it – his lover. She held out her hand with the yellow freesias to Max's having just-risen – like slow, warm-blooded, just-risen whales – lover, not beautiful though, youngish but already balding, with a pronounced overbite and a mole on his head that his receding hair uncovered. He had answered the door.

From the kitchen Max called out gaily and asked if she would like a hit of brandy in her coffee. Against the cold. Of course she would like it. Against the cold. Sugar? called Max.

Yes. Sugar, she said to Woody. Did you say your name was Woody?

Yes, Woody. I take my coffee black, said Woody who could not have looked less Woody-like if he had been a woodpecker. So to speak.

A thing like that – Corinne went on stupidly – sugar in your coffee, does not change overnight.

After this initial blundering, bovine beginning, however she carried it off. With panache, actually. (Panache and daring were Max's two favourite words. Anything without panache and daring could only be dismal.) Actually, she was relieved. Even rather buoyed. Because it meant that Max had not spurned her, Corinne Mackenzie, in particular. But women in general. She could not take offence or have her feelings hurt at that. It was not personal. Quite the contrary. Her friendship with Max testified to ... to ... to whatever it was friendship testified to when you did not go to bed together. Women were not Max's cup of tea. It made sense that he had dated as long as it was politically incumbent on him to do so, but he had not bedded these women because they were not his cup of tea. He might even have phrased it exactly thus. Did. His wrist flicked and the starched cuff peeked out and the cufflink gleamed. He was, even then, the most civilized man in America.

But Max didn't live in America any longer because it was crass and commercial and shallow and nothing worked and England was impossible because nothing worked there either and they picked your pocket in Italy. All Europe was living on its glorious past, nothing else. Europe laid out its past like a giant, still-feathered carcass for the Americans (and now, of course, the Japanese) to prey on, peck its dead, unseeing eyes and

She sat down on one of the wooden platform benches, breathless, after her incessant pacing and looked up the empty tracks and wires leading away from Empoli toward Pisa. And the airport. Escape. She rubbed her throbbing temples, took off her hat and shook her dark hair, undid the top button on her coat. There. That was better. The easier to breathe. Inhale. Exhale. Inhale. Yes. And of course it was silly to – Exhale – get worked up about it because she would simply look Max up in the address book. She would not have left something that important behind in the centre desk drawer. She would call Max before she flew out of Pisa because he was someplace in Europe. Some cold place. He had moved someplace where things presumably did work. Switzerland or Scandinavia. Or some cold place that had an air of efficiency. Rather like a hospital.

II

As in a slow and noisy, random dance, the passengers for the train to Firenze gathered on the platform, their advent and recession predictable as the tide, as easily known by the timetable posted low, eye-level on the wall outside. And one inside, high above the ticket booth. High and low. Ebb and flow. The Firenze train blasted in and passengers got swept on and dusted off (because the Empoli station was nothing if not well maintained). These passengers ebbed from the platform after the train left, into the station, the bar, or simply, like the porters, leaning against the peach-coloured arches, smoking, waiting, like actors whose cues are a long way off.

She was chilled clear through and realized she must have been outside for a very long time. The thought of coffee appealed to her but not the cosy, crowded bar with its bottles filled with experience she would never taste and the door that led to the town of Empoli. She stood and walked to the waiting-room. It had only one door. To and from the platform.

The waiting-room was broad, high and drafty, lined on three sides with polished benches and a single inadequate heater. The marble floor was so clean you could see your reflection and though the walls were bare, they were not painted institutional green but a sort of pale vanilla colour with fluted plaster piping at the ceiling. Whimsical. A single slab of sunlight cut into panes fell from the door and Corinne unbuttoned her coat and sat within its picketed confines, amongst, oh, possibly a dozen other people scattered along the walls. No good-looking men, though. With or without newspapers.

A cleaning-woman hunkered in a corner with her broom and barrel, daring anyone (with her eyes) to dirty her floor. One young man (a German judging from the stickers on his backpack) did, tossed a used ticket down. She swooped on him, crying out for all the world to hear that this young man had come from a family of pigs. Look at him! No respect! Young people today were thoughtless and thankless. The cleaning-woman turned to three old huddled grandmas, two with the single-seam mouth of the toothless. They solemnly corroborated her assessment of young people in general, this German in particular. He stalked out of the waiting-room. Amongst themselves the three old dragons and the cleaning-lady agreed it was good riddance to bad rubbish. They exchanged heated views on the general uselessness of the young, how in their day

Oh yes. Corinne could have told them a thing or two. How truly vile young people can be. All they want is sex and money but no responsibilities. And thankless? Thankless! Here we are, offering them a programme that allows them to study art in Italy. A sacred opportunity! Truly! What do they do? They defecate on it. No, it's true. I swear. One of them actually crouched, squatted in the hall, oozed *merda*. And his peers – no better. The girls laughed. Crass. In my day, things were different. I do not say we were angels, but we revered art and life and love. These kids – but it is a mistake to call them kids. They are not cute and little. They are adults. They are a menace. Listen, in America you get three of them on the bus and people get off. It's true. On the subway, you clutch your bag and keep your eyes on the ads. You step aside at this offensive arrogance. They thought it was funny, that – that pile, the *merda*. Could I continue to deal with such dogs? Dogs might defecate on the floor, yes, but they would not laugh. And now, I shall return to the university and they will fire me and it will be very hard to get another job at my age – I left the museum to take this one and they won't hire me back because they'll know I broke my contract, just walked out on my responsibilities. Well, that is not one of my responsibilities. I'll point to the contract and ask: Where does it say a thing about *merda*? Where?

The centre desk drawer. I left it there along with the address book and Giorgio Carruthers will paw through that too. (Giorgio is as American as they come, even if his mother couldn't speak a word of English. Giorgio is insufferable.) But he will paw through the desk and my underwear. I can't do anything about it now. I took what I could. I was lucky to escape with my skin.

She rubbed her cheek thoughtfully. Sadly. As Max had said his father touched his. And after more than fifty years, what could it possibly matter if Max lied, if his father had slapped him? After half a century, *acqua passata, non macina piu, si?* She smiled at the three old black-clad women staring at her with piercing eyes, the absolutely unabashed gaze of dragons. No one to fear. No one to answer to. These women reigned supreme over as much of the world as they cared about. Corinne bit her lip. 'I've been thinking aloud, I guess. Well, you can imagine the shock of it. To come in and find – terrible. Terrible what these young people will do.'

The cleaning-woman returned to her barrel and the old dragons hunkered down amongst themselves and words blew up from their enclave like smoke, like three crones huddled, hunched over a boiling pasta pot. *Strega Nonna*. Grandma Witch. The three fell, as witches will, to fearlessly muttering of death, husbands, children, weddings, errant girls and wayward boys, difficult births and swift, fatal illnesses. Corinne understood. All. She wondered if she put on a black dress and thirty pounds, took five inches off her height, added a few years, abjured the dye bottle, might she too qualify as an old dragon? Like them she had had husbands and weddings and difficult births – well, one, a daughter, that wayward girl, Allegra. She had known men, lain down with them at night, risen with them in the morning, lied to them, lied for them, cried for them, bent double and beat her head on the floor for them. Oh, not for her first dim and ineffectual husband, Allegra's father, but the others. Lovers. Cherished, vanished lovers, lied and cried and wept for them and for the other husband: Dennis.

For Dennis (and at an age when such passion is utterly unbecoming on a woman, which is to say, in these last few years, when a woman was supposed, expected – the hell you say, *required* – to exude grandmotherly serenity unto senility) Corinne Mackenzie had bent double, beat her head on the floor, gasped, hurt, took so many sleeping-pills she saw double when she got up in the morning. She got stoned, not on the pills, but stoned, beaten, hit – face, back, belly, groin – with chunky Latinate phrases from Dennis's lawyer, stoned like the woman taken in adultery would have been if Jesus himself had not intervened. Though it was the man, Dennis, taken in adultery. Taken. Smitten. Succumbed to adultery and moved right in with her, married her as soon as the divorce was final from Corinne who tried everything she could think of to hang on to him. Money. Moral obligation. The grandeur, sweep, passion and longevity of her love. Every lofty principle and every low trick in the Book of Love. (No need to wonder Who Wrote the Book of Love. Not any more. Lawyers. They wrote it, relished it: the swine.) Corinne lay stoned and bleeding, making long, expensive, transatlantic calls to Max on those crackling phone lines that always make you feel like you have to shout: I'M DYING, MAX.

No, you're not. You've known he was cheating on you for years.

NO! I NEVER KNEW.

You never wanted to know. There's a difference. Everyone thought you were so brave, tolerating his infidelities.

I NEVER TOLERATED THEM!

You deluded yourself then. And it's all the same thing, Corinne.

WHAT IS?

The truth of it is, Corinne, that what people call strength is only an endless capacity for self-delusion, for imagining things otherwise.

I'M NOT DELUDED! I'M TIRED OF BEING STRONG. I WANT . . . I WANT . . .

All you need is a new man. Someone new to occupy your imagination. Someone other than Dennis. That's the trouble.

THAT'S NOT THE TROUBLE! I'M TOO OLD FOR A NEW MAN.

Bullshit, my dear.

I'M DYING OF THE PAIN! I MAY ALREADY BE DEAD.

Corinne only knew for certain she was not dead when there came to her office at the museum a wholly unexpected phone call from the university and a man asked her to have coffee with him that afternoon at a downtown restaurant to discuss the Institute for Italian Art they were founding in Tuscany. They needed a Director.

'You come highly recommended as a Renaissance authority and an administrator,' said the wispy, bald man before her. He had an overbite and a mole at what was once his hairline. He passed the sugar. 'You take sugar, I believe.'

'Woody?'

'Max says you are the perfect Director for our programme. He says you have a first rate mind, that you are fearless, imaginative, able and speak fluent Italian.' Woody sipped his black coffee. 'He says you have panache.'

'He is fond of that word.'

'But sparing in his praise. I thought it best to approach you informally in case you did not wish to leave the museum, after all these years, for what would be a brand new undertaking in every sense of the word.'

'I would welcome the new undertaking. I do welcome. I

Do, she said to Italy, the land of Honour Artifice and Presentation Being Everything. The perfect place for Corinne. The perfect job. Perfect. Except for the students. Unused to dealing with students, Corinne did not know (as Giorgio did) that students want – need, demand, insist – to be courted-up and coddled. Corinne did not see them as winsome youngsters but as adults, refused to indulge them or pat their little hands or bottoms, was appalled at their bad manners as guests in a foreign country. It seemed clear to her that you should have good manners in someone else's country as you would in someone else's house. They had no manners at all. Giorgio made excuses for them but Corinne thought him a great toady to offer himself as chum, trouble-shooter and all-around Good Guy. She thought Giorgio downright spread-eagled himself to the students. And of course that's why the turds were not at his door. The pile of indignancy and obscenity was at her door. Oh, was there ever

'Lady? Hey, Lady – are you all right? Can I get you something, Lady? Can I help you put your coat back on?'

He was a young man, a student, clearly. You could tell. He was the age of Adam Black and for a moment she feared it was Adam Black and he was about to squat and

'Lady, can I bring you something from the bar? A glass of water, maybe?' He reached out and brought Corinne's coat up over her shoulders. 'You're shaking all over, Lady, and I could hear your teeth chattering all the way down there.' He nodded down the bench where his girl-friend who had stringy hair and wide, frightened eyes, watched. He patted Corinne's shoulder. 'I knew you were an American.'

'Of course I'm an American,' Corinne snapped. 'I'm more American than you are! I have had to define myself every day for two years as an American. For two years, every day, someone says how well I speak the language and I must be an American and I have to say, Yes. *Yes!* I am an American!' She glanced from the young man to the three Italian crones, looked from one to the other as though she'd been asked to choose with whom she best belonged. Define. Defend. She was suddenly very tired.

She patted the boy's hand and smiled. 'Thank you. It's nothing. It's been cleaned up. Thank you' very much, gentlemen, but I shall not leave this post under an undeserved cloud. My reputation, my whole professional life is at stake. You believe that since the *merda* has been cleaned up, I should have stayed. How very American of you. How very American to think that the past, once addressed, however shallowly, in whatever sort of namby-pamby manner you care to call good faith, that in and of themselves such paltry efforts will vanquish the past. You believe that in tidying and dusting the past, you can defeat it. How American. To say *It's all in the past* is exactly the same as if you'd said, *It never existed at all.* This is as American as the Pledge of Allegiance. It might as well *be* the Pledge of Allegiance: *It's all in the past, dear, and so it cannot matter and will not touch us, or change, or contaminate us if we clear it up, turn our backs and march forward ever forward because the present creates itself afresh each day, springs forth on the half shell. The pristine present.*

I stand before you, gentlemen, to testify to the

contrary. Giorgio may have hired someone to clean up the *merda* – oh, let us say it! Let us say it was shit, *shit*, gentlemen, there before my office door. Giorgio may have cleaned it with his own fair hands. But the shit existed and we must deal here, gentlemen, not simply with the shit itself but with the *notion* of the shit. We must address it. Because the past can contaminate the present. The future. The past often does and only Americans believe to the contrary. It is not enough to clean the shit up, gentlemen, you have to wrestle with the notion of it. To vanquish shit, the past, you must do more than hire it cleaned. You must do what Max did: you must twist and writhe it, clip and force and make the past fit the present you envision. It is not a matter of cleaning it up but a matter of imaginative conviction.

I do not wholly indict you, gentlemen. I am an American too. I am more American than you could ever dream of being, there in your safe little university berths. I have been defining and defending myself and my country – daily for two years to people like those three dragons over there. Look at them, gentlemen. In Italy, *Strega Nonna* is a powerful person. In Italy, these old women (on the graceless side of fifty) are fearless. Ride any bus and see what I mean. The young people snap to around these old women. But for me, Adam Black leaves his shit at my door and his peers concur in this action, even if they did not themselves squat. Adam Black will go unpunished. But I shall be punished because he shat in front of my door. I did not imagine this, gentlemen, I heard them, laughing and chatting, their endless coarse and boring babble all the way down the corridor and into the street, riding the bus and even at home as I so hurriedly packed, because nothing could make their voices stop except the pills I knew would drop me down down down into that sweet and dreamless well of forgetting the centre desk drawer and the laundry on the balcony and the hot water heater. Because *to clean it up* – and I do not mean to mock poor Giorgio's voice unduly – but to clean up the shit is *not to say it never existed*.

III

They announced the train to Pisa would be delayed. Several travellers in the waiting-room jumped up (as travellers will) as though their jumping up and making a great fuss will somehow hasten to make some other damned bit of difference. The American boy who had been so kind looked patiently at his girl-friend. The girl-friend took the maternal line (wouldn't you know it? – the little twit) and patted his hand. The three old women went on obliviously with their smoky babble. Dragon talk. Either they were not going to Pisa. Or, they knew the train would get here when it got here and there was not a damned thing they could do about it. It simply didn't matter.

It certainly didn't matter to Corinne Mackenzie. No plane tickets. No plans. No foreordained destination with someone waiting. Only one thing matters to the refugee: escape. Escape from the students and the centre desk drawer and Giorgio. The dreaded thought occurred that having missed her originally, Giorgio had phoned ahead to have them hold the Pisa train while he jumped in his car and drove like a wild man to Empoli. Knowing she would change at Empoli. Everyone changed at Empoli. She could see him now, parked illegally before the station, flying in with his coat like wings, appealing before her on bended knee (like some skinny, unlovely Annunciation angel) to return so he could keep his comfy berth as toady and assistant and not have to be the responsible Director.

Nothing can induce me (oh, that was grand, fine, simple, distinguished) nothing can induce me to return, Giorgio, even if you tell me you will find my underwear waving bye-bye on the balcony, even if you go through my flat as though I had died, moving towards the centre desk drawer where there, right there amongst the paper clips and pens, I put it yesterday (it could not have been yesterday), I put it there: that last anguished letter from Max who guessed, who knew from the night of the dead bird dinner party (knew, not guessing – knew) even if you find the hot water heater on and the flat unlocked. I have escaped. I have fled, Giorgio. I have given a hundred-and-fifty-thousand lire to the greengrocer across the street who will never in a million years mail my books but keep the money, knowing he will never see me again, never mind that he has always been courteous, friendly, gentle and forthcoming for two full years. Never mind. That's how those Italians are, Giorgio; pickpockets! Peasants! They kneel at the feet of the Virgin while they rob you in the church.

'Signora, prego!' He took her arm, this man, gently but firmly, and led her out.

'I must find the porter. It's time for the Pisa train. I must have my – '

'Signora, guarda – ' He pointed to the sign.

Two choices presented themselves to Corinne. She could blush, falter, *die on the spot* – that she had wandered into the men's room while looking for the porter. Or – rather like an old dragon – she could assume she had a perfect right to go wherever she wished. She chose to graciously allow the man (whose hand was light on her arm, a whiff of wine on his breath) to escort her to a bench outside. As they walked she chattered with him in her fluent, musical Italian and then he was all deference and understanding. Oh, after that, he was all paste and wax. The wax would give the paste substance. The paste would hold the wax when it wanted to melt. Men were like that. All men.

He asked her to wait on the bench and returned with the tiny muscle-bound porter who explained that it was too early to bring out her bags for the Pisa train. Had she not heard? It had been delayed. Yes, delayed again, if you like, Signora, but delayed. She should go into the warm waiting-room until it was announced. She should not sit here on this outside bench where it was so cold and

It wasn't though. The wind had made a noon-time truce with the sun. Or perhaps the sun seduced the wind, lulled it into submission. In November it would be a short seduction, but why not? How nice, the prospects of *il pranzo*, that lovely big meal followed by *il riposo*. Soon, one by one the shops would close and everyone would go home for *il pranzo* and a nap, the affirmation of the personal life. Commercial life would not resume until four when the awnings rolled back up. Till then there would be no life on the streets, only noise from the restaurants and cooking smells, perhaps sleepy children's voices, perhaps tender laughter from behind the shutters of second storey windows. *Il pranzo* and *il riposo*. Was that why so many of them – like Paolo, the young bartender, like this man, whoever he was, though he had gone now, even like the old dragons, they all had the look of people who had risen from contented beds? Because they rose from those beds twice a day instead of once; they returned to work late in the afternoon and then meandered home at eight?

Hopelessly inefficient. That's what Max said of the Italian way of life. He had come to visit her just a few months ago. August. Late in August and for one afternoon only and would not hear of staying a moment longer. One afternoon before turning around and going right back to wherever it was he had gone to. They had a slow, pleasurable lunch on the shaded balcony, clothesline down altogether, thank you, everything spruced up, looking its best for Max. Presentation Being Everything. The potted geraniums waved languidly, responsive to whatever miscreant breeze might care to come up from the street below. The narrow street was lined with sinny crêpe myrtles, their pastel, papery blossoms the colours of sashes on young girls' dresses a hundred years ago, said Max. Or maybe a hundred thousand years ago.

On the white table-cloth tiny tears of spilled Chianti stained. They each held an amber glass of *vinsanto* and the sticky dessert plates lay in a kind of afterglowing afternoon abandon between them. The sun, in its late August arc, peeked and teased through the lattice, lit up Corinne's fuchsia cotton dress, caught and tinted the smoke that rose from Max's cigarette which he held in the European fashion, though she knew very well he affected this. Max was more American than he cared to admit. Though the effort had cost him a good deal of imaginative energy, he had effectively vanquished his refugee past, the life of squalor and necessity, living over a stinking furrier's shop, his father pulling up suspenders, pulling on a moth-bitten sweater and going downstairs to work in the furrier's shop because without the English language, all his German learning was worthless. His father was stubborn and did not wish to learn English, did not learn it at all until after his mother – lacking paint, cello and family – had died. She worked for the furrier too. She kept his books. Max, politic as he was polite, shrewd as he was charming and beautiful, put all of them and all of that behind him. Swiftly and without regret. So tidied, dusted and cleaned-up was the refugee past that it might never have existed. The slap transmuted – transmogrified – transubstantiated into a caress, far more fitting for the most civilized man in America. Probably the most civilized man in Italy now. On her balcony. They watched the greengrocer across the street reopen his shop.

'Hopelessly inefficient,' said Max, as the greengrocer's awnings rolled up in a thunderous rattle. Old Signor Vitti began hauling his boxes of produce out again at four as he had hauled them at seven this morning, stacking them neatly, artfully in front of his shop. Hopelessly inefficient. 'He should stack them all at once in the morning,' Max said. 'Put in a few more hours and go home for a nice long uninterrupted evening of it. Not do that twice a day.' Max pointed to Signor Vitti who (unaware of their eyes) stood wiping his brow.

'That's very American of you, Max.' Corinne retorted. 'But in Italy you have to relinquish efficiency and shrug at the future and tolerate, even savour the past and the present. As it were.'

'Oh, my dear Corinne. Only you, you alone of women could take that ridiculous phrase – "as it were" – and invest it with such – what? Seductiveness. Truly. You make it sound like an invitation.'

'Don't flatter yourself,' she replied breezily. That was the sort of tone you took with Max after a quarter of a century, after you guessed but did not know. Did not want to know. Guessed all the things you did not want to know.

'Italy suits you, Corinne.'

'Italy saved my life. You did, actually. After Dennis. Getting me this job.'

'Oh, it was nothing. A word to the wise. I was not lying. You are superb. Anyway, you wouldn't have died. You're being dramatic.'

'It felt like death.'

Max smoked thoughtfully. 'Love is like that. Overrated. Like travel or Godiva chocolates.'

They watched as Signor Vitti huffed and puffed in the August heat, heaved his bins of Tuscan tomatoes out to the sidewalk. His son came by with his little daughter. They gave the child a peach and the son told the father to go into the cool of the shop. The son, light, lithe, well proportioned, moved effortlessly, brought out the bins and boxes, muscles straining against his damp shirt.

'You should have been a man, Corinne. You have lived the way a man lives.' Max spoke without a false note and the ring of utter sincerity sounded foreign in his voice. 'Men do as they please. They always find a reason, if one is needed, before or after, but they live as they please. Women don't. Women always live the way someone else wants them to. They conduct their lives along a sort of railway timetable. They must do this, or that, or the other, at a certain time and in a certain order. But men say to the world, You can't confine or constrain me by what you think I ought to be. You've lived like that, Corinne.'

'It has cost me,' she said evenly and after a deep breath.

'Of course it has! It will cost you more as you get older. That's the inverse rule: things get easier for men as they get older. Things get harder for women.'

'Dennis, I suppose, is a case in point.'

'Don't look at me like that, Corinne. I didn't make the rule. I'm only reciting it.'

Smoke curled from his nose and a smile curled on his lips. He put his cigarette out. The sun moved through the lattice and struck his cheek.

'I knew you should have been a man when I first met you,' he continued. 'Oh, it's not a sexual judgment, for God's sake, it's intellectual. Really.'

'And how did you know?'

Max chuckled. 'All those Renaissance angels. Most women who go in for art, they flail and coo over the Impressionists, which – ' he snorted contemptuously, '– what a bunch of sissies. The gorge rises. Only a woman with real balls takes on the Renaissance.'

'I don't recall having taken it on.'

'That's why you should have been a man! You were, you always have been unaware of your own courage. You're quite beautiful to watch. Not at all posturing the way women usually do when they undertake something brave.' His voice minced high and false: '*Oh, look at me! I'm being so brave!* You, Corinne,' – he put out his cigarette by breaking the ash off. A clean break – 'you simply did it. You see, when people talk about the Renaissance, they offer up all that textbook tripe and humbug about humanity and the human body and so on. Bullshit. All of it. The Renaissance was not about Man or Mankind. It was by, for and about men. Men's bodies and men's thoughts and men's laws and battles and politics and the religion men fashioned. Men, not mankind. And certainly not women! All those Botticelli beauties aside.'

'That's quite a large aside.'

'No. It isn't. You know exactly what I'm talking about.' He lit up again. 'Don't you?'

'Why didn't we have this conversation in graduate school, Max?'

'There was no need to then.'

She sipped her *vinsanto*. 'Do we need to now?'

Max fanned the smoke and laughed his jagged laugh. 'Think of all those Renaissance Annunciations, Corinne. Does the eye rest on the vapid Virgin about to get the news? No. Of course not. It's the angel that draws, keeps, delights the eye. The angels' sinews, those strong-fingered, strong-winged angels with bodies of men, their rippling torsos, their strong, flat plains made in God's image. But still, the unmistakable bodies of men.'

Signor Vitti's son finished with the cartons of produce, swung his little daughter (now finished with her peach) up easily on his shoulder and with a cheerful farewell to his father, set off down the street.

'Most women haven't the stomach for the Renaissance for that very reason, Corinne. That's how I knew you were remarkable from the beginning. Of course, then, all those years ago, I did not know, I could not guess you would be ongoingly interesting. You have been, you know. I have watched your life with ongoing interest.'

'You have done more than watch,' she said dryly. Adding, 'But less than you might have.'

The sun, inching forward, fell full on Max's face: bony, the skin thin and fragile, mottled. His hair was entirely grey and not at all blond. Dark splotches dotted his hands which he quickly wrapped in his napkin.

'Perhaps we've been fortunate, that you weren't a man, Corinne. Our friendship has been fortunate in that.'

'Perhaps *you* have been fortunate,' she said with more bitterness than she intended.

He seemed not to notice, chose not to. He continued. 'If familiarity breeds contempt, you can imagine what intimacy breeds. You've had lovers. You've had husbands.' He did not take his steadfast blue eyes from her. 'You've lived the way a man lives and that's why you've suffered so much. That's what your lovers, your husbands could not abide in you. Your courage and imagination, your passion. They could not abide the courage and imagination that goes with it. Must. Of necessity go with it. They hated your courage and imagination and passion. I loved them. I loved you. They are the things I most loved and admired in you. But most men can't abide that in women. Anything else they will tolerate. Literally, Corinne, *anything*. But not that. That's why they left you, my dear. From that first, dreary, what was his . . .'

'Barry.'

'From him till Dennis. Everyone in between and everyone since.'

'There hasn't been anyone since.'

'Pity.'

On the street below the other merchants ran their awnings up on rackety metal runners and in this quickening, noisy afternoon allegro, Corinne said, 'You never loved me.'

'Of course I loved you. Didn't you know that?'

He looked at his watch. His cufflinks gleamed in the light. Even in the heat of a Tuscan summer, he wore cufflinks.

'But I must leave now. I have a train to catch if I'm to get the plane at Pisa.'

'You're sure you won't – '

'I'm sure.'

She rose. Odd, she should just now notice they were virtually the same height. He always seemed taller.

He'd grown so thin she probably outweighed him. 'You change at Empoli,' she reminded him. 'That train will take you directly to the Pisa airport.'

'Comforting.'

'I didn't know that, Max.'

'But you just told me – "Change at Empoli and that train will – "'

'I didn't know you loved me.'

'Of course you did. You've always known it. You just didn't know I'd say it. Ordinarily, I might not have.'

'Let me come with you.'

'Absolutely not! I can find the door, Corinne. You stay here so when I get down to the street, I can look up and see you here on the balcony with a glass of *vinsanto*. Pour another glass of *vinsanto*. Please. Do as I ask. Let me see you here at the last. Let me take this picture of you with me to the

> . . . grave, that is my next, my foreordained destination. But please, do not for one moment mistake this for some sort of tacky, vulgar suicide note written in a drunken stupor. I am as sober as I can be, what with the pain and the pills. That's why I came here in the first place. I heard they had a cure. Perhaps I did not hear quite cure. (Perhaps I only wished I had.) I might have heard treatment, maybe not that even. Maybe I heard drugs they do not allow in America. So I came to this cold, efficient place and I shall do the efficient thing.
>
> Ultimately one wishes for efficiency. Dying is very difficult, ugly, graceless, ungainly, inefficient. Whereas death – what could be simpler? There are some moments in life when all that is left to you is gesture.
>
> I am about to become, once again, a refugee. This

time I will not escape with my skin. I shall take it off – the flesh – like the tattered, dirty, crumbling old shirt that it is.

Do not fear for me, my dear. It will all be swift and easy. Do not cry, my dear, my love.

Love,
Max

The three old dragons roused themselves from the clean, warm public splendour of the waiting-room and every porter not engaged in the active cadging of tips, hopped to, lifted their bags for them as they hobbled to the platform. Corinne rose from her bench, hoisting her own two suitcases and joined the other passengers as the train to Pisa was announced. People seemed suddenly to emerge from all over the station, clustering forward expectantly, listening for the approach of the train. You could tell, just at a look, who was getting off at Pisa Centrale and who was going to the *aeroporto*. Look at those people – a family of five surrounded by a perfect forest of baggage. Americans, of course. No European would pack up that many children and think it fun to travel. Europeans would only do that if they had to, if they were refugees, lucky to escape with their skins.

Corinne peered forward, looking for the Pisa train, happy, confident that Giorgio would never catch her now. Perhaps she was wrong and he had not even pursued her to Empoli. Perhaps he was, even now, at her flat, pushing open the unlocked door, walking through deserted rooms, the bedroom, the study, bathroom, sitting-room where he had found the laundry flapping on the balcony line, on into the kitchen, turning the hot water heater off. Walking in and through her flat, her life, the things she'd left undone, Giorgio, treating her things, the letter in the centre of the desk drawer, as though she had died. Like Max had died, already dead by the time the note came. Day before yesterday. Already dead.

'Ah well,' she turned to the old dragon by her side. The woman came up to Corinne's shoulder. Corinne smiled. 'Acqua passata, non macina piu, si?'

Strega Nonna agreed it was all water under the bridge, though she could not have known it was a very American sentiment and ultimately correct. Literally: in the end, correct. The process of living is that of accumulation: friends, lovers, family, goods, experience, memories. The process of dying is that of letting go. Not in any orderly or efficient fashion but simple release. The change, from one process to the other, was that of a curve in time; you rounded this curve in time and the one process was behind you; life lost its savour and nothing – not food, not wine, not sex or music or men or women or the pleasures of paint or words – would ever be as good as it once was. You got on this train and you could not get off. You rounded the curve whether you wished to or not. Did people know when they rounded the curve? Did most people know? Such a fundamental moment. You would think so. Although perhaps it came on you slowly and slowly the things you'd accumulated fell from your life and the people you'd accumulated fell from your life, and the experiences you'd accumulated fell from your life, the knowledge, the significance of memory. And then your life fell from your life.

The train for Pisa galloped into Empoli, hurtling, thrashing, a great swirl of noise and smoke, impatient, as though it had no wish to stop. It was already crowded. People were standing in the aisles.

Corinne followed the three old dragons on. As soon as

they entered the car, four people stood so that the dragons might have a seat. The dragons accepted this gesture with a nod. Nothing more. Corinne took a place opposite, a single place beside an old man who farted loudly, lifting one buttock for effect. The sound was that of the flaccid snap of a deck of old cards. One of the dragons motioned to Corinne: *Come, join us, there is room here with us*.

The old man looked pleased. He had farted this seat empty all the way from Firenze.

Overhead there was room for only one of Corinne's bags. She smashed the other under foot, folded her hands over her purse and held her breath against that moment of combined, heightened expectation, irrevocability: when the train goes into motion, pulls out of the station and your chance to go backwards is forever lost and now denied you. When time dissolved like a great lozenge in a bath of *what if*.

What if, for instance, Paolo had not waved his sad and simple farewell this morning? What if he had got back on the train? Would Corinne be with him now (his rippling torso, his strong flat plains made in God's image) in an Empoli hotel room? What if she had said to the young bartender, there in the station bar, pointing to each of the thirty or forty liquors she had never tasted: one shot of each. I don't care what it costs and I don't care how long it takes. Now *that* would have been a grand gesture! Immensely satisfying. Worthy. Courageous and not to be mistaken. This – the mere desertion of Giorgio, the Institute, her job and the filthy students – would have paled beside a gesture like that! Line them up, she should have said, all along the bar. One bottle and beside it, one glass. I shall taste them in order, one after the other. I shall savour each. I shall not be rushed, but move slowly as a just-risen, warm-blooded whale through this experience. It is absolutely *non importante* to me how long it takes. *Niente*. I may even fling open the front door and step, irrevocably, into the streets of Empoli because, after all, I have no plans as yet. No tickets. No one waiting for me at some foreordained destination.

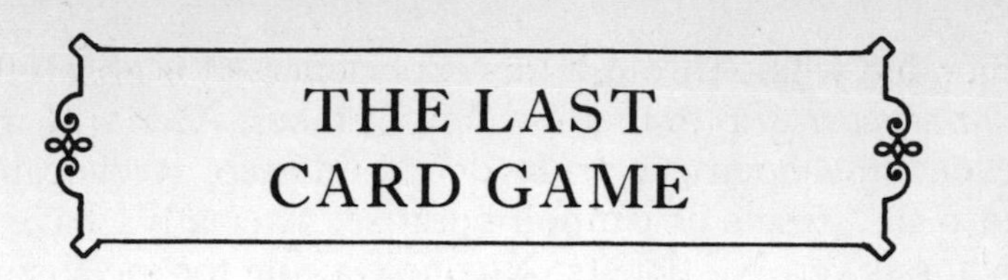

THE LAST CARD GAME

Balraj Khanna

It was bitterly cold. The snow was turning to ice and a chilling silence prevailed as it would on a morning like this. Nothing moved – only a few school-children at the bus-stop, throwing snowballs at each other; and a postman trudging along from door to door, delivering mail. It was a typical post-Christmas, early New Year morning.

Madho blew into his hands as he walked Lona's terrier, Teddy. Madho loathed these walks and he hated 'this son of a bitch', as he called Teddy, to Lona's annoyance. A dog was a dog where Madho was concerned. But not where Lona and Teddy were. For Lona and Teddy were made for each other. They owned each other and they lived for each other. It disgusted Madho when Lona fed Teddy with her fingers as she would have the child they never had, and then touched the food with them. It revolted him when the bastard jumped into her lap at meals, dipping his nozzle in her plate and, sometimes, his. It made Madho mad when the little bugger hopped into their bed as if it was his. Madho had loved dogs as a boy. But that was a long time ago in India where a dog behaved like a dog and was treated like one. But here the four-legged creature was your master – like Teddy. Teddy had made Madho a dog-hater. But Madho had to walk him every morning, evening and, often, in the middle of the night – such was the reality of their life. Otherwise madam would scream. And boy, madam could scream.

Madho walked to the wharf. He would walk another

couple of hundred yards along the embankment. This he liked – being so close to the river filled him with joy. When he arrived at the bridge, the tree there was Teddy's favourite, he would turn back.

Near the bridge, Madho noticed something untypical about the morning. In fact it was something extraordinary: the strangest sight he had seen in all his thirty years in London. A black man as tall as him, six-foot-three strolling leisurely along. The man was of his girth and weight, which was sixteen stone. He wore what looked like an ancient Roman senator's toga – a flowing white robe which covered only half of his big black hulk. His head and hands were enormous and so were his feet. His feet – Madho's eyes popped and his lower jaw fell – were bare! He resembled some great Masai or Zulu chieftain without his war-paint and without either, it seemed, a worry in the world. He walked barefoot in the snow and ice as if he strolled on a grassy clearing in his ancestral jungles. A few passers-by also saw him. But they moved politely on – they knew these weirdo types.

Madho also moved on but he watched from the corner of his eye and saw the Zulu chief take the slope leading to the river-walk that went along the river for some distance. On his way back, five minutes later, Madho stopped at exactly the same spot where the Zulu had taken the river-walk. Open-mouthed, Madho looked. There was not a speck in sight on the clean white quayside. The black yeti had vanished into the proverbial thin air. His footprints were there and that was all. The river-walk ended abruptly into the curve of the embankment a hundred yards away. Those promenading there simply had to turn back. The black yeti had not turned back.

Back home, Lona stirred as Teddy jumped into bed with her. Madho knew he shouldn't wake her up – his young continental wife loved to sleep late in the mornings and once she woke up, she couldn't go back – but he couldn't help it.

'Guess what I just saw?' Madho said, in spite of himself.

'Umm . . .' Lona said, shaking her legs in the quilt.

'A coal-black negro . . .' Madho said.

'Umm-mm . . .' Lona groaned angrily.

'He was walking barefoot on ice.'

'Shut up. Let me sleep,' Lona screamed. When Lona screamed it chilled Madho's spine. It also filled him with anger.

'Even in her sleep she can scream,' Madho muttered. He was hurt. He was annoyed. He had to tell her what he saw at the river – it was so utterly bizarre, unbelievable. 'Even in her sleep she can make me miserable.' She wasn't like that when they had first met four years ago and in the beginning of their so-called marriage. 'Some bloody marriage.'

'But things were still exciting then,' Lona used to say now.

Madho hit her when she screamed unnecessarily (and she screamed unnecessarily all the time now). Only that stopped her. But then she wouldn't talk to him for days. That made him more miserable.

'Let the sleeping bitch lie,' Madho said in his throat and went away to bath and get ready. Tonight was the big night. He didn't want to do or say anything to annoy her – anything and everything annoyed her these days. Madho wanted to make sure that she would be on his side tonight, that she wouldn't sabotage the evening which she was perfectly capable of doing. Much depended on it. When ready, he downed a cup of tea and left a note for Lona: 'Adore you – as usual.'

As Madho was about to leave, Lona screamed again,

'Don't forget my dress.' She had bought it in the sale at an expensive shop in Clifford Street in Mayfair. It needed something done to it. It was to be ready today.

'Won't, your Ladyness.'

The morning was busy; Friday mornings always were. But the picture of the noble African savage treading barefoot the snows of Europe kept invading his thoughts. Just before lunch Dixit phoned. In an excited, high-pitched voice he asked if everything was all right.

'Everything is. Hope you are in one of your losing streaks. Hope everybody is,' Madho replied in his confident, almost bluff, Punjabi way.

Dixit, ten years younger and also a Punjabi, was awed by Madho's all-pervasive confidence. Everybody was. For such was the manner and voice – deeply metallic – of the man, made all the more impressive by his stature. Why, he should have been on stage, Dixit used to think. He would make as good an Othello as Olivier's.

'I am in a special streak. A special mood,' Dixit said.

'And what's that?' Madho asked.

'Ball-chopping.'

'That's interesting because so am I. What about Pran and the Pretty Boy?'

Dixit didn't know. But minutes after he hung up, Madho phoned Pran, a contemporary of his and a friend from the good old days back in the Punjab.

'You'd better be coming with a lot of lolly,' Madho said. It sounded like an order.

'Any particular reason, may I ask?' Pran said with mock humility.

'You may. Reason is man wants to fleece you.'

'Man always does. Fucking man,' Pran laughed.

Madho didn't expect to hear from the last of the card quartet, Vishwanath, or Vishi, as he was called, like the

Indian opening bat. Madho had given him another name – Pretty Boy – because he was the prima donna type. The son of a minor Punjab Hills rajah, he was the same age as Dixit, good-looking and aloof. He didn't phone you. You phoned him. It was the same with the girls. He didn't run after them. They did all the running. And he had a way of looking at Lona which made Madho burn with jealousy. At their first meeting at the scrap-metal wallah Lalvani's party in Wembley, Madho had observed that his dear wife couldn't take her eyes off him. Later, after some guarded grilling by her jealous husband who didn't want to appear to be jealous, she had flatly denied that and had said she didn't find him attractive: 'Not a bit. What's the matter with you?' Of course, Madho knew she was lying and lying through her teeth. Madho always knew when Lona was lying – suddenly she became very girlish. Next time they met him – was it at the hotel-chain wallah Guptara's or at the silk damnfool Bansal's? – it had been the same story again. Lona and Vishi had looked at each other as if they were lovers, or wanted to be. Soon after that their circles had mixed and their card games started. They began to see a lot more of Vishi. Madho noticed that now the two of them had stopped looking at each other, as if something had happened. This bothered Madho even more.

But just before the end of the afternoon, Madho had a surprise. Vishi rang up. Jennifer, the branch secretary, took the call.

'It's Dishy Vishy. Just back from Paris,' Jennifer said, smiling. She was teasing. She knew Madho didn't like her to call Vishi 'Dishy Vishy'.

'How was France?' Madho said, taking the call.

'Cold,' Vishi replied.

'And the women?'

'Very French. I hear man is in one of his fleecing moods.'

'Somebody spreading rumours. But they are only true. What sort of a mood is the Pretty Boy in?'

'To make *animelles frites* of you tonight.'

'What the hell is that?'

'Tell you later.'

'All right. Bring lots of cash. Brightens up the night.'

'How much is lots?' Vishi said in an off-hand sort of way, putting Madho at some unease.

'Don't know. Ten?' Madho didn't know why he had said that. It was sheer bravado, Punjabi style – speak first, think later (or not at all). Tonight's game was going to be a big one. Nobody knew why. But they all wanted it to be. They were playing after a long time – six weeks. So it would be. So let it be. The figure ten seemed fitting. At least to quote. But all told, Madho had managed only about two which, under normal circumstances, was enough. A story had been circulating that Vishi hadn't done badly out of this French deal. Madho saw no harm in saying how much was lots.

'Done,' Vishi said and hung up. Madho went back to work. At four he picked up his greatcoat to go out.

'Going to pick up Lona's dress. Back at half-past,' Madho said to Jennifer. It would not take longer than half an hour from Hatton Gardens to Mayfair and back. But when Madho returned with the dress it was five-past-five, five minutes too late for the safe which was on an automatic time-switch. The other staff had left – everybody left on the dot on Fridays and sometimes even before. Only Jennifer was there, waiting for him.

'Oh, Madho. You've done it again.'

'Traffic. Total murder. Oh, damn.' Madho kicked a chair.

'And it's Friday.' It meant the cash would have to be

taken home for the weekend. Mr Patel, the boss, was very strict about it. His orders were: in such a case not a penny was to be left outside the safe. He was not insured for that sort of thing.

'How much is it, Jen?' But Madho knew exactly how much it was.

'Not a lot. A little over ten thousand.'

'Not a lot she says!' Actually it was not as far as it went. But for Madho it was. He had never taken so much cash home before. A few times in the past, for one reason or the other, he had failed to be back on time for the time-switch. And as the boss had happened to be away, like this weekend, he had done what he had to do – taken the cash home for safekeeping. But the amount in question had seldom been more than two or three thousand. Madho had kept it in the room next to the one in which the card games were held. But he had never touched a penny of it.

Why should I have to tonight?

It would just be there, a few feet away, linking him to it with an invisible cord, giving him just that much extra confidence, and confidence was what these games were about. He would never draw on it. Madho was good at cards. He never lost. Or almost never.

'I hate taking it home, Jen.' Madho had a pained look saying that.

'There is something else we can do. Run away to somewhere nice and sunny, like the Seychelles.' Jennifer laughed as she stood at the door.

Madho told her about the Zulu chieftain and dropped her off at Hyde Park Corner. Madho had heard of Indian sages and Maharishis walking barefoot in the snows of the Himalayas in search of nirvana and such like. But a shoeless negro on a frozen Thames side? It didn't make sense.

'People walk barefoot on beds of flaming coal. People can walk barefoot on London snow for all I care.'

But why?

'Maybe his wife is also a screamer.'

Back home from work every evening, Madho slipped into something comfy – long, flowing, silk robes which he had specially made in India whenever he went there with or without Lona – she had to be dragged out there, she couldn't stand its poverty. These garments were loose and airy. They were supposed to be comfortable. They were also supposed to hide – which in the event they only accentuated – his girth. His favourite one had huge emerald and orange flowers all over it. It was gaudy. Lona detested it. Madho often wore it for that reason. But tonight he wanted to do nothing that might upset her. Tonight he wore a plain white one. As he inspected himself in the mirror, he saw the black yeti of the morning. And to complete the picture, Madho was barefoot – he never wore shoes at home.

Here it is called three card brag. Back home it is called *teen pati* – three card game. It is easy to play. All you need is money (lots of it, preferably), nerve and luck. Madho never had lots of money. But he always pretended that he had – pretending is an important part of the game. It is called bluffing. Some people are good at it, some are not. Some people have the nerve for it, some don't. Some people are lucky at cards and, as is well known, most are not. Madho was good at bluffing. He had the nerve. He was also lucky. Vishi too had the nerve and he bluffed – he was a gambler. But he was not lucky.

Madho liked to catch whoever was bluffing,

especially Vishi. He always did, as if he had secret knowledge that the Pretty Boy was bluffing. It was uncanny. If the two of them only were left in the game and if Vishi was bluffing, Madho always won. But Vishi never gave up. He longed to teach Madho a lesson. Some people like to burn their fingers, or, to put it another way, they never learn. Vishi never learnt.

That night Vishi decided he would play straight; that is, he would be true to the cards, reminding himself of the gamblers' dictum – if you are true to the cards, the cards won't cheat you. Tonight he would play on the strength of his cards. And tonight the cards did not let him down. He got good hands all through the evening and he didn't go wild and he kept winning. Nobody liked that; Madho liked it even less. The thing about him was he always appeared to believe in whatever he was doing. This had its effect on those who were not sure of what they were doing, especially if they were playing on with an indifferent, weak hand. Madho knew the other gambling dictum – you can never win vast sums unless you take risks. To accompany all that, God had given him a veritable gift, his enormous, clean-shaven face. It was always blank. As usual, Madho saw to it that everybody had what they liked best and, as usual, quantities of it: whisky for himself, champagne for Lona, cognac for Vishi and beer for Dixit and Pran. As the night deepened, as bottles went down, so did, for once, Madho's face. The habitually light Punjabi tint went a shade and a half darker.

Dixit and Pran were 'fleeced', 'skinned', 'peeled', 'f'd dry', according to the table jargon. Though not by Madho for a change. But they continued playing, on credit now. Lona too. She usually did that – played on credit. (If she won, she took the money. If she lost, it was OK. The boys, being Punjabi, said 'Never mind.

Forget it'.) Only Madho and Vishi still paid with cash, although Madho didn't have much of it left.

It was time for a snack. Lona had in readiness a selection of cheeses and French bread. She brought the tray to the table and cut the bread with a large bread-knife. Madho did not want anything. It was unlike him, for normally he was hungry at this time of the night. It meant he was angry. It was quite late and everybody was quite drunk. Everybody except Madho who never got drunk. He drank more than everybody, at least a whole bottle of Black Label, but it never showed – neither on his mug nor in his behaviour. He remained as calm and lucid as ever, and ever so sure of what he was doing. Vishi used to admire him for that. He was also irritated by it.

With everybody's money burning holes in his pocket, Vishi began to take liberties. 'Don't, you fool, don't,' he kept saying to himself; Lona, too, who sat next to him, by kicking his foot under the table. But the fool was no longer able to put the brake on himself. The snack eaten, he dealt again. As was the table's habit, everybody played a couple of rounds of blind moves. Then Lona picked up her cards.

'Sheet,' she hissed, dropping them. Teddy slept in her lap. She lifted him up and held him against her long, sleek neck for comfort.

'Double sheet,' Pran said, imitating her speech and gesture.

'I'll join you two musketeers,' Dixit said, throwing his cards down like them.

Another couple of blind moves later, Madho picked up his cards. After seeing them, he doubled the bet.

'Twenty pounds,' he said.

'Twenty pounds,' Vishi said, pretending to take a look at his own cards. He did not see them. For reasons unknown even to himself – the combined effect of the sterling combustion in his pockets and the inspiration of the gold of the cognac elsewhere in him was working full blast – Vishi did not want to know his cards. He pretended to be looking at them the gamblers' way – taking an oblique, 45-degree peep at their corners. In fact he didn't see them. But everybody thought – well, naturally – that he had, everybody except Madho. Madho knew the truth. He also knew that his opponent had reached the stage when a gambler plays, not necessarily out of bravado, desperation or panic, without seeing his cards. Nobody knows why he does that, least of all himself. Maybe it is the result of the death-wish which Dr Freud invested us all with, especially the gambler.

So Madho knew. He also knew that Vishi did not know that he knew. And Madho had great cards. He had 'the Fairy', a straight – Ten, Eleven and Twelve, or Ten, Jack and Queen – of the same suite. The Pretty Boy was caught. And the beauty of it was that he himself had set the trap. Who's *animelles frites* now? The question, however, was would Vishi play on?

'I say, I've only a few of these left now. Have you any cash tucked away upstairs or downstairs to lend?' Madho said to Lona, pointing with both his huge hands to the remaining twenty-pound notes in front of him.

'No,' Lona replied. It was a silly question. Why did he ask it?

'In that case, why don't I put this lot in one go? Madness putting in twenty after twenty after twenty. What does the table say?' Madho said. Twenty was the maximum bet allowed in a normal game. To go higher one had to have the table's permission.

'If you want to commit hara-kiri . . .' Vishi said, '. . . no objection from this part of the table.' Now why did he say that? He knew Madho had a good hand. Otherwise he wouldn't bet away his last penny.

'There. Twenty twenties.' Madho put in all he had. It meant that if Vishi wanted to stay in the game he had to match the amount. And if he wanted to see Madho's cards, which he must now, he had to shell out eight hundred pounds.

'Eight hundred,' Vishi said, counting out the money and gently placing it on the table. 'Now why did you do that, donkey-arse?' he asked himself.

'Eight hundred!' Pran and Dixit gasped.

Madho panicked. But there wasn't a flicker of a muscle on his face to suggest that. The question was what was he going to do? He had banked on Vishi not looking at his cards properly and going out of the game, leaving him all that money. Maybe Vishi had seen his cards after all.

An imperial rule of the game was that in such a make–break case like this, only cash did the singing. No IOU notes, no cheques, no jewellery . . . Only cash and strictly cash. Or you went out of the game.

'Son of a so-and-so,' Madho said to Vishi with feigned affection. He said so in his confident Punjabi way. Then he told them all about the barefooted black man in the snow, betraying only the slightest hint of worry by the way he said 'son', 'so-and-so' and 'snow' – the S slipped. But nobody showed any interest in it whatsoever. Madho was surprised, even disappointed – he equated their lack of interest in his strange story with a lack of interest in him. He felt insulted and angry. More so by and with Lona. He had been angry with her all evening because she had gone and sat next to Vishi. However, one thing was clear to him. He had to do something and do it fast. He stood up.

'Madho!' Lona snapped. Teddy yelped.

'Oh, this son of a bitch,' Madho said. He filled Lona's glass with champagne bubbles, Vishi's with cognac, his own with Black Label and placed cans of beer before the other two. Then he went next door. Lona and Teddy followed.

'You gone mad?' Lona screamed, standing between him and the cupboard where the company money was.

'I know what I'm doing. I've got cards.' Madho pushed her aside.

'You are mad.'

'I've got Ten, Jack and Queen of Spades. What has the Pretty Boy got? Besides, he hasn't even seen his cards.'

'Patel will have you put inside if you lose.'

'I can't. I know what I'm doing.'

'You make me seek. You always have.'

'I know, baby. But tonight is my night.'

'You are raving mad . . .'

Madho didn't let her finish. He snatched the money from the cupboard.

'Sixteen to see you, you said?' he said in Punjabi, returning to the game.

'Man's hearing giving man trouble? Man should put oil in his ears. Mustard oil is best,' Vishi said in Punjabi.

'*Gandoo sala*.'

'English spoken here,' Lona said.

'Sixteen it is then. Sweet sixteen. But not to see you,' Madho said in English.

Eyes popped and mouths gaped – nobody had seen anything like it.

'Story: a goat wanted to be eaten. But she didn't go to the cook. She went and tied herself with rope to the butcher's door. True story,' Vishi said. He was thinking. He was thinking fast. At the same time he was not thinking at all.

'Story also is that hangmen in certain civilized countries let their victims do their job for them. They give them a long, long rope,' Madho said.

'That so?' Vishi faked a smile. He knew what he had done – made a right ass of himself, walked into a trap. He was three grand into the game which was as good as lost now anyway. He should look at his cards, throw them away and get out of this bloody mess. But . . . But Vishi couldn't do that. Not tonight. Tonight he had what he seldom had – money in such quantity. 'All right then. Sixteen from yours sincerely as well,' he said hoarsely and laid down thirty-two fifty-pound notes.

'I like that,' Madho said, rubbing his hands with glee. It was the glee of a man whose spade was only inches away from the buried treasure-chest. Quietly, he added another sixteen hundred to the mountain of notes in the middle of the table.

'I am going to be seek,' Lona shrieked. Teddy echoed her outburst with a spluttering bark.

Madho's right hand twitched – it was reflex action. But he resisted the temptation of hitting her. He stared at Vishi. Vishi was staring at Lona. His stare said, 'Well, you wanted this to happen. It is happening. You wanted one of us to be broken. I am being broken. But I won't go down before I make him shit in whatever he's wearing. You'll see.'

'The goat cometh. She cometh. And *Monsieur le Boucher* is waiting and ready,' Vishi almost sang, pulling out another sixteen hundred from his pocket.

'Become *Monsieur* the Butcher now, have we? Each man to his vocation. And why not? Free country, dammit.' Madho grinned and added sixteen hundred more to the already enormous pile. It looked obscene. Everybody knew whose money he was playing with. This made the whole thing disgusting.

'This is utterly ridiculous. Utterly. You two have gone bananas,' Dixit yelped.

'One of you got to see the other,' Pran said.

'Yup. But tonight it ain't gonna be me,' Madho said.

'What can you do when the goat insists on being eaten?' Vishi said.

'Who, me? Me, I'm giving the rope tonight,' Madho said.

'Fucking bastard,' Lona yelled.

'Keep your hair on, baby. What's the matter with you?' Madho said.

'What's the matter with me? Think, you fat bastard.'

This time Madho couldn't check himself. He lashed out. But Lona pulled her face away in time.

'Madho sahib!' the three men cried in one voice.

'Keep your arse out of it,' Madho said to Lona with clenched teeth.

A long, prickly silence followed like a broken wreath of thorns.

'Madho sahib, what happened to the rope and all?' Vishi finally said. He hadn't wanted to say it – he was thinking of Lona. But he hated Madho. More so tonight.

'Are you playing or wanking with words?' Madho snapped.

Things were clearly not what they usually were. Usually, there was never an argument, not even a cross word, and never ever flaring up of tempers. Whether one won or lost, it was always good-hearted, sportsman-like.

'I'm watching the goat. The goat is coming,' Vishi said, putting down a wad of notes. It was three thousand and two hundred.

This was unbelievable. Madho's huge face suddenly seemed a little swollen. He darted a quick spiky look at

Lona and thumped another bundle of notes on the table. He could play only two more hands with what he had left, or ask to see his enemy's cards. But his bravado had enlarged with the promise of a great fortune even if it was lined with the threat of potential doom. He had done his arithmetic. He knew how much the pretty face had won all evening; more than twice of that he had already put into the game. The question was how much more he had on him. Certainly not as much as Madho had.

'So Dishy Vishy wants a thrashing? And he's going to get it,' Madho said.

'From you, presumably?'

'You're right, dear boy. From me . . .'

'Shut up, Fatso. See him and finish the damnfool story,' Pran shouted. Pran was an old friend. He could call him what he liked.

'I will finish him all right,' Madho grunted and put down sixty-four hundred. This was all he had. He knew Vishi couldn't match it.

'See him! See him!' Pran and Dixit shouted.

'No. I won't.'

'Sixty-four, eh, Fatso?' Vishi said.

'Tongue, young man, tongue. Needs trimming,' Madho barked.

'Why don't you bastards take out knives?' Lona hissed.

'Not a bad idea. What does the young man say?' Madho said, pointing to the bread-knife.

'The young man listens to a frustrated old man. And the young man plays on,' Vishi said.

'Enough . . .' Dixit shouted angrily. '. . .Enough is enough. Stop this madness. Take back what you've both put in and call it a day.'

'Nobody quits. What are you saying, Dixit sahib? Lot of money here. My money,' Madho said.

'Your bloody company's money,' Lona howled.

'Shut up, Ladyness.' Madho hit out again. This time his hand found Lona's face. The other men held their breath. They were struck by the same feeling of foreboding, that the game had hit a blind alley, that the only way out of it was through something awful.

'Beg you, Madho. Beg you, Vishi. With folded hands. Divide and quit,' Dixit said with folded hands. 'Divide and quit.'

'That's what Jinnah said to Mountbatten – "Divide and quit India." But this is money. My money,' Madho said.

'So what are you going to do? Play on? See me? Call it off?' Vishi said. Was his voice weakening? He knew how much he had left – just enough for one more hand. Did Fatso have as much? If he did, the Pretty Boy knew he was done for.

'Your move,' Madho reminded him, as if he needed reminding.

'Sixty-four, then.' Vishi piled up the money.

Madho had a 220-kV shock. He had not expected this. He was sure that Vishi would either get out of the game or, if he was that foolish, which he obviously was, see him. So it came as the gravest shock of his gambling life when Vishi just played on. For Madho had only a few hundred pounds left. He could neither carry on, nor call to see the shit-mouth. Madho had had it.

'So, big boy?' Vishi said.

'Big boy is in big sheet. Serve him right,' Lona said. Madho aimed another back-handed slap at her. But Lona ducked. A sinister silence hung in the room heavier than the cigarette smoke that filled it. It seemed to be screaming just one word – disaster. But disaster for who?

It became obvious that Madho had no money left to play on.

'So I take what is mine. And all this is mine,' Vishi said, embracing the table with his arms.

'No, you don't,' Madho said. 'I see you. I know you haven't seen your cards. You've been bluffing all along.'

'True. Too true.'

'So I see you.'

'You produce the money – twelve thousand eight hundred – and you see me.'

Madho's confidence abandoned him. The change came swiftly. He began to grovel.

'What in this house do you want that will stand for twelve eight?'

'Nothing.'

'The diamond in this ring is worth six or seven minimum as you know. This Omega watch is equal to twenty-five hundred. Those Mogul miniatures are not less than one grand each. I'll put down six of them. Plus this ring. Plus the watch. Plus . . .'

'Cash. Strictly cash.'

'I'll put the house in, you bastard, to see you.'

'Don't want that.'

'Then what do you want?'

'Shall I tell you?'

'Yes, damn you. And hurry.'

'Her. For the night,' Vishi said.

Consternation. And silence.

'You hear that, Lon?' Madho called her Lon when he wanted a favour from her, when he was tender.

'You disgust me,' Lona answered.

'She is on. She is in. Now show your fucking cards.

Beat this?' Madho said, turning his cards one by one. 'The Fairy. Ten. Eleven. Twelve.'

Vishi felt a jab in his chest as if someone had given him a sharp blow there. It was all over.

'All right, Fatso. You win. So what?' Vishi said. He picked up his cards and was about to throw them away when Lona struck Madho right across his cheek very hard.

'You are sheet,' Lona screamed and Teddy went berserk.

'I told the Pretty Boy not to try it on me. I knew what I was doing,' Madho said, ignoring Lona. Then he leaned over patted Teddy with what was decidedly genuine affection for once.

'But let us at least see your cards, *yaar*,' Dixit said to Vishi.

Broken-hearted, Vishi turned his cards one by one and 220-kilovoltage struck again, this time everyone present. Ten. Jack. Queen. All of hearts. Another Fairy. Madho thumped the table with his massive fists. All the glasses flew and fell, some even broke. Cognac mixed with champagne and beer. Madho, having been the one to call, had lost. Now what?

There was so much money on the table that it looked like the desk of a very untidy newspaper editor. Vishi once knew a magazine editor. The magazine didn't sell well. His friend's desk looked just like this table, except that the bits of paper in his office were only bits of paper.

Now what?

Dixit and Pran rose and left quietly. Vishi and Lona stared at each other; Madho half-way up a white wall, at nothing in particular. Madho had lost. He was lost. His face was yellow. It was yellow with the fear of tomorrow. Tomorrow was polite plain-clothed policemen, handcuffs, a ride in the police car and . . .

Madho cleared his throat and stood up. He rearranged his white silk toga-like robe with the ease of a pregnant woman arranging her sari over her swollen self and moved away, muttering, 'You bastard.'

'This dough,' Vishi called him back from the door. 'Take what is yours.'

'Shut your face. Do *it* and get out,' Madho said.

'That what you want?'

'Yeah.'

'That's what he wants. So let him have it,' Lona said.

'Listen, Fatso. Take what you took from the company. How much was it?'

Madho did not answer. But Vishi had a good idea. He pulled out twelve grand and piled it up in front of Madho's chair. He stuffed the rest into his pockets. 'Christ had a last supper. You had a last card game.'

'Take her . . .' Madho said and went out of the door.

'I don't need your permission. I won her.'

A little later, Vishi and Lona stood face to face with each other in the guest-room overlooking the garden. For once Teddy was not by her side.

'Bastard,' Lona said, undoing the little cord in the neck of her new dress. The dress slid down her long, lily-white body. It fell neatly in a circle around her naked feet. She lit two cigarettes and placed one between Vishi's pursed lips. 'Bastard.'

'You always said I had to win you, or "wine" you as you'd put it. I have – won you or "wined" you.'

'Bastard.'

'Who are you calling a bastard? Me or him?'

Lona drank from her glass and sat down on the edge of the bed. Vishi stood only inches away.

'What now?' Lona said.

'What now?' Vishi said.

'I always wanted you. From first time I see you. But not like this.'

'Then how?'

'I not know. I not know anything any more. And I not care.' Lona took his cigarette and put it next to hers in the ashtray. Then she took his hands in hers and placed them on her bosom. Vishy cupped her beautiful, round breasts in his hands and looked deeply in her green–blue eyes. Lona shut her eyes and undid her bra. It dangled tantalizingly from his hands. He raised her to her feet, holding on to her breasts. Lona stood up, her eyes still shut and a faint, enigmatic smile playing on her lips. She opened her eyes and pulled her bra away. Then she bent over and pulled her underwear down to her knees. Steadying herself by holding Vishi's shoulder, she pushed her underwear with a foot and stepped out of it. She stood naked before him, her eyes closed again and that smile on her lips.

'And you?' Lona said, loosening his tie and undoing his shirt buttons.

'I want to go somewhere,' Vishi said.

'You know where it is. Hurry.' Lona threw herself on the bed. She opened her arms and lay there, waiting.

Vishi went to the bathroom. He closed the door behind him and came and stood in front of the mirror by the window.

'Bastard,' Vishi said to the mirror. Next moment he opened the window and stepped into the garden, gently closing the window behind him. It was snowing again. But it was a powdery snow. It was falling quickly. Vishi shivered and fastened his tie and did up his shirt buttons as he walked up the sidewalk that led to the front of the street. His car was parked a few doors away. A black cat came from somewhere and started walking alongside him.

'I am going home. Where are you going?'

Back at the card table, Madho sat staring blankly at the neat pile of money. His cheeks throbbed and his chest wanted to explode. For no reason at all he swung his massive head around. His glazed eyes rested on the long, sharp bread-knife in the cheese tray. Thirty seconds later he was at the door of the guest-room at the back of the house. It was open, Madho hadn't expected it to be. Inside, Lona lay spread naked on the bed. She was fast asleep. Knife in hand, Madho approached her. As he came to her, there was a movement on his left side. He turned and saw the black yeti, the abominable snowman of the morning glaring at him from the full-length mirror by the French window. Madho's hand opened of its own accord and the knife fell noiselessly on the thick woollen carpet. He straightened up and opened the window. Closing it behind him, he walked in Vishi's footsteps and walked on to the wharf. He took the same pathway that led down to the river, the same pathway the Zulu chief had taken the previous morning. A heavily-clad man walking a little dog by the bridge saw him and thought he presented an odd sight. As he and his dog came clear of the bridge and passed the slope, his heart missed a beat when he examined the footprints. They were enormous and they had been made by bare feet. When he looked around for him who had left them behind, there was not a speck to be seen on the clean white quayside. Only one-way footprints.

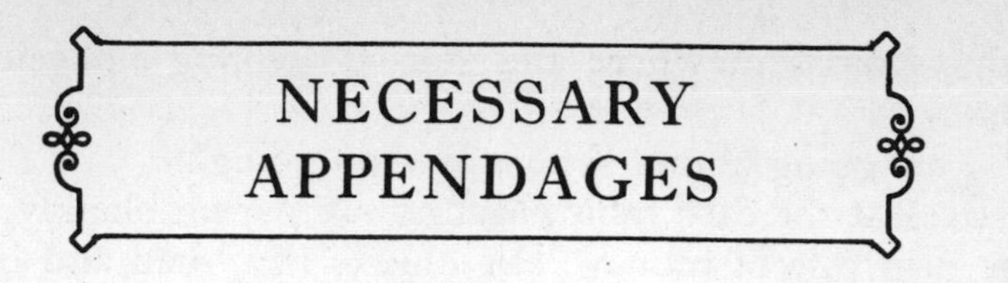

Tony Peake

'But what about Toby?' asked Graham, staring down at the swaddled shape of their seven-month-old son. 'It's a five-hour crossing and at least another five on the other side. Will he cope?'

'Will I cope, you mean,' smiled Laura, bending over the cot and tucking a final quilt over the sleeping Toby.

'Well, will you?'

Laura straightened up. 'Of course he'll cope. Babies are more resilient than you think.'

'And you?'

Laura closed her eyes, though whether in resignation or so as to conceal some other, more complex emotion, Graham couldn't be sure. 'I thought we'd decided. We both want it. And we need a break. Why go over and over the same old ground?'

Graham shrugged. 'You say we both want it. But do we, really? And Richard? What about Richard? He may hate the idea.'

'Richard', said Laura, stepping back from the cot, 'will jump at the idea. Believe me.' She slipped an arm around Graham's waist. 'All you have to do is pick up the phone.'

Later, after their usual Thursday supper of pasta and salad, and after he'd shared the last of the wine between their two glasses, lining them up side by side so as to be sure of giving them each the same amount, she said, 'Right. Ring him now.'

He looked across the table at her. In the dim light of the dining-room alcove the details of her face were indistinct beneath her helmet of hair, only the precise, red line of her mouth standing out with any clarity.

'You're sure this is what you want?'

She lifted her glass to her lips and took a small, deft sip. 'Surer, it would seem, than you.'

'You're not just doing it to please me?'

She returned her glass to the table. 'Ah!' she said. 'So that's what you think! Just being obedient, am I? The perfect wife.' She challenged him with her eyes. 'It hadn't occurred to you that of the two of us, I might be the one who fancies Richard most? That it's not entirely yours, this fantasy we're plotting?'

He got up and went to the phone.

'I only hope', he said, starting to dial, 'that we know what we're doing.'

'What we know', she countered, 'is what we want. What we don't know is whether we'll get it.'

The phone at Richard's end began to ring.

'Wouldn't you say?'

But before he could answer, Richard's mellifluous voice was purring in his ear.

'Maloney speaking.'

'Richard! It's Graham.'

'Graham! How are you?'

'Fine, fine. And you?'

'Can't complain.'

'Listen! Laura and I were wondering . . . We've been offered the use of this house . . . Winbourn it's called . . . In the west of Ireland . . . We're thinking of going over for Easter and we wondered if . . . Well, if you'd like to come too.'

There, it was out. He waited, numbed, for Richard's response.

'Winbourn? Isn't that Gary Stewart's house?'

'Yes.'

'How the hell do you come to be offered the use of Gary Stewart's house?'

'Well, his daughter Sally's been working at the theatre, and one day last week I happened to mention that since coming to London I've always wanted to visit Ireland, and she said her father's house stood empty most of the year – he's always in Hollywood – and if we wanted to – well, we could have it. There's an old couple, apparently, who live in the grounds and keep an eye on things but otherwise – well, it just sits there.'

'Gary Stewart! Shit!'

'So?' queried Graham. 'Can you come?'

'Can I come?' echoed Richard. 'Of course I can come! Gary Stewart! Jesus! When do we leave?'

Out of the corner of his eye, Graham became aware of movement in the alcove. Laura had been clearing the table and now she was preparing to take their dirty plates through to the kitchen. He waited until she drew level with him, then gave her a thumbs up.

There was, in her answering smile, a flicker of triumph so personal, so private, that he was left feeling oddly superfluous. 'What we know', she'd said, 'is what we want.' Did he know, though, had he ever known, what it was that Laura wanted?

They'd met and married in Cape Town, he in the second year of his drama degree, she half-way through an MA in history. Their courtship had been swift and surprising, a mere three months separating the day he'd collided with her diminutive form on the library steps, sending her notebooks flying, and the day they'd presented themselves, he in his only suit, she in a borrowed dress, at the Register Office, entering the building as two, giggling individuals, and emerging from it, a quarter of an hour later, still giggling, but as one.

'Wasn't he horrible?' she'd said, wrinkling her nose. 'The registrar? His breath smelt. Did you notice?'

Something about the way she said this, the mere fact that she'd said it, caused him a moment's unease, made him wonder if her displeasure was really aimed at the registrar. What did he know, after all, really know, about this small, neat and disconcertingly intense woman who'd turned his world inside out by welcoming him with such alacrity into hers, who made him blush, sometimes, the way she stared at him, and who called him her knight in shining armour, as if she needed him to rescue her from something?

'You don't think we've done the wrong thing?' he asked worriedly.

She giggled. 'Well, so they all tell us. But they can't hurt us now. Not now we've got each other.'

'They' were their parents, both sets of whom had reacted with horror to the news of the wedding: hers because, as rigid Afrikaners, they objected to an English son-in-law; his because they viewed twenty-five-year-old Laura as the older woman in embryo, come to trick their impressionable twenty-year-old of his freedom and future.

'Fuck all parents!' she went on. 'Fuck all parents for the way they try to stifle you. But most of all, my love,' – and here she lifted her giggling face coquettishly to his – 'fuck me.'

They'd made love a great deal in those early months, exploring and devouring each other with an intensity that left him feeling not sated but emptied, not more himself but, mercifully, less. Laura's obsessive need for him, coupled with the delight she took in his, to him, lank and awkward body, momentarily stilled all his usual neuroses and uncertainties, even that sick and secret part of him that leapt to life at the sight of men in summer shorts, their muscled thighs brown from the sun, or on the beach when, stripped to a triangle of black, these same men hurled themselves into the curling Atlantic breakers.

'You make me so happy,' he'd whisper in her ear as they lay entwined in their chaos of sheets. 'So very happy.' Meaning, of course: so normal, so very normal.

For almost a year he hardly gave the men of Cape Town a thought, and never visited the little shop at the end of Long Street where, in a rack at the back, there was a section on sports: magazines on naturism and body-building.

Then, gradually, insidiously, like water finding out the fracture in a vase, his interest in men began to seep back into his life. He would, in the street, be helplessly drawn to the curve of a labourer's neck, or on the bus to the line of an arm lying lazy along the back of a seat, and before long he was visiting the shop again and poring over the magazines. It being South Africa, the men in the magazines were never entirely nude, and not that attractive – slackly middle-aged in the naturist titles, popping with muscle in the others – but he pored over them all the same, until, shamed into action by the watchful Greek behind the counter, he would buy one and add it to the growing collection in the back of his briefcase – which was where, hunting for their joint cheque book on the anniversary of their wedding, Laura came across them.

She didn't react immediately. All day she kept whatever it was she was feeling to herself; and that evening, as they sat on their balcony savouring the champagne she'd bought and watching the sun sink behind Robben Island, even if Graham's eyes hadn't been on the sunset, his thoughts on the irony that the lump of rock silhouetted so fetchingly against the sky should be the country's most infamous prison, he wouldn't have noticed anything more than a certain watchfulness in Laura's manner, a certain wariness. It was only when they made their way rather tipsily to bed that he realized anything was amiss – for there, in a neat little pile on his pillow, were the magazines.

'What the hell . . .?' he began.

Laura, who'd slipped into bed before him, cut across his bluster by reaching for the top magazine and opening it at random. 'Show me your favourite,' she said.

He took a step backwards, snagging his ankle on the bedside table. 'Laura, please! You must let me explain.'

'Him, for example? Do you go for him?'

'Laura, please . . .'

But she merely patted the coverlet. 'Angel, please! You can't see properly from there.'

She made him guide her through each magazine, pointing out the men who most appealed to him, which legs he found most sexy, which arms, which stomachs, which chests. When he'd finished, she said simply, 'So much nicer if we share them, don't you think?' – and slipping her hand between his legs, pulled him on to her and whispered in his ear, 'That man in the last magazine. The one in the white costume. Didn't you love his eyes?'

And because, for all his squeamishness about the situation, he had been excited, too, by looking at the magazines with her, he responded eagerly to the pressure of her hand, was more than ready to be taken into her.

'You mustn't mind,' he said afterwards, running a hesitant finger along the set of her jaw. 'I'd hate you to think they were that important. The magazines, I mean. You're what matters. Not them.'

'I don't mind,' she said, 'as long as we share them.'

'You mean that?'

'Of course.'

And it seemed that she did. In the days that followed she made no further reference to the magazines, nor did she seem in the least bit strange or distant. If anything, she was more affectionate than usual, more tender, and she didn't shrug him off, or look at him askance, when he reciprocated her tenderness.

Until, with the advent of summer, on perhaps their third or fourth sortie to the beach, she dug him in the side one morning, and gesturing towards a surfer carrying his board down to the sea, surprised him with a question. 'Now tell me. The guy with the board. Could you go for him?'

It took him a moment to see where she was pointing, by which time the surfer was almost in the water.

He shrugged. 'He's too far away. And anyway, why do you ask?'

'I like to know what turns you on,' she said. 'What makes my baby tick.'

'You,' he said. 'You make me tick.'

She leant over and pinched him, sending a stab of pain up his arm. 'Show me!' she hissed. 'Show me who turns you on.'

He sat up and began scanning the beach. 'All right. That one there. With the brown hair.'

'Why him?'

Now he was embarrassed. 'I can't say.'

'Of course you can.'

'Well, it's – no, I can't.'

'Of course you can.'

'Well, it's partly the shape of his bum.'

'Why his bum?'

'It's firm and it's neat.'

'What else?'

'His pectorals and the hair on his legs.'

'What else?'

'Laura please, I can't.'

'Go on.' It was a command, not a request.

'And he looks . . .'

'Looks what?'

'Well hung.'

Her eyebrows rose. 'That's important?'

'Yes.'

'Very?' She was staring at him with an odd expression.

He wormed his toes into the sand. 'Well . . .'

'Very?'

He hung his head. 'Pretty much.'

'I see.'

At the end of the day, returning to the car, she caught his arm on the spot where she'd pinched him, making him wince, and whispered, 'There's someone for you. He's – what do you say – well hung.' But though she giggled as the man in question passed them, his light-blue jeans bearing ample testimony to her powers of observation, there was something in her tone that unsettled him, an edge of resentment, anger, even disgust. And in the car on their way back to town, it wasn't entirely frivolous, not altogether a joke, the song she made up:

'Keep your thoughts to yourself
And your cock in control
Keep your beady eyes on the crotch ahead.'

'Don't!' he snapped.

She darted him a look of mock surprise. 'You don't like my song?'

'You're making too much of it.'

'I'm making too much of it? You let slip that anatomically I'm deficient, that I lack a rather necessary appendage, and now you're cross because I sing about it?'

'Laura, please! You're you. I don't want you like them.'

'Ah!' she said. 'But imagine how much more you'd love me if I had a cock!'

They'd drawn up at a set of traffic lights, and she took his arm and gestured towards the man beginning to cross the road. Although the man was carrying a shopping-bag which partly obscured his body, there was no mistaking why he was being pointed out – nor any escaping the fact that Graham had spotted him first, had already clocked, with a practised side-long glance, the promising bulge in his shorts.

'On a scale of one to ten,' said Laura, 'I'd say that was a seven. Yes?'

Graham didn't reply.

'Too much?'

'No, no,' he said woodenly. 'Spot on.'

'This game I like,' she said. 'Especially if we keep score.'

Crotch-watching, she dubbed it; and as the summer engulfed them in its heat and languor, she took to playing it with a vengeance, not only on the beach but on their shopping trips to town, at the movies, strolling along the sea-front, anywhere, in fact, where there were men. And although with time he grew more adept at hiding his discomfort, the more obsessively she played the game, the more uneasy it made him, the less he liked her invasion of this particular fantasy – and he was greatly relieved when, towards the end of summer, and hot on the heels of his graduation, he was offered a means of escape: the job of stage-managing a multiracial theatre in Johannesburg.

'Isn't it fantastic?' he crowed. 'My first application, and I land the job! At one of the most innovative theatres in the country too!'

Though best of all – better, even, than the job, or the fairytale cottage they managed to find within a week of their arrival, or the fact that Laura had no difficulty in acquiring a new supervisor for her thesis – best of all was that at a stroke, the move seemed to work the spell he'd asked of it. Laura gave up crotch-watching, and with her obsession went his. Men ceased to be the focal point of their existence.

'I was right,' he thought to himself. 'It was a stage, a tiny part of me, unimportant.'

And in his relief at being thus released from himself, he showered Laura with gifts, was more than usually attentive to her: the perfect husband.

It lasted eight months. Then two things happened. Laura fell pregnant and Graham went to bed with a man.

The man was Graham's assistant stage-manager, a short, dark nineteen-year-old, a silent boy who went quietly about his work, not seeming to take much notice of the outside world. His name was John, he'd recently moved flats, and Graham had promised to help him put up a bookcase.

It was a Saturday and Laura had gone shopping with a friend, leaving Graham the car and instructions to be back by six because, she said, she might have news for him.

John's flat was in Hillbrow, on the sixteenth floor of a once sleek, now decaying block over which, like the smell of failure, there hung a faint but persistent smell of food. John had only moved in the week before and the flat was still barely furnished – two chairs and his stereo in the living-room, a mattress and a tea-chest in the one bedroom, nothing at all in the other.

The fridge, however, was well stocked with beers and they drank a couple and looked through John's record collection before turning their attention to the bookcase, a do-it-yourself affair in cheap, streaky pine which John had bought as a kit. They worked silently and in expert, practised unison, and it wasn't long before the bookcase was up and Graham was helping John unpack his books.

'*Giovanni's Room*,' he said. 'What's that?'

'It's about two guys, an American and an Italian, in Paris, in this room, they get involved . . .' John tailed off.

'You mean they're queer?'

John shrugged. 'It's about love, certainly.'

Graham felt a sudden constriction in his stomach, an unexpected and unwelcome surge of excitement and lust. He opened the book at random and read: 'He seemed – somehow – younger than I had ever been, and blonder and more beautiful, and he wore his masculinity as unequivocally as he wore his skin. He made me think of home – perhaps home is not a place but simply an irrevocable condition.'

He shut the book quickly.

'You can borrow it if you like,' said John.

Graham shook his head and stuffed the book onto the shelf. 'I've already got something on the go.'

They finished unpacking the books.

'There,' said Graham. 'Looks good.'

'Yes,' said John gravely. 'Thank you.'

Then he stepped forward and, taking Graham's face in his hands, stared intently into his eyes – and reading there what he expected to read, pulled Graham towards him and kissed him.

Although he stiffened, Graham didn't pull away, nor did he protest when John took his hand and led him into the bedroom, where he unbuttoned Graham's shirt, unbuckled his trousers, then undressed himself and, pulling Graham onto the mattress, nestled his short, furry body against the larger contours of Graham's pale, hairless one.

They lay in silence for a long time, not moving, then John felt between Graham's legs.

'What is it?' he asked with soft, caressive concern. 'Don't you want to?' And when Graham didn't reply: 'Well, that's fine by me. We can just lie here. That's nice too.'

The hour hand on the clock by the bed went from two to three to four; and gradually for Graham, the almost nauseating excitement he'd felt when John had begun to unbutton his shirt settled into a sort of peace, a sense of rightness, as if his whole life had been aimed at this point, everything he was and everything he'd done designed to bring him here to John's room to lie in John's arms, and when John eventually felt for him again, he was ready.

When the clock reached five, he said, 'I have to go.'

John lifted himself onto his elbow and stared into Graham's eyes.

'You're beautiful,' he said quietly.

'I must go.'

'That's all right,' said John. 'I know.' And he jumped up and threw Graham his clothes.

At the door to the flat, he touched Graham's arm. 'Wait a minute!' He vanished into the gloom and returned with *Giovanni's Room*. 'Here,' he said, 'take this.' He pressed the book into Graham's hand. 'You'll find it interesting.'

'Thank you,' said Graham. 'That's very sweet of you. Thanks.'

Though no sooner had he reached the street, than he dropped the book furtively into the nearest bin.

Arriving back at the cottage, he was relieved to find Laura still out. He wouldn't have been able to cope, he realized, had she been there to greet him. It made him feel quite odd enough, not wholly himself, displaced, just to see her knitting on the arm of her chair, the remains of their morning coffee on the tray by the sofa. He ran himself a bath, and getting into it, began to wash himself meticulously. He was still in the bath when Laura burst through the door crying, 'Guess what? I'm pregnant!'

The euphoria lasted a month. Laura was so patently thrilled, her customary spikiness and occasional bad temper, her uncertainty and her fear of strangers, transformed into such cat-like contentment that he couldn't help but be pleased too – and he discovered within his pleasure a nugget of something else, an atavistic delight in the fact that he was continuing the family-line, that he was doing what sons were brought into the world to do.

Then, at the end of the month, and coinciding with the onset for Laura of morning sickness, an unaccountable unease took hold of Graham. With Laura pregnant, he knew he had to get away from the theatre, from all that was known and familiar. Now that he was going to be a father, he had to start anew.

He broached the subject one evening as he and Laura were taking a dip in their neighbour's pool.

They'd dived in together and as they swam for the

shallow end, he said, 'I think we ought to move to London.'

'London?' In her surprise, Laura took in a mouthful of water.

'Well, I've got a British passport and now you're pregnant we have to think again about South Africa. Things are changing, I know, but not that fast. This isn't a good place to bring up children. Imagine if it's a boy. He'll have to do his military training on the border.'

'There may not be a war on the border by then.'

'But we have to think of these things.'

They reached the shallow end and Laura stood up, shaking the water angrily from her head.

'Why are you saying this really?'

'Don't you think it's a good idea?'

'What about my thesis?'

'You can do that by correspondence.'

'And your job? How will you get a job in London?'

'I've got contacts.'

'But London's horrible. Everyone says so. Cold and wet and crowded.'

'That's only what they say.'

'How can we bring up a baby there?'

'How can we do it here?'

'But this is paradise!'

'On the surface, sure. But visit Soweto and what do you find?'

'We don't live in Soweto.'

'What happens in Soweto affects what happens here.'

She looked at him. 'So we're going to London then?'

'Don't you think it's for the best?'

'And when will we stop running?' she asked. 'Or does it go on for ever? A new city each time you can't face yourself?'

Their parents took the news equally badly, but nothing anyone said could change Graham's mind. He found out about flights, he got the manager of the theatre to write on his behalf to a handful of London theatres, he wrote himself to the people he knew about accommodation, and when he'd done all this, even though nothing definite had come back, no word of a job or a flat, he booked the tickets.

'Contrary to what you think,' he said to Laura, 'I'm doing this for the baby. For you and the baby. Not me at all. So please be with me.'

'Oh, but I am,' she said. 'That's exactly it. I'm your wife, after all. With you all the way.'

They arrived in London in the autumn and stayed with a friend in Chiswick, in a large house off the high road, where they were told they could have the attic for as long as they needed it. Fortune smiled on them, though, and within weeks Graham had found a stage-managing job and a flat in Tufnell Park.

'See!' he said. 'I told you things would work out.'

Even the weather treated them kindly, running, on their arrival, to a fortnight of Indian summer followed by almost a month of crisp, clear days during which the trees in the parks began, with slow magnificence, to go over.

'See!' he repeated. 'I'm not such a lousy husband.'

They were well entrenched by the time the weather changed and a dull, grey sky came down to trap the city in its own cold and misery. Though by then they hardly noticed, for Laura was almost due – and on the 17 December she gave birth to seven pounds four ounces of screaming, healthy baby: Toby Jonathan Andries;

the Toby for them, the Jonathan for his parents, the Andries for hers.

They had a perfect Christmas and New Year, cocooned in the flat by the weather and Toby, taking it in turns with the feeds and the nappies, and coming, sometimes, to stand jointly at the bedroom door just to stare in wonder at the cot and the fragile, miraculous proof it contained of their future.

Then, in the second week of January, Richard exploded into their lives. A new show was coming into the theatre and Richard, twenty-four and just out of drama school, had landed the job of understudying the star.

Graham was coming down the stairs from the dressing-rooms on the morning of the first read-through, a clipboard under his arm, when, barrelling up the stairs, came a matinee-idol in a massive and somewhat moth-eaten fur coat.

'Maloney!' he panted. 'Richard Maloney. Not late, am I? For the reading?'

There was something so touchingly defiant and out of place about the tattered opulence of Richard's coat that Graham warmed to him immediately.

'No,' he said, laughing. 'You've plenty of time. Follow me.'

Within days they were friends, nipping out together to the pub for a lunchtime drink, fetching each other sandwiches or cups of tea from the café on the corner, gossiping in the stalls. Graham learnt that Richard came from Ireland, but had lived in London since the age of ten, had gone from school to Hamburg, where he'd managed a band before deciding he wanted to act because, bowled over by his looks, a stranger in a bar had come up to him and said he had a face the camera would love. Returning to London, he'd landed a place at LAMDA, from which he'd just graduated. He had a bedsit in Islington, rode everywhere on a bike and, the fur lobby notwithstanding, was inseparable from his coat, harbinger of the life-style to which he aspired.

He'd recently broken up with his girl-friend and though he affected not to mind, Graham sensed that he was lonely – and because he and Laura, Toby apart, were lonely too, he said, 'Why don't you come for supper on Sunday? Nothing special. Pot luck. But you can meet the family.'

And so it was, that Sunday, that Richard came to supper – and so successful was the evening, so immediately did Laura and Richard take to each other, that they asked him back, and before long they'd become a fixture, their Sundays together, and expanded into a ritual: a lunchtime drink at the Flask, a walk on Hampstead Heath, then tea at the flat, supper and an hour or two of television.

Laura broached the subject first. 'Tell me something,' she said over breakfast one morning. 'Do you fancy Richard at all?'

'I beg your pardon?'

'Richard. Do you fancy him?'

'Well, he's awfully nice and he's frightfully good-looking, but I really . . .'

'Don't be coy,' she said. 'You know what I mean.'

'Why?' said Graham. 'Do you?'

She didn't reply but that night, in bed, she slipped a hand between Graham's legs and said, 'I wonder how he's hung?'

Graham began to watch Richard in a different way, to study the particular and pleasing configuration of his face, the way his voice seemed to caress the words he uttered, the startling power and grace of his body.

'You know what I think?' Laura said one Sunday

after Richard had left and they were washing up. 'I think you're a little in love with him.'

'Nonsense.'

'Your eyes,' she said. 'They're what give you away.'

'I like him, sure. He's a good friend. And yes, I find him attractive. But to suggest I'm in love with him!'

'I wouldn't mind, you know,' she said. 'As long as we shared him.'

'I'm not enough for you?'

She looked at him. 'Did I say that?'

A fortnight later Sally Stewart offered Graham the use of her father's house.

They met, as arranged, at Euston, boarded the train for Holyhead and, after an unscheduled delay of two hours at the other end, were decanted at midnight on to a ferry that carried them, pitching, through a turbulent sea to Dunlaoghaire. They landed at dawn, tired but triumphant, picked up their rented car, and with Graham at the wheel, Richard navigating and Laura jiggling a fretful Toby on her lap, headed west. They reached their destination mid-afternoon.

They stopped in the local village to shop, then, following Sally's directions, took a narrow road that skirted a lake until they came, as promised, to an imposing set of wrought iron gates and, turning through them into a tunnel of rhododendrons, followed the drive until it opened out before a large, square Georgian house, its brick façade warm and inviting in the afternoon sun. To the right of the house the land fell in a series of lawns to a boat-shed and a jetty, whilst to the left it had been transformed, by turns, into a garden, a tennis court, a pool.

'My God!' breathed Richard. 'This is unbelievable.'

The front door opened and a small, pert woman with greying hair appeared.

'Welcome to Winbourn,' she said. 'I'm Mrs Worral. Now don't you be worrying with your bags. Mr Worral will fetch those later. What an adorable baby! How old is he? Or is it a she?'

They were led inside and given a tour of the house. The ground floor consisted of an L-shaped drawing-room which overlooked the lake, a book-lined study, a dining-room that boasted twelve foot of gleaming, mahogany table, a billiard-room, a snuggery and, at the back of the house, a scruffy games-room. Upstairs, there was a glut of bedrooms, all *en suite*.

'This one's Mr Stewart's', said Mrs Worral, 'and Sally uses this one but any of the others are yours. You choose. It's no skin off my nose where you sleep. All the beds are made up.'

They chose rooms opposite each other at the far end of the corridor, and then coming downstairs, met Mr Worral in the hall. He'd brought in the bags.

'Now you just tell me', he said, 'if you'd like to use the boat and I'll show you where everything is. The tennis rackets and croquet things are in the rec room by the tennis court.'

'And if you'll come with me, miss,' Mrs Worral said to Laura, 'I'll show you the kitchen.'

'We're in the house behind the pool,' said Mr Worral. 'You've only to call if you need anything.'

Richard and Graham took their cases upstairs whilst Mrs Worral ushered Laura into the kitchen.

'I still can't believe it,' said Richard, coming into Graham's room. 'It's like a fairy tale.'

'Pretty bloody grand, eh?' smiled Graham.

'This is what acting's all about.'

He crossed to the window. Graham joined him.

The grounds fell in a series of plateaux to the lake, to be echoed on the other side by a purple mass of mountain, lightly iced with snow.

'Stunning, eh?'

Graham nodded.

Richard turned, and taking Graham in his arms, gave him a sudden, sharp hug. 'It's good of you to have asked me.'

'It's great you could come.' Graham's voice was thick in his throat.

'We're going to have a ball.'

'An absolute ball.'

Later, after Graham had bathed Toby and Laura had fed him and put him down in his carry-cot in a corner of the kitchen, they opened a bottle of wine and set about preparing an elaborate supper.

'We must do this in style,' said Laura. 'Otherwise we'll offend the house.'

They ate at the massive table in the dining-room, giggling at each other across its gleaming length and marvelling at the silverware, the crystal, the gloomy oils on the walls.

Afterwards they settled in the drawing-room and tried to feign nonchalance about the snap shots dotted about on the sideboards and mantelpiece: Elizabeth Taylor standing where Graham was standing by the fireplace; Richard Dreyfuss and Dustin Hoffman on the jetty; Mary Dunaway, Gary Stewart's first wife, striking a pose by the pool.

'The very rich', intoned Richard, 'are different to you and me.'

'I'll say,' said Laura, investigating a cupboard in the corner. 'They have better liqueur for a start. Look at this.' She produced an expensive-looking brandy. 'Shall we?'

'Why not?' said Graham, and giggling again, he poured them each a glass.

'A holiday to remember,' toasted Laura.

'A holiday to remember,' echoed Graham.

Graham and Laura slept until Toby woke them at six. Going to the window, Graham drew the curtains on a perfect day: a powder-blue sky and lake, the promise of sun.

Descending to the kitchen to make tea, he found Mrs Worral putting some milk in the fridge.

'From the farm,' she explained. 'And I've put some eggs in the pantry. Will four pints be enough?'

Graham nodded. 'Looks like it's going to be a perfect day.'

'You've struck it lucky, all right,' said Mrs Worral. 'In the seventies they say it'll be, before the week is out.'

And indeed, it was already warm by the time they'd had breakfast; and when, later that morning and with some help from Mr Worral, they took the boat out on the lake, both Richard and Graham were able to take off their shirts.

'Such views on this boat!' said Laura. 'I wish I had my camera.'

That afternoon they walked to the little church they'd sighted on the hill beyond the house and that evening they ate another elaborate meal in the dining-room.

After supper Laura said she fancied a stroll.

'I'll listen for Toby,' said Richard.

Laura and Graham went out on to the lawn. Although there was no moon, their eyes soon adjusted to the dark, and they followed the fall of the lawns all the way down to the jetty.

'Well,' she said, 'when are you going to ask him?'

'Ask him what?'

'You know.'

'When the right moment presents itself. I can't just spring it on him.'

'Why not?'

'I just can't.'

'And what if the right moment doesn't present itself?'

'Then we do nothing.'

'You mean we come all this way and do nothing?'

'If the right moment doesn't present itself.'

'What a waste.'

'Why? Aren't you enjoying yourself?'

'Of course I'm enjoying myself.'

'So what's wrong with this? Just as it is.' Graham gestured to where, high above them, brilliant cubes of light spilled onto the lawn from the drawing-room windows.

'It's not what we want,' she said. 'It's not what we came for.'

The next afternoon Laura announced she was tired and was going to take a nap.

'In that case,' said Richard, 'I'm going back to the church to take some snaps of the graveyard.'

'I'll come too,' said Graham, 'if I may.'

'Of course,' said Richard. 'That would be nice.'

Graham sat on the wall and watched whilst Richard moved like a cat between the gravestones, clicking away with his camera. Then, out of film, he joined Graham on the wall.

'I really needed this break,' he said. 'I know we're always whinging, and you must be sick of it from work, but it isn't easy being an actor, always waiting on others, at their beck and call. You and Laura are very special to me.'

Graham cleared his throat. 'I'm glad', he said, 'because you're very special to us.' He kept his eyes fixed on his feet. 'In fact,' he went on, 'we would have been heartbroken if you hadn't come.' He didn't dare look up in case he met Richard's eyes. 'In fact, we'd both like it, Laura and I, if we could all go to bed together. You know, sleep together. If you'd like to, that is. We don't want to force you.'

Graham found he couldn't go on. He tailed off and there was silence.

'Well,' said Richard eventually, 'I hardly know what to say.'

'You don't have to say anything,' said Graham hastily. 'You don't have to do anything. Not if you don't want to. We just wanted you to know.' He slithered off the wall. 'It's up to you. Entirely up to you.' Now, at last, he was able to meet his friend's eyes. 'I suppose we'd better be going back.'

They didn't say much on the way back, and when they got to the house, Richard went to his room. Laura was in the kitchen making tea.

'I've spoken to him,' said Graham.

'And?'

He shrugged.

'What did he say?'

'Not a lot. But he didn't seem too horrified.'

'What next?'

Again Graham shrugged. 'Don't ask me.'

'We must behave', said Laura, 'as if nothing has happened.'

'Isn't that a touch British?'

'It's the only way.'

That evening at dinner none of them made any reference to the afternoon and though there was a slight tension in the air, a few less giggles than normal,

Laura's prescription worked: they got through the meal unscathed.

After dinner they played snooker, then they watched television, then Graham stood up and said, 'Well, time for bed.'

'Indeed,' said Laura, standing up with him.

Together they looked at Richard.

'Me too, I guess,' he said. 'This country air. It tires you out.'

They turned out the downstairs lights and went upstairs. In the corridor outside their bedrooms, Richard said, 'Well, good night, you two!' – and planting a clumsy kiss on Laura's cheek, darted into his room.

Graham looked at Laura and shrugged. He opened their door and turned out the passage light. Laura followed him into their room.

'He's shy,' she said. 'That's all. You'll have to go and invite him.'

'I already did,' he said. 'As good as.'

'You have to make it absolutely clear.'

'Why me?' he said. 'Why not you?'

'It has to be you,' she said. 'You're the man.'

He began to undress. 'No,' he said, 'I don't want to.' But when she got into bed and reached across for him, his body betrayed him.

'So what's this, then?' she crowed. 'Of course you want it.'

'All right,' he said, throwing back the covers. 'I'll go.'

He went into the bathroom and fetched a towel.

'Check on Toby,' she said as he came back into the room.

He went to the cot. 'Out like a light.'

He went to the door.

'What am I going to say?' he asked.

'Just invite him over. That's all.'

He went into the corridor. There was a line of light under Richard's door. Graham hesitated a moment before knocking. There was no reply. He knocked again, a little louder this time, and Richard said, 'Yes?'

Graham opened the door. Richard was lying in bed, propped up on one elbow, reading.

'We'd like it', said Graham, 'if you joined us.'

It came out more as an order than a request and it didn't surprise him when, almost meekly, Richard folded down the corner of the page he was on, closed his book and stood up.

He was naked, and Graham caught his breath at how neatly Richard's body contained its own masculinity, how perfectly, how succinctly it announced itself. Graham's masculinity, or so he'd always felt, leaked rather than emanated from his untidy, gangling frame.

Expressionless, Graham walked to the door and, taking Richard by the hand, led him, like a child, across the corridor and into their bedroom.

Laura had thrown back the covers and was lying full-out on the sheets. When he and Richard reached the bed, she lifted her arms and said, very softly, 'Come!'

Richard let go of Graham's hand and leant over Laura. Her arms came up and clasped him round the neck. He fell on to her, their two bodies merging into one.

Graham remained standing by the side of the bed, suddenly at a loss at what to do. Then, rather hesitantly, he lay down next to the rise and fall of their bodies.

'Yes, yes!' Laura was whispering in Richard's ear. 'Oh yes, like that, like that!'

Graham extended a tentative hand and encountered Richard's back. He let his hand slip to the globe of Richard's bucking buttocks, and from there to his inner thigh. He met no obstacles to his exploration of

Richard's body but neither did he feel it to be welcome. He removed his hand, whereupon Laura clutched at it, her nails digging painfully into his flesh.

'Oh, yes, yes, yes!' she was moaning. 'Like that, like that!'

The pressure from Laura's nails increased, the springs of the bed began a vulgar creaking, and then, just when he thought he couldn't stand the pain any longer, Laura's hand went limp, there was a long sigh, and he heard her say, 'Oh, that was good. I needed that. Thank you.'

Graham reached out for Richard, but as he did so, Richard rolled off Laura and got to his feet. 'I'm sorry,' he said. 'I think I should go back to my room.'

'Not on our account,' said Laura. 'We'd like you to stay. Wouldn't we, Graham?'

'I don't think I should.' His body dematerialized into the shadows.

Graham heard the door click shut. He lay very still for a long time and then, very hesitantly, he put out a hand to feel for Laura. As he touched her, she twitched away from him, and lashing out with her foot, kicked him sharply on the shin.

'Laura?' he queried.

But there was no reply.

He lay absolutely motionless after that, not moving at all, until at five o'clock he heard Toby stir in his cot, and getting up, took his son downstairs to warm his bottle.

At breakfast the next morning, both Laura and Richard were very subdued. When he attempted to give Laura a good morning kiss, Graham found himself kissing not her cheek but the empty air, so quickly did she side-step his embrace; and Richard was equally loath to be drawn into early morning pleasantries.

After breakfast, Richard said, 'I promised I'd ring my agent. Do you think they'll mind if I use the phone?'

And after five minutes in the study, he reappeared in the doorway and said, 'You won't believe this but I've got to go back. I'm up for a part in the new Simon Gray.'

'When?' said Graham. 'When must you leave?'

'This afternoon. Isn't that a bummer?'

'It's because of last night, isn't it?' said Graham.

Richard laughed. 'Of course not. Last night was just fine.' He came properly into the room, and walking over to Graham, gave him a clumsy hug. 'You're a lovely man, you should know that. You too,' he said to Laura. 'I'm honoured that you like me. Good God, flattered! But you know how it is. Work is work. Now what about trains?'

Laura, who was winding Toby, said simply, 'Mrs Worral. Ask Mrs Worral. She'll know about trains.'

They had an early lunch, after which, in virtual silence, they drove Richard to the station, where, despite the sinking sensation in the pit of his stomach, Graham managed to be reasonably matter of fact about their leave-taking; every bit as matter of fact, he noticed thankfully, as Laura.

As they pulled out of the station forecourt, he patted her on the knee and said, 'For the best, I suppose. I mean, where would we have gone from here? When you think about it, I mean.'

She didn't reply, just said, in a low, dull voice, 'I'd like to see where you asked him.' So he made a detour to the little church and they went into the graveyard and he showed her where he and Richard had sat on the wall. She ran her hand slowly along the stone then turning to the baby in her arms, said, 'Well, Toby, time for your supper, I suppose.'

Back at the house, she went into the kitchen to

prepare Toby's supper whilst he went upstairs to prepare Toby's bath.

'Don't forget,' he said as they went their separate ways in the hallway, 'we still have each other.'

He heard the scream as he was bending to turn on the tap. For a second he thought his ears were deceiving him; then, as the scream – high-pitched and agonized – continued and grew, he knew that they weren't, and dashed downstairs and into the kitchen.

The first sight to greet him was Toby in his feeding-chair, his chubby hands waving, conductor-like, in the air: a miniature maestro coaxing his mother through her aria of grief. Then, beyond the baby, huddled like an animal at bay in the corner of the room, he saw Laura, her eyes fixed blankly on a point in the middle distance, her mouth open in the scream.

He ran up to her and shook her, but that didn't stop her; it was as if she hadn't felt his hand on her shoulder, was oblivious to his presence. He took a step back and slapped her hard across the face. Only then did she stop screaming.

'Laura,' he began, 'my angel, you mustn't . . .' But even as the words formed on his lips and other words queued up to join them, he realized that nothing he could say could ever make good the damage.

'I'm sorry,' he whispered. 'I'm so sorry.'

Still she didn't acknowledge his presence, so crouching down opposite her, he took her hand and pulled her upright, and putting his arm around her shoulder, guided her towards the table where Toby, perhaps to fill the silence that had settled so oppressively on the room, had set up a howling of his own. With his free arm, Graham scooped up the baby, and it was thus that Mrs Worral, who'd come up from her house in the grounds to investigate the scream she thought she'd heard, saw them: a perfect family grouping, mother, father and son, thrown into glowing relief by the late afternoon sun streaming in through the window.

Clare Colvin

The cherubs, like over-fed children, sprawl insolently along the balustrade of the staircase that leads to the mirrored hall. Their stubby limbs, petrified in mid-cavorting, impede your hand's smooth progress over the marble. They sprout from every available surface; puffing with gilded faces from the cornices of fluted columns; displaying dimpled chubbiness as they encircle the beautiful woman reclining on the permanently vaporized cloud on the ceiling of the hall. She gazes past their juvenile obesity at something more pleasing in the middle distance. The dark eyes in the pale face that blushes pink on the cheeks search out her love. She gazes towards the marble floor fifty feet below.

You can tell from the portrait of him, with its visionary eyes, that Archduke Wolfgang Otto of Herzenburg must have been an obsessive man. The proof of it, of course, is in the palace. His statement is in every wall, every ceiling. 'When I build a palace for love, I build a palace for love.' The cherubs, the pastoral scenes of nymphs and shepherds, of gods and goddesses pursuing their desire proclaim a world where romantic love rules. Into that world, his Palace Bellamora, he brought his bride from Mantua, Maria Caterina. She arrived with a band of entertainers from the court of her uncle, the Duke, for she had noted in the portrait they had sent before the first meeting the melancholy in Wolfgang Otto's long face and pale eyes. Her bridal coach was followed by four others, the first containing her servants, the second and third musicians and singers, and the fourth, a quartet of dwarfs.

Maria Caterina need not have feared her arrival in a barbaric land for Herzenburg was a beautiful city because of its position on the Danube, surrounded by hills, and because of the Archduke's passion for architecture. Herzenburg was the cradle of early baroque and year by year white and yellow buildings with curlicues like whipped cream replaced the medieval timber. Maria Caterina settled into the palace of love, reassured by the beauty around her, and requested only that some special apartments, like those in Mantua, should be built for her dwarfs, for they became unhappy if they were surrounded all the time by hugeness.

'We shall build apartments that will rival any in Mantua,' said Wolfgang Otto. He had known nothing about the dwarfs until he had seen them scrambling out of their carriage, shouting to each other in Italian, but if Maria Caterina wished to be entertained by these tiny grotesques, then he was happy to accommodate them on as small a scale as she wished.

The dwarfs entertained with the ferocious energy that was contained in their short bodies. They tumbled, fought, sang, danced as if their lives depended on it. As no doubt they did, for a dwarf's life outside the protection of the court was precarious. Wolfgang Otto grew to feel a special warmth for these little men but for the saddest of reasons. He loved Maria Caterina with a passion he had never known before and she loved him with the passion she had promised she would give her husband. But the day after the court had celebrated the news that she was with child, she had been suddenly racked with pain and then a terrible bleeding, and the child had been lost. Less than a year later the same events were repeated – an expected child, celebrations, the loss of the child. And a few months later, again, but this time without the celebrations. Wolfgang Otto became nervous of approaching the woman he adored, of inflicting through his love the certainty of pain and the possibility of death. The dwarfs, gambolling on their short legs in childishly ribboned costumes, became substitute children. Wolfgang Otto and Maria Caterina, walking in celibate closeness through the gardens of the Bellamora, would watch fondly as the dwarfs tussled with each other over possession of a football. When it was heard that the Archduke was a soft touch for the little men, the original four were joined by Austrian dwarfs and there were as many as seven or eight at the court.

The Archduke's passion for building began to take a sombre note. He had constructed in the gardens a memorial to the unborn children, and then he asked his architect to design a monument to contain the family sarcophagi. A gilded dome arose in the park adjoining the gardens, its walls a mosaic of coloured marble. On its ceiling was painted a heavenly scene, of Wolfgang Otto and Maria Caterina seated together on a celestial throne, flanked by angels. Below the picture of the happy pair was a bronze sarcophagus of double size, for the Archduke did not intend that they would be separated in death. The bronze was carved into folds, like the silk coverings on the ducal bed. Upon the sarcophagus reclined the bronze figures of the Archduke and Archduchess, their likeness taken from portraits painted at the time of their marriage, so that they could gaze at each other throughout eternity in nuptial bliss.

It was the death of one of the dwarfs that precipitated Maria Caterina's crisis. Gianni, one of the original Italians, had been ill with pneumonia, for the clear air that had made the first sight of white and gold Herzenburg so enchanting was the result of the frequent rainstorms attracted by the surrounding mountains. Maria Caterina had been calm at the funeral but when the Archduke unveiled the bronze statue of the dwarf in what had hitherto been the rose garden, she burst into tears in sight of all the courtiers. Gesticulating at the patchwork of squares edged with privet, she cried, 'Are these waiting for other statues? Is this yet another graveyard you have created?'

Confused by her outburst, for he had thought she would be pleased by the honour to one of her favourite dwarfs, Wolfgang Otto explained, 'But eventually the other dwarfs will die as well and this will be their garden.'

She sobbed and fell against him, her fists beating at his chest. 'All you give me is death. I want life, I want children.'

The courtiers turned their faces away in tactful sympathy and stayed a discreet distance behind them as Wolfgang Otto and Maria Caterina walked back to the mockery of the gilded cherubs. That night Maria Caterina anointed her body with the essence of frangipani which had been sent from Italy and waited for Wolfgang Otto to say good night, as he always did, before he retired. He came into her bedchamber hesitantly, his mind preoccupied with a speech on accepting the will of God, and his nostrils were filled with the perfume that made his senses reel.

'Otto,' she said, as he was about to speak, 'I do not want to hear what you have to say. I want your love, Otto, I want your children.'

He fell to his knees in front of her, his arms holding her to him, his face against her groin. He stayed the rest of the night in her bed, and the next night, and the next. He stayed until she found herself with child again. This time there was no miscarriage and she carried the child to its full term. But nature, which had refused to let her pregnancies continue before, had been right. She was not made for childbearing and the birth killed her.

A sumptuous funeral, the like of which Herzenburg had not seen before, was arranged. The Archduchess was laid on a bier of lilies in an ebony hearse drawn by six black-plumed horses with purple cloths below the black and silver harness. The hearse was followed by coach upon coach of Herzenburg relatives, whose veiled faces could be dimly seen through the rain-spattered windows. The Archduke himself was exposed to public view as he rose beside the bier on an iron-grey stallion, his eyes staring bleakly through the rain that dripped on to his black doublet and lace cuffs. The Herzenburgers looked respectfully at his face, as unmoving as one of the statues. What a man was the Archduke, they said to each other. What a man! After the funeral, the Archduchess was brought from the cathedral to be interred in the great bronze bed, while the Archduke returned to the palace to wait for the day when he would join her.

Imagine growing up in a palace like this, toddling on unsteady feet along what must seem like acre upon acre of polished floor, seeing in the distance the painted clouds, the gilded cherubs, the scenes from classical legend – Apollo eternally reaching for Daphne, Venus with Cupid, Leda and the swan. If you left the painted clouds for the real ones outside you were still in a world of artifice, of geometrical paths, precisely clipped hedges, stone statues with unseeing eyes. What messages must have been absorbed unconsciously by Isabella's young mind, what dreams? Yet in all her childhood years she was aware of only one picture that disturbed her. It showed a young girl in the grasp of a saturnine man who is drawing her towards the darkness. In the bright centre of the picture a beautiful woman, wreathed in flowers, is oblivious to the girl's distress. Isabella was fearful of passing by the picture after dark, especially after her nurse explained that it was the legend of Persephone and that was what happened to girls who strayed from home.

A child loves buildings scaled to its height, and Isabella would retreat to the security of the dwarfs' apartments. In their small-scale baroque rooms, she would be entertained with sweets and strudel on dolls' plates. The dwarfs became her childhood companions, for her father had neglected the world outside, his thoughts taken up by the hereafter and by the memory of Maria Caterina. Isabella grew up in a world of vast ornate space and its miniature mirror image.

Imagine her now, walking through the staterooms towards the mirror hall, in the stiffly embroidered court dress that you can see in her portrait, its starched collar framing her face. Her clear skin is unmarked by time or emotion, her eyes are open as windows to an uncomplicated soul, and her fair hair is caught up by ribbons. She is walking hand in hand with one of the dwarfs and they pause as they see Wolfgang Otto gazing up towards the ceiling of the hall into the eyes of Maria Caterina.

The girl smiles to see her father on his rounds again. First the mirror hall, then the monument. Only after that can he attend to the living. The pain of fifteen years ago has lessened, and he can now acknowledge her as a source of muted joy, a sign that there is life even in death. 'My daughter, Isabella,' he breathes. 'Bianca Isabella.'

The dwarf bows to the Archduke. He is relatively new to the court. He has an intelligent face with high-bridged nose and firm chin, and walks with confidence rather than the compensatory swagger that some of the dwarfs adopt. Most of them have known only poverty and then the riches of the court, which were theirs if they clowned and gambolled, but Stefan has come from a family who were officers in the Imperial Army. Long after the doctors had despaired, his father insisted that his son would be a soldier and had even managed to get him a commission.

Stefan has courtly manners, he can play the lute and sing, but what Isabella likes best is being held spellbound by his tales of a soldier's life at its wildest and most dangerous. She never tires of them and they often walk around the garden together, as he talks of the places he has seen, the adventures he has had. They sometimes sit in Isabella's favourite lily-pond garden, which is always warm and sheltered, surrounded by a thick box hedge. She watches his face as he talks, or looks across at the dark mirror of the water which reflects the lilies. When they sit side by side on the stone bench overlooking the pool, you would imagine them to be a similar height, until you glanced downwards at their legs. Stefan's do not reach the ground. Curiously, Isabella considers herself to be the oddity, for once she was the same size as the dwarfs. It was she who had changed, not they, and she is disconcerted now that she looks down at them. The years of being surrounded by stone cherubs and dwarfs have shaped her sense of normality.

The vastness of the main courtyard is overwhelming. Surrounded on four sides by the height of the palace, yet so large it is not often entirely shaded, it is built to receive convoys of carriages, though it was rare to see even one. Prince Niccolo's visits, once every three years or so, were an exception. He stayed several weeks and threw Herzenburg into turmoil, for he brought with him upwards of fifty men-at-arms, a posse of pages, servants and pack mules. The clatter of many hooves echoing through the streets, the jingle of harness, a commotion of people, carriage wheels on cobble-stones signalled their arrival, and then they were milling around in the courtyard. The walls echoed with noise, steam rose from the horse manure deposited at intervals on the paving, trunks and crates were dragged over the stones in the direction of different doors. From the carriage that bore the Mantuan coat-of-arms Niccolo emerged, his face streaked with grime, his clothes crumpled and travel-worn.

This time, as always, Wolfgang Otto was waiting there to greet the brother of his dear wife.

'*Grüss Gott*, my good brother,' he cried stepping forward to embrace him.

'*Grüss Gott, mio fratello*,' said Niccolo, then swiftly disengaged himself, exclaiming, 'I must have hot water, I must have clean clothes; *I cannot speak until I have changed*.'

The Archduke's servants hurried him to his apartments from whence he emerged two hours later, bathed, clean-shaven, in fresh linen, scented with pomade, his courtly persona restored to him. Slight of build, like many of his family, he dressed for effect in dark velvet, magenta-sashed, and a short cloak that swirled behind him as he walked. The buckles on his shoes glowed with rubies. He walked through the staterooms to the library where the Archduke awaited him for the private audience with which they began each visit. Niccolo had determined this time to broach the subject of his niece's marriage, though her father again shrugged with incomprehension.

'She is only fifteen,' said Wolfgang Otto. 'Hardly more than a child.'

'She is nearly sixteen,' said Niccolo. 'Unless you arrange a betrothal for her, she will choose someone for herself – and she will choose badly.'

'She leads a cloistered life and meets no one,' the Archduke replied, but Niccolo was not to be deterred. For the next hour they debated the merits of various noble families and their sons, and eventually Wolfgang Otto conceded he had at one time thought of young Franz Christian, son of his cousin Gustav von Rebnitz-Freiberg. He had come to Herzenburg with his parents a year ago and had seemed a fine boy; good manners, a healthy country upbringing.

'I think we can find better than young Franz Christian,' said Niccolo, looking through the list he had drawn up. 'You should further your strength with the house of Hapsburg. Is this son, for instance, contracted yet?'

Wolfgang Otto looked at the names on the paper and regretted his seclusion which now, it seemed, had put his daughter at a disadvantage.

'You are right,' he said. 'It is fitting that Isabella should marry well. It is the least I can do in memory of her mother.'

Niccolo sighed and laid the paper to one side. 'Where is La Bianca Isabella?' he asked. 'I must talk to my niece now that we are deciding her future.'

In the garden, taking the air of the bright April afternoon, Isabella was walking towards the palace from the lily-pond garden. The dark hedges and the green of the new leaves emphasized her white and gold. Niccolo, watching her attentively, said, 'She is old enough,' and then, 'Why is she wearing a farthingale? Only elderly *grandes dames* wear them nowadays.'

Isabella waved to them, her other hand clasping Stefan's. Niccolo asked, 'Is that a child with her?'

'It is one of my dwarfs,' replied Wolfgang Otto. 'He arrived a year ago and is a favourite companion of hers.'

'Dwarfs,' said Niccolo, thoughtfully. 'You still have dwarfs, do you? Troublesome little beasts.'

Isabella let go of Stefan's hand and ran down the path to Niccolo with a joyful cry.

'Uncle, I have missed you,' she said, taking his hands in hers. 'When you are here there are parties and banquets and then all is quiet until next time.'

'Is it me that you miss or the parties and banquets?' asked Niccolo. His arms encircled her and his eyes, looking over her shoulder, met those of the dwarf. As he laid claim to Isabella, he saw in the dwarf's eyes ambition, jealousy, and then, as the dwarf evaded his gaze, a need for concealment. Niccolo glanced at Isabella's blithely happy face and then at Wolfgang Otto. What an idiot my brother is, he thought. But then Otto, with his head in the clouds, knew nothing of the ambitions of small men. He waited until they were in the privacy of the library, taking a glass of Tokay before joining the Herzenburg relatives for dinner, and said, 'On reflection, you may be right to favour Franz Christian. We know he is available and that his family will be delighted, so we should therefore make an approach. I should say that we had not a moment to lose.'

The smoke from a thousand candles drifted upwards from the chandeliers to the ceiling of the mirror hall, thin columns like votary offerings to the Archduchess who reclined on her cloud surveying the scene below her. Earlier there had been a banquet and Isabella had been seated next to Franz Christian. She had been glad of the quantities of food, for Franz Christian was young and tongue-tied. A pleasant enough boy with an outdoor complexion, snub nose and eager-to-please eyes. But his talk, how boring that had been! His horse, his dogs and the weather. As the conversation faltered they had devoured ever more of the food – roast pheasant, venison with wood mushrooms, slabs of beef in dill sauce. She had looked up from her plate briefly to see her uncle Niccolo watching them. She saw the dark eyes in the face that reflected the Medici strain in his ancestry, the deeply etched lines at the side of the mouth, outward marks of years of living amongst a court that intrigued against the Imperial powers. Niccolo raised a goblet of wine and smiled at her. She had asked the boy, 'What is my uncle planning?' but he had blushed and become inarticulate.

It had been a relief, then, to adjourn to the hall where conversation was no longer required. Now the musicians bowed to the guests and began the overture to Monteverdi's *Orfeo*. It had been the first opera to be performed there when Maria Caterina had arrived as a bride, a prophetic choice in its story of love and of death. Isabella sat with Franz Christian at her right side, her father at her left. A buzz of conversation continued at the back of the hall from those oblivious to the heart-pulling strains of the music but Isabella listened enthralled to the soaring notes of the singer. Replete with food, her face warmed with wine and the heat of the candle flame, she let her glance slide past Franz Christian to the doorway closest to the musicians, where Stefan was standing. She smiled at him as he turned and saw her. How sweet he looked in his blue suit with the white collar and what a noble, sensitive face he had. She looked at him with affection, then raised her eyes to the mirrored wall and found she was gazing straight into the eyes of her uncle, who was standing behind her, watching her in the glass. Her face was young and open, and all her thoughts were exposed. Suddenly, for the first time in her life, she understood the need to mask emotions that till then had seemed simple and happy.

The next morning they told her she would marry Franz Christian and that there was no reason, now that had been decided, for the marriage to be delayed. Isabella had always assumed she would gladly obey her father and marry whoever he, in his wisdom, chose, but now her spirit rebelled and she shouted, 'I will not have Franz Christian. He is dull, he is stupid, he knows nothing. Why are you in such haste with this marriage? What is behind it all?'

'We are only anxious for your happiness,' said her father.

'I do not believe you,' she cried, then turned her back and walked out of the library, down the great staircase and out into the gardens. As the distance between her and the palace increased, her pace gradually slowed and she felt calmer. She walked as far as the lily-pond garden, knowing that the water which reflected the waxen stillness of the lilies would calm her soul.

The midday sun bathed the garden in warmth, releasing the scent of the box hedge. She lay back on the grass, the sun warming her skin through the stiffly-laced dress. Lacing and whalebone and petticoats, how cumbersome they all were and how much she would like to be rid of them! And why had she been so angry when they had talked of her marriage? Why was her happy nature becoming stormy and agitated?

She heard the sound of approaching footsteps and raised herself on her elbow to see Stefan. She smiled up at him and saw the joy in his face. How affectionate he was, she thought, and called, 'Stefan, I am so glad you are here. My father and my uncle have been annoying me and I want to be distracted from my thoughts. Will you tell me one of your stories?'

'Which story would you like?' Stefan sat beside her, his eyes taking in the smoothness of her skin and its youthful bloom.

'Tell me about the campaign against the Turks. How you rode into battle at the head of the Army.'

Stefan laughed. 'It was not quite like that.' But then none of the stories he told were the same as reality. He did not tell her how he had hoped when he had enlisted that he would be a real soldier and how his body had always let him down. When he fell from his pony, one of his comrades had to dismount to help him back into the saddle. With the best will in the world, his battalion could not have in active service a soldier who needed a helper, and so they gave him the role of mascot, a talisman of what they were defending. It made him feel that the better part of him was not being used but at least he had seen the battles and in his imagination he had ridden with them, his sword cutting down the infidel.

'It was not quite like that,' said Stefan and embarked on a tale of finding himself in the thick of a horde of turbanned Turks in the dust and confusion of a desert battlefield. The sun blazing overhead, the thirst, the noise and cries, the sound of the Turkish captain's horse falling to the ground a split second after the Turk had raised his scimitar, glinting in the sun and poised to descend on Stefan's head . . .

Isabella listened, enthralled, and then as the story ended, she sighed. 'If only I could have such adventures. But my life is going to be dull.'

'How can it be dull? You are beautiful, you are the

daughter of a noble house. Your life is rich.' And then he asked, 'What did they say to you that made you angry?'

She told him of their proposal that she should marry Franz Christian, and as he listened a pain struck him in the region of his heart, so intense that he almost cried out. His Bianca Isabella married, taken away from him, his best friend, his avid listener, the delight of his eyes. He looked at her, saw the breasts constrained by the stiff bodice, and felt as if his harvest had been snatched from him. He was filled with rage at the injustice of fate that held out such happiness but not for him. Unable to control his feelings, he cried out in pain. She reached out a solicitous hand and he clasped it, and the next thing he was aware of was of clinging tightly to her with his arms, his legs, like a human limpet, unable to let go.

'Stefan, please,' she whispered.

'They must not take you away,' he cried. 'I love you, Isabella, I cannot let you go.'

He kissed her face, her eyes and her mouth, claiming possession of her. Her mind filled with disbelief and yet her arms held him to her. She felt the rasp of his cheek against her smoothness, felt the heat of his mouth against hers, and then her lips parted in response to him and a sweet feeling passed through her to her depths. She knew then the rapture of the gods and goddesses on the painted walls and she was certain that she loved him.

Prince Niccolo departed for Vienna, taking with him a party of twenty men-at-arms and four pages. The rest of his entourage kicked their heels in Herzenburg, annoying the citizens as they sought ways of relieving their boredom. Wolfgang Otto talked quietly to Isabella about her duty. Franz Christian, he said, was a good-natured boy and, though a little shy at the moment, he would improve. It was a match with which, he promised her, she would be happy.

What she told him then came as a revelation of such awfulness that he could hardly speak for several moments. Her eyes shining, she said, 'Father, I could never marry Franz Christian because I love Stefan.'

The Archduke fell into a fury, which did not move her, and then into despair when she said, 'I shall marry Stefan or I shall marry no one. If you do not let me marry him, I shall enter a convent.'

A letter, written by the Archduke's own hand so that no one should know of its contents, arrived at Prince Niccolo's apartments the next day. Niccolo delayed his return to Herzenberg for three days in order to attend a banquet given for the Emperor. There he met a charming countess from Buda who invited him to a soirée the next evening and finally, six days later, his coach clattered through the archway into the great courtyard of the Palace Bellamora. He found Wolfgang Otto sitting in the library, staring at the fire, his face haggard with despair.

'I have betrayed Maria Caterina,' he said to Niccolo. 'I have not taken care of her daughter and now she is beyond my care.'

'It is witchcraft,' said Niccolo, his eyes glittering with anger. 'The dwarf has bewitched your daughter. Have him sent to trial.'

The Archduke said, no, the shame, the scandal, and Niccolo, changing his tone, said, 'You are right, it is not a serious matter, just a childish whim. Dismiss the dwarf and Isabella will soon forget him.'

'I said he must go and Isabella said she would go with him. I have been distracted these last few days. I wish, brother, you had returned earlier.'

'Why do you not buy the dwarf's agreement?' asked Niccolo. 'Give him a handsome sum of money and a fine coach to take him away, and lock up your daughter so that she cannot follow.'

'The dwarf was proud and said his love meant more to him than all the riches in the world. They are both immovable and vow that they will marry.'

Niccolo shrugged and smiled. 'There is always a final solution when people are inexcusably obstinate. Poison the dwarf. I can arrange that quite easily.'

Wolfgang Otto shook his head vehemently. 'No, it would be a sin against God. Not here, not in the Palace Bellamora. And besides, Isabella would be broken-hearted.'

'Then we must find a way of making Isabella's heart whole again,' said Niccolo. 'Where is she now?'

'I do not know. She hides away for hours in her unhappiness.'

'At this time, of all times, you should have a watch kept on her,' snapped Niccolo. He left the library with some impatience, and walked through the state apartments, past the mirrored walls with their rococo borders, past the lacquered panels, past the portraits of Herzenburg ancestors posing in ruffs and slashed doublets embroidered with pearls, down the cherubs' staircase, and out on to the balustraded steps that led to the gardens. To the right and left of him stretched a complex pattern of gravel paths, borders and hedged walks, flat as a chessboard in its artificial formality. Two courtiers were walking with mannered grace along the paths, pausing before they changed direction with gestures of polite inquiry. Niccolo's face lightened as an idea, sublime in its simplicity, came to him.

He returned to the library, his briskness dissipating before him the shadowy gloom, and demanded, 'Tell me about Freiberg where Franz Christian lives. What sort of life do they lead?'

'It is thirty miles away as the crow flies and yet a world apart,' said Wolfgang Otto. 'Schloss Freiberg is built with turrets and towers, guarding the pass to Vienna. Architecturally it is nothing. The countryside is wild and mountainous. My cousins ride and hunt, and hunt and ride. There is nothing else to do.'

'A perfect place,' asserted Niccolo. 'Do you not think that Isabella should see Franz Christian in the place he knows and where he is at home?'

Wolfgang Otto saw the wisdom of this proposal which would take Isabella from the influence of Stefan, but her face set obstinately when they told her and she said, 'I will not go there without Stefan.'

The Archduke looked towards his brother-in-law for guidance. Niccolo smiled and said, 'Let him go too. We would not have our Isabella moping for her Stefan.'

Wolfgang Otto protested, 'But, brother, is that wise?'

'Trust me,' said Niccolo.

Three days later the courtyard resounded with noise as two parties left in separate directions. Driving to the mountains, the Herzenburg coach, containing Isabella, her two ladies and Stefan. Milling south to Italy in a convoy of men-at-arms, packhorses, and assorted pages and servants, Prince Niccolo's coach, with the Mantuan coat of arms. The citizens of Herzenburg watched the Italian party clatter out of town and heaved a communal sigh of relief. At the palace Bellamora the Archduke spread out before him thc plans his architect had brought him two weeks earlier and which he had not had the heart to look at before. Now, examining the precise black lines on the manuscript, he saw in his mind's eye graceful domes of cream and gold. A church built to the Saints Maria and Caterina, to add the crowning touch to Herzenburg.

The road to Freiberg is submerged in pine forests until suddenly it runs into open countryside and before you the schloss towers in all its craggy glory against the sky. A barrier of woods surrounds the castle and beyond are the alpine meadows in their summer covering of green. It is, as the Archduke observed, a world apart from Herzenburg but it has its own architectural merit as one of the finest castle fortresses of its day.

A different world for Isabella. Before her, a great hall where she could see a confusion of dogs and people through the smoke haze. Exuberant wolfhounds pulled at her cloak, resonant voices shouted. On the walls, a jungle of antlered heads of stags, wild boar, muskets, halberds and swords. Cousin Gustav, large and four-square, descended on the Herzenburg party, arms extended in greeting, followed by Franz Christian's brothers and sisters. Then Franz Christian himself came forward, shy and tongue-tied, and bowed his head over her hand in the only courtly gesture he knew.

Isabella responded with exhilaration to this world. Through midday heat or sudden summer storms she followed her cousins on their hunting expeditions. Their purpose in life was two-fold – to nurture their own animals and to hunt down the wild. On the upland pastures their herds of goats and cattle grazed peacefully, while in the woods and mountains the creatures of the wild cowered to the trample of hooves and the jingle of horses' harness.

On horseback Franz Christian became a centaur. In leather jerkin, his brown hair flowing like a mane in the breeze, he and his chestnut horse were one. As they scrambled up the steep slopes, his body swayed with the horse's pace. He turned to call encouragement to Isabella, and his teeth flashed white in his ruddy-complexioned face, his brown eyes sparkled. Niccolo had seen it all . . . in the mountains Franz Christian was in his element.

Stefan, veteran of imaginary battles, trailed at the back of the hunt, for his pony was small and ill-tempered. Ahead he saw Franz Christian on the chestnut and Isabella on the grey riding side by side like lifelong companions. Once she turned and came back to him, asking if he was tired. He said, 'No, but I have been given a pig for a horse. Do not try to wait for me.'

'Poor Stefan,' she murmured, looking concerned and amused, and the words were bitter in his ears.

'Let us have some time together without your cousins, without the endless hunts,' he demanded.

Guilt nudged at her conscience, for she remembered how insistent she had been that he should accompany her.

'Have you been very unhappy here?' she asked. 'Then tomorrow they can go hunting without us.'

The wood surrounding Schloss Freiberg is silent, muffling footsteps in the layers of pine needles that cushion the ground. The dark trees soar upwards and light slants through the gaps in long beams as through a cathedral window. Isabella and Stefan walked hand in hand along the path that led to the alpine meadows, Stefan carrying a basket of food and wine which Isabella had gathered from the kitchens.

Quietness and stillness around them, and each of them silent with their own thoughts, subdued by the woods and by unexpressed fears. Ahead of her Isabella saw lightness and her heart lightened too as they approached the gap that led to the meadows. To the right and left were thorn hedges, and in front of them a gate, chained and padlocked, barred the way. Through it they could see a shimmering pattern of green and gold. The grass shivered as a breeze ran through, two blue butterflies like fragments of sky skimmed over the golden cups, and a lark spiralled upwards, its joyous song piercing the air. Isabella's heart filled with joy too and she yearned to be in the meadow, to lie on the grass in the warmth of the sun.

The gate was high and thorns had woven through the slats. She hitched up her skirt and petticoats and clambered over, jumping down to the ground the other side. Then she waited for Stefan but he could not get on to the gate while holding the basket. He put it on the ground and tried again, but this time the height of the gate, the surroundings of thorns and the uncertain tread frustrated his efforts. Isabella climbed back over the gate to help him. This time it was more difficult for, after her initial enthusiasm, she felt the thorns scratch at her legs. Stefan struggled but the thorny gate remained invincible.

'We will find another way through the woods,' she said, looking at the meadow which seemed ever more enticing, waiting for them in the sun. A shadow fell on her mood, and as they walked back down the path, the thought drummed through her head, 'He could not even get over a gate . . . could not get over a gate . . . could not get over a gate . . .' And then, suddenly, 'All the stories he told me were . . . stories.'

They walked in silence towards the castle and she no longer held his hand.

The firelight and the burning torches cast a flickering glow over the great hall. The gypsy fiddlers played relentlessly; high, keening notes like strings that pulled at the limbs of the dancers. Impossible not to dance, and Franz Christian was in the centre of the circle, never stopping for breath. His face shone with sweat but his body never tired – lithe and muscular, bounding with animal health. He danced with Isabella, who had stood in front of him, her hand extended as if for a minuet.

'None of your court dances here,' he cried and whirled her round in a wild gallop. The watchers clapped and cheered as Isabella, her pale face flushed, hopped and tapped her toes with the rest. Faster and faster, until dizzy and out of breath, she stopped Franz Christian, gasping, 'I cannot dance any more.'

He led her from the clamour and smoke of the hall into the cool of the night air. She rested a hand, to steady herself, against his chest and felt through the doublet the pumping of his heart. She looked up at his face, which glowed with the heat of the dance, and with tenderness and desire. In wonderment, she pressed her hand against his heart.

'Cousin, I can feel your heart beat.'

He bent his head towards her and she said, 'No, wait, cousin, you are too hasty,' and she took her handkerchief from her bodice and pressed it to his brow.

'There, that is better,' and she waited until he put his arms around her, drawing her to him, and she could feel him breathing in time with her. She looked into the darkness of his face above hers and whispered, 'Cousin, we are well suited.'

The marriage of Isabella and Franz Christian was

celebrated in the style Herzenburg had grown to expect of their Archduke. Fanfares of trumpets heralded a procession that brought the entire city to a standstill. Isabella, in a coach decorated with gilded cherubs and drawn by six greys, wore a gown of gold and white, embroidered with diamonds and pearls. Her coach was preceded and followed by a convoy of Freiberg and Herzenburg relatives, and a regiment of the Archduke's own soldiers. The citizens gawped at the silks and the jewels, the trappings and horses, and chorused their approval. Accustomed as they were to living amongst the cream of baroque, they would not have been content with anything less. The celebrations continued for two weeks, depleting the entire area of game and venison, and then the newly-wed pair departed with Prince Niccolo to spend the rest of the season in Italy.

In the midst of the rejoicing Stefan had retreated to a corner in the dwarfs' apartments. His distraught presence was merely tolerated by the other dwarfs who blamed his condition on the folly of trying to step out of the mould. Stefan mourned the passing of Isabella as the Archduke had mourned Maria Caterina. When the dwarf died, from a heart attack that came on him suddenly soon after the bridal party had left, the Archduke felt a pang of grief for his suffering. He ordered a statue of Stefan to be cast in bronze and placed next to the others in the dwarfs' garden. Four years later, soon after the birth of his second grandchild, the Archduke finally and thankfully closed his eyes on the world, and was laid to rest in the sarcophagus next to Maria Caterina.

Palace of Bellamora, palace of love, the idyllic setting

for lovers. Picture Franz Christian and Isabella, surrounded by children, living there happily ever after. But fairy tales end at the wedding, before the endlessness of married life. Look at the portrait of Franz Christian, only ten years after their wedding and already foursquare and redfaced like his father. And there is Isabella, mother of three, yet in the full ripeness of her beauty, her eyes still searching out love. Here is Isabella's private drawing-room, to which she retreated when tired of the court. Swagged with plaster roses, pastoral paintings and, oddly, the picture of Persephone that had so frightened her as a girl, she has turned it into her haven. Imagine her sitting there in the evening, while Franz Christian is away hunting, tired of court life, yet tired also of life with Franz Christian. He did not, alas, become more intelligent with the years, and has lost the youthful litheness that had won her heart. Where is the perfect love for which the Palace Bellamora was built? Interred in bronze? Petrified in the garden?

Prince Niccolo is often with Isabella of an evening, for after years of wrangling Mantua fell to the Imperial troops and life is more comfortable here. She has taken to confiding her thoughts in him and he listens sympathetically. He cheers her with gossip from Vienna or Venice or wherever he has travelled. She sighs, 'What adventures! I must go there and see for myself.'

One warm summer's evening, over supper together, she became restless and sad, her thoughts going back to the early days with Franz Christian.

'Oh, Uncle,' she said, 'can you tell me, why did my love die?'

'It was some sort of shock to his heart, I was told,' replied Niccolo.

She gazed at him, puzzled and yet half-comprehending. 'Why do you suddenly talk of Stefan? I was speaking of my love for my husband.'

He looked at her across the table, as he had ten years ago, when their eyes had met in the mirror. He said, 'Perhaps you need to be reminded of how the dwarf loved you. Do you remember that day? In the heat of the afternoon? Under the eaves of the palace?'

She had been eating a leg of partridge which she held in her hand, and now she stared at him, the partridge still raised to her mouth. That one afternoon when she had pledged herself to Stefan, his murmurings of love, his insistent hands, and then that moment when he had lost himself in the world of her petticoats and she had lost herself to him. The colour suffused her cheeks and she asked, 'How did you know?' and then, 'Why are you telling me now, all these years later?'

A silence in which she could hear only the clock ticking and the sound of her breathing. He smiled and she saw in his face that of the saturnine god.

'My Bianca Isabella,' he said, 'I know the secrets of your heart and now you must know mine.'

Then he carefully took the partridge from her and raised her fingers to his mouth.

Was this then the perfect love for which the Palace Bellamora was built? An ageing roué with his compliant niece? And yet they achieved a sublime happiness, untouched by the misery of others. Picture them now, a few years on, in the mirror hall as the musicians play Monteverdi's new opera, *L'Incoronazione di Poppaea*. The voices of the singers soar to the heights of the purest emotion as Nero and Poppaea pledge their love, which has been achieved over the bodies of others. As the notes reach up to the heavens, Niccolo and Isabella smile at each other over the slumbering form of Franz Christian. Later, after her husband has retired to his chamber to sleep off the wine, Isabella sits before her mirror brushing her hair and Niccolo watches. He catches at a strand of gold and winds it round his hand.

'Uncle,' she says, 'why did you marry me to Franz Christian?'

'We thought it best for you then,' said Niccolo, drawing the hair towards him so that her raised head meets his eyes in the glass.

'For me? No, Uncle, it was best for you. You were claiming me for yourself, even then, and you knew that Franz was no rival.'

She sees from his eyes, unmasked in the mirror, that she has at last touched on the truth.

'Oh really, Uncle,' she says, laughing softly, 'I am beginning to see right through you.'

The Palace Bellamora, built as a paradise, is permeated with a sense of failure. Is it because of the heights to which the palace aspired compared with the fallibility of those who lived there? Nothing of their lives remains, only the setting. You can see Stefan's statue as you enter the garden, striking a brave pose, gazing steadfastly before him. The portraits of Isabella, the Archduke and Franz Christian are to be found in several rooms. But none of Prince Niccolo, and there are none of him either in Mantua, where most of the pictures were sold or destroyed. Archduke Wolfgang Otto at least was right to have built and built, as if immortality depended on it. Lives vanish as if never lived and who is there to remember them for you?

The Archduke is remembered today for his white and gold city, inhabited by people considerably less beautiful than their surroundings, who dress in dirndls and loden. The palace belongs to the city and many musical events are held there. Music and money go together for Herzenburg. The latest festival celebrates the Baroque, with a concert of Monteverdi, Vivaldi and Gluck to be held in the great mirrored hall.

We ascend the staircase of cherubs to the hall where neat little chairs are ranged in rows on the wide polished floor. The chandeliers, adapted from those of the time, bathe the gilding in a hard electric light that flattens its rich subtlety. It is all so restored, it looks *nouveau*. We sit on the upright chairs and my husband reads from the programme.

'"In 1607, Archduke Wolfgang Otto, founder of the present city of Herzenburg, built a palace for his bride, Maria Caterina – Palace Bellamora, the palace of beautiful love."'

'How very romantic,' I say. 'I wish you would do the same for me.'

'There's something perverse about building a palace for love,' says my husband. 'Much good it did him, in any case. She died four years after they married, it says here. Perhaps that's why their love was so perfect. It's easy to love a dead wife.'

My husband comes out with these crashing remarks. I remain silent, because I know how easily we can quarrel. It is not his fault that he bores me. We married too young, before I realized there were others.

The musicians arrive in white tie and tails and bow to the polite applause. My husband, still reading from his programme, says, '"A feature of the palace is the dwarfs' garden." We've seen that. It was rather sad. Not much else about the history here.'

'It's all in the walls,' I say, without thinking. 'The walls and the portraits.'

'"Beautiful scenes of mythical love,"' reads my husband. 'What guff. Most of the scenes are rape or abduction. Gods pouncing on underclad nymphs.'

'Be quiet, they're beginning.'

The musicians strike up and the sound of several centuries ago is transmitted through reeds and strings to our ears. The thoughts and emotions of then are accessible to us now. My husband has closed his eyes; the better, he says, to hear the music. I keep my eyes open and look around me, for the surroundings are part of the sound.

I am listening to the music and taking in the room: its gilded cherubs, the ornate carving, the mirrored walls that reflect us. We applaud the Vivaldi, then the musicians begin the overture to Monteverdi's *La Favola d'Orfeo*. The plangent sounds of the strings, the haunting reeds of the flute sound their harmony of love and death. I am aware of being watched by someone just beyond my vision. I almost catch the glance in the mirror, but not quite. I look away, then back again quickly, but still they elude me, those eyes that anticipate thought. Then look, if it pleases you, I tell them. The walls around me seem more alive than the people. The walls watch, they listen, as they have for near on four hundred years. Isabella sat here where I am sitting; Bianca Isabella, and the eyes in the mirror watched her. The music suffuses me with its notes of lightness and darkness, the room gathers round me, the light dims. As I look towards the ceiling, I see the smoke of a thousand candles drifting up from the chandeliers.

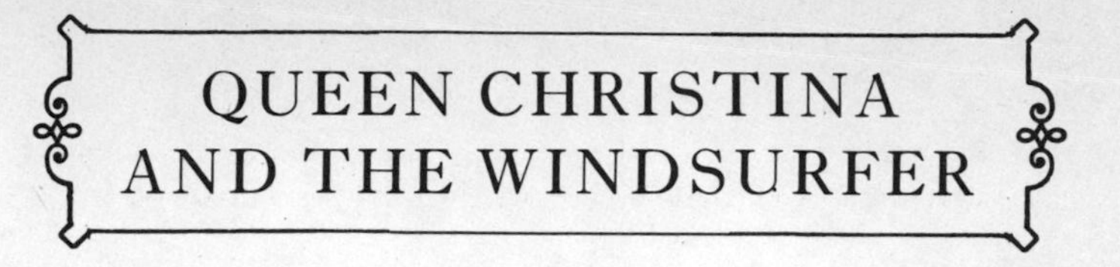

QUEEN CHRISTINA AND THE WINDSURFER

Alison Fell

The big ferry steamed past the mouth of the bay, stately, discoing, lit up like a castle. In the broad white wake Poseidon's daughter lurked unseen, as one by one coke cans plopped into the waves around her. She watched a pretty German girl stretch out her long brown neck to be kissed; watched how the German boy lifted the glossy sheet of hair and twisted it up on to the crown of her head while he touched his lips to her nape. The hair was toffee-dark with the wheaty sheen of sun, and straight as the farthest horizon.

Swamped with envy, Poseidon's daughter rolled on to her back, and sighed, and sank. Down in the green deeps of the palace nothing was straight, and everything was uncertain and wavered: or so thought Poseidon's daughter as she combed out her tough black curls in the mirror, and glowered her thick brows, and blew small rainbow bubbles of disgust.

Presently she swam up to her mother and circled hopefully, waiting for an opening.

'Am I pretty, Mother?' she demanded at last, with as much petulance as she dared, for Amphitrite was harassed and crusty and had little patience with such energetic despairs.

Amphitrite glanced up from her housework and frowned. It was the holiday season again: six million tourists to shit and piss in the sea. From strayed missiles to ham sandwiches, everything fell from the air and the water rotted it, and try as she might to sweep and sort, to recycle and dispose, the Mediterranean was fast becoming a garbage bin. Amphitrite hurled three thonged sandals and a Daytona beach T-shirt into a large cockle-shell, and for a moment thought rancorously of Aphrodite – she who rose from the foam and never did a day's work thereafter.

'Any young girl with clean hair is pretty,' she said testily, thrusting a broom at her daughter, and her daughter, silenced, took it and the two women set to work in concert, sighing, as women do.

On the beach of Plati Yialos, in Nicos' Taverna, Hanni the windsurfer was watching television. Hanni the windsurfer was salt-streaked and golden; his jeans were cut off at the knee and the snakelets of his hair were crystalline blond. At night Hanni camped on the beach and ate water-melons filled with rum, and each morning early he would run to the shore and mount his surfboard in one bold bound, and the sail would take the wind and the light board leave the surface and skip from wave-crest to wave-crest until it was virtually flying.

Poseidon's daughter had watched all this, daily, from the first flush of summer to the harsh height of it, had watched Hanni's mouth taste the wind and the wind trickle through his hair, watched also the slim girls with cigarettes in their mouths who on the sunburned beach shielded their eyes with their hands and gazed out to sea, waiting for his return . . . had slipped, finally – in love and frustration – under the keel of his board where, clinging on by the tips of her fingers, she had flown beneath him for mile upon ardent mile, all green and unseen in the dappled shadow of the sail.

Down in the deeps Poseidon's daughter swept and

swept and the white sand flew in clouds and the startled inkfish scuttled off to safety.

'Am I as pretty as . . .?' she brooded, frowning so fiercely that she was no longer pretty at all. 'Am I as pretty as . . .?'

At last the question weighed so heavily that she threw down her broom and entered the throne-room and asked without preamble, 'Who is the most perfect woman in the world, Father?'

From the uncomfortable heights of his throne Poseidon listened unwillingly, tapping his foot on a ramp of seaweed. Above the waves a new moon was rising and at the palace gates his golden sea-horses pranced and whinnied, eager to be off.

'Why, Aphrodite,' he said absently, and then, with a guilty glance over his shoulder, he corrected himself. 'I mean Amphitrite, of course.'

'But apart from her?' said his daughter crossly.

Poseidon stroked his long beard for a moment, considering. 'Helen?' he pondered, but in truth he had hardly given the matter a thought for the last few centuries. 'Why don't you ask your uncle,' he suggested at last. 'Zeus always did have an eye for the ladies.' Then, relieved to have discharged his fatherly duty, he bade his daughter a quick good night and, jumping into his waiting chariot, drove at full speed around the curve of the coast. At the flat rock of Krissopigi Poseidon slithered out of the sea and trained his telescope on the farthest moons of Uranus: Miranda, where blue snows of nitrogen arched and plumed from furious geysers; Triton, with its sheer cliffs of ice more than twenty miles high. As his eye strained to pick out the lovely details, his thoughts strayed to his brother, and he let out an involuntary sigh which stirred the waves to a tumult and spattered the lens of his telescope with spray. For, try as he might to accept his destiny, he could not help feeling that his own inheritance was in every way inferior. However you looked at it, water was simply not as virile an element as earth or time, as fire or air. Down in the green gloom it was easy to become dispirited, whereas out here the air was sharp and the stars so still and clear you could have cut them out with scissors and pinned them to your breast for all eternity.

Back at the palace there was the habitual fuss and bother as Amphitrite made ready for the night. Libations had to be offered up; potions had to be ground and bound and mixed with ambergris and applied to her face and hands; silver hairpins fell from her hair and had to be retrieved from the soft white sand. Restraining her vast impatience, Poseidon's daughter did her duty, combing and soothing, until at last her mother's head drooped on the pillow. Then with a flick of her tail she fled the bedroom and swam fast towards the shore.

With her nose just above the wooden landing-stage of Nicos' Taverna, she could easily spy on Hanni in the lit interior. A television blared from a high shelf above the bar. The film was black and white and old, and accompanied by the scratchings of an invisible orchestra, but Hanni's full brooding attention was fixed on it. From her secret vantage-point Poseidon's daughter watched two ringleted young men make merry swordplay in more snow than she had ever seen, even on the highest summit of Mount Olympus. Later, one of the two young men was revealed as a woman, and then the old men in the café slapped their thighs and all the small ouzo bottles romped and rolled on the café tables, and when Poseidon's daughter whispered Hanni's name to the lapping waves it was a small sound, quite drowned in the uproar of wolf-whistles.

Before the sun rose next morning Poseidon's daughter was arrowing towards the high cliff of Kastro, where her uncle Zeus received minor deities and petitioning mortals in the first light of dawn. But as the sun rose red over the eastern seas she scanned the high rock and the lemon groves and saw only the silent cocoons of several sleeping-bags, and a stray goat rooting hopefully among the scattered rucksacks.

Back at Plati Yialos, the sand was brazen yellow and the first tourists were stumbling on to the terrace of the taverna, calling for foreign breakfasts. A small snort from the mouth of the bay signalled the arrival of the first boat-load of day-trippers, who presently clambered out on to the jetty by the church and marched in a straggling crocodile along the curving sands, past the few Greeks at their fishing nets, towards the small blue tent where Hanni, patient and cross-legged, awaited prospective pupils.

'*Kalamares!*' cried the English, conscious of the need for politeness in foreign lands, and if the Greeks were surprised to be thus greeted with the word for octopus, with the great tact of their nation they gave no sign of it. '*Guten Morgen!*' cried the Germans with Goethe in their knapsacks. '*Ciao!*' bubbled the Italians in their slight and slippery swimsuits.

At last, scanning the throng, Poseidon's daughter caught sight of her uncle exercising on a stone jetty at the far end of the beach, where the Germans congregated. His biceps glistened with oil, his stomach was pulled in tautly, and his grey–black hair was gelled straight back from his noble forehead. All around him the Germans threw down their rucksacks, cast off their clothes and thundered mother-naked into the surf.

'Uncle Zeus,' cried Poseidon's daughter from the waves. 'Who is the most perfect woman in the world?'

'Don't "Uncle" me,' hissed Zeus, swivelling his pectorals towards a naked Nordic girl who stood knee-deep in the surf with her face turned up to the sun. 'The name's Stavros.'

Poseidon's daughter was undaunted, however, and, tugging at his ankle, repeated her question.

'Well, Greta Garbo, of course,' said Zeus, with a jealous glance at Hanni's tent, which was by now quite surrounded by Euro-beauties, so that nothing could be glimpsed of Hanni but the topmost tuft of his blond hair and a faint blue curl of cigarette smoke. He had been lobbied, recently, to make Garbo an immortal, although just at that moment he could see little advantage in immortality and indeed would gladly have exchanged the entire inheritance of Kronos and Ouranos for one sole afternoon inside the sleek hide of that taciturn youth.

Disconsolate, Poseidon's daughter swam ever-widening circles in the broad bay. Under the surface ripples of light wavered over the rocks, and the anemones opened sleepy brilliant eyes to watch her pass. By now it was almost lunchtime; the caiques with their ballast of water-melons rode at anchor by the quay, and charcoal flared under the griddle on the taverna terrace.

On a promontory near the entrance to the bay she spied her aunt, Athena the owl-eyed, battering squid against a rock to tenderize it. Filled with that urge to confess which love inspires in us, and eager to indulge in the compensatory thrills of chatter, Poseidon's daughter swam up strongly and surfaced in the hot noon air. Besides – although she herself had no spinsterly aspirations – she genuinely did admire her aunt, who, unlike her mother Amphitrite, had proved that she would be a doormat to no man on earth or in heaven.

'Aunt Athena,' she murmured languorously, lying along a wave and all prepared for confidences.

'Don't tell me,' said Athena in a voice that knew everything and tolerated much of it. 'You're in love with that beach-bum.' Raising her eyes to heaven, she slapped the squid hard against the rock and pronounced, 'For youthful folly it is the most hopeless thing to entangle itself in empty imaginings. The more obstinately it clings to such unreal fantasies, the more certainly will humiliation overtake it.' And then she patted Poseidon's daughter kindly enough and saw her off with a firm admonition to look to her studies and develop herself.

That night, when he had drunk too well and was dreamy with retsina, Hanni the windsurfer wandered down to the shore and stretched his fine frame out on his surfboard. Flat on his back he watched the moon rise: his mouth was open, his hands dangled in the wavelets. Presently, lulled by the soft sound of the wind in the tamarisk trees, he fell into a deep sleep. Hidden by a wreath of sea-wrack, Poseidon's daughter gazed on him longingly, until at last, astonished by her own temerity, she tugged lightly at the prow and drew the board down from the sand until it floated entire in the shallows.

Now, of all the talents that the gods had apportioned to Poseidon's daughter, the only one she had taken pains to nurture was the capacity to see into dreams. And so she lay below the board, watching, nibbling at Hanni's fingertips like a hungry minnow. Meanwhile, Hanni dreamt on, oblivious: dreamt of a full sail, of waves like white stallions. Stealthily, so as not to wake him, Poseidon's daughter pressed her wet lips to his dry ones, and hoisted herself on to the board, mouthing words of love. But in the dream she saw that the words blew like froth or spume from her lips, and seaweed streaked her white face, and Hanni shrank back from this apparition from the deeps and shuddered piteously in his sleep. Fearful that he would fall splashing into the shallows, Poseidon's daughter steadied the board with her hand, until the dreamer sighed and settled again. The wind of the dream recovered and blew breath into the quickening sail, and now there was a woman with her straight back braced against the mast, but it was not she, not Poseidon's daughter, not a thick-browed girl with stormy curls, but a woman of cool bones and superior deep eyes, and she knew then, most certainly, that this was the most perfect woman in the world. And as the dreamer stretched out his arms to the lovely paragon, Poseidon's daughter dived ever deeper into the bitter waters of her jealousy, and she would have given all the world to wrap her own form around the woman like a cloak, so that it would be her face Hanni sought and her body his arms reached out to with such speechless longing.

Of all the skills the gods possessed, it was Zeus alone who knew the trick of snipping the rope that holds the dream to the dreamer. Once – or so her aunt Athena had told her – incensed by the intrusion of aeroplanes into the peaceful Attic skies, Zeus had made fearful mischief. Looking above him, he saw that each plane towed the dreams of its passengers behind it, like a trawler tows its netted catch. Inside the blond fuselage the travellers, having kicked off their shoes and bound velvet masks over their eyes, had slept their way across the troubled Gulf, across Syria and Turkey, so that when the plane turned north-west and struck out across the Ionian Sea their dreams were in full flight – or rather in full dive; for although it is commonly believed that dreams rise up from the dreamer like word-balloons in a cartoon strip, the truth of the matter is that by their very nature they seek out those slower watery elements which blur boundaries and mix one thing up with another, and although, in these rapid times, few are the dreams that find their way there, those that do so live and leap most happily, like dolphins, in the shifting seas. So it happened that when Zeus took his silver scissors and snipped at the cords, the dreams were cast out across the sea and drifted there, higgledy-piggledy, like waterskiers who have lost hold of their tow-rope, and the plane flew on with its perfectly straight jet-trail and its perfectly empty-headed passengers. And some of the dreams Zeus seized by their tails and flung like thunderbolts, so that they fell into the orange groves of Lebanon or shrivelled unnoticed on the salt strands of the Red Sea. Only much later, when the passengers had scattered to their various destinations and slept several nights of empty sleep, did the dreams which survived swim blindly back towards their owners. But as fortune or Zeus would have it, there was no way of telling which dream belonged to a Catholic mission-nurse *en route* from Calcutta, and which to an investment analyst from Kyoto, so that the dreams were forced to seek parents quite at random, like orphaned penguin chicks on the rocky shelves of Patagonia. And Zeus, seeing the broker fall on his knees to ask forgiveness, and the angel-faced Sister take out options on holy relics, laughed so loud in his lemon grove that the rock of Kastro shivered, and cracks appeared in the stepped white streets of the village, and memorial urns fell marvellously asunder in the chapel. Or so her aunt Athena had told her; Athena who had no patience with capriciousness and who made no secret of her opinion that in all respects she was better suited than Zeus to command the company of the gods.

But although Zeus was both boastful and unpredictable, he could also be generous, and it was with this hope in her heart that Poseidon's daughter swam for the second time to the white rock of Kastro to throw herself upon her uncle's magnanimity and beg from him the trick of dream-conjuring.

Under the lemon trees Zeus opened his eyes; beside him the lovely German girl stirred in her sleeping-bag, and her lovely mouth murmured the name 'Stavros'. Zeus stroked the silky pelt on his chest and was well pleased with the night's work. When he saw the rough head of his ragamuffin niece break the surface of the bay he laughed indulgently.

'What now?' he cried, throwing a handful of figs at her. For a daughter of the meek and myopic Poseidon she was certainly demanding.

Affecting not to notice the sleeping girl, Poseidon's daughter drew herself up and made her request with as much dignity as she could muster.

'Stop wanting, start having,' said Zeus, flicking the silver scissors casually up into the air, where they hung suspended. Poseidon's daughter leapt like a porpoise to catch them, but not until she had made a solemn promise to return them after seven nights did the scissors fall into her eager hand.

And so every night for seven nights Poseidon's daughter waited and watched by the jetty, and each time the foreign woman flickered into Hanni's dreams she took the silver scissors and cut her out completely. And Hanni snorted with distress in his sleep, and in the mornings was fretful and clumsy, like a woman at her monthly time, and took to sitting crouched under the tamarisk trees, surly and unspeaking. But if the beauties who had clustered around him so admiringly were disgruntled and drifted off in search of more responseful men, so too was Poseidon's daughter farther from her goal than ever. For although she could cut the Nordic woman out of Hanni's dreams and scatter her images as far as Africa, try as she might she could find no way of filling the gaps that the woman's face had left. For her own dream was not clear enough, was boundaryless and wavered, and would not be fitted in.

From her rock promontory Athena saw her niece swim asymmetrical and distraught towards the high rock of Kastro, saw also the dangerous flash of the silver scissors in the light of the setting sun; and from her erratic path in the sea Poseidon's daughter saw the clean-cut limbs of her aunt Athena, who knew how to develop herself. Athena set down her weighing-scales and stopped bargaining with the fishermen, and called her niece to her. But as she listened to the girl's unhappy tale, and as she stroked the stormy curls on the unhappy head, all the time her eyes rested with longing on the silver scissors, and despite itself her mind filled with plans to steal them from Zeus, although – or so she persuaded herself – her only desire in so doing would be to put an end to his ungodly nonsense. In her mind's eye all Attica lay before her, just and fair as her own daughter-city of Athens, and the vision glittered as her voice spoke comfort and resolution to Poseidon's daughter.

She spoke of the power of the will, and how it must be tended like the melon seed in its earthy bed or the speckled egg in the belly of the heron, and she waxed long and lyrical in this vein until she had quite forgotten her less honourable intentions.

Finally, remembering herself, she said, 'But you are young yet and only learning. So I will pit the power of my own will behind yours and, believe me, we will send Hanni the dream that he deserves. Only you must give the silver scissors to me now, for safe-keeping.'

At first Poseidon's daughter demurred, saying that she had made her uncle a solemn promise, but the fireflies winking at her from the juniper bushes said that indeed she was young and weren't promises for adults to keep, and finally she was persuaded and handed over the silver scissors.

That night Poseidon's daughter did not go to the jetty but slept soundly in her palace bed, and in her dream her aunt Athena was a wise and whiskered fish which plied peacefully in and out of the windows.

Athena, meanwhile, took up her knapsack and hiked through the spinifex under the whitest of moons until she looked down upon the silvered rock of Kastro and the sleeping form of Zeus. Zeus lay outstretched on a marble boulder, his arms flung above his head like a child who has never known fear. Under cover of a cloud which shadowed the moon Athena crept up on the sleeping figure and knelt beside him. She gazed at his right hand, at the soft palm upturned, at the squat thumb, and lastly at the elongated pointing forefinger, the finger of pride, the finger which stabbed out such arbitrary commands. Then, full of resolve to separate the finger from its knuckle and the god from his pride, she took the silver scissors from her knapsack.

But before the blade encountered the golden skin, Zeus, without opening an eye, let out a great snort of triumph and seized Athena's wrist, so that her ambitions were quite confounded.

Athena, however, was above all a stateswoman, and possessed at all times an understanding of the political weaknesses of her opponents; understood, for instance, that Zeus could ill afford to see the citizens of Athens roused against him. And so she folded her hands in her lap and bowed her head with all appearance of meekness while Zeus paced the lemon grove till the red dust rose, and in his heart wrath struggled with expediency.

But what of Poseidon's daughter, then, with the night over and the butterfly-blue morning just beginning, the morning when Athena would pit wits and will behind her quest for Hanni? She stretched out her limbs in her cockle-shell bed, imagining how Hanni too would be waking now, stretching his lissom brown form, rubbing sleep from eyes slaty–green as a lizard's back; in luxurious superstition she mimicked every move he might make, down to the tiniest moue of the mouth and the most exquisite twitch of the toe.

When the conch shell sounded at the palace gate Poseidon's daughter could hardly contain her excitement. However, it was not her aunt Athena who was ushered in but – with much pomp and ceremony and pawing of horses – her eminent uncle Zeus. Zeus waved aside the deferences that were due to him and fixed a ferocious eye on his unruly niece, who, seeing the silver scissors safe once again in his belt, threw herself at his feet and was much afraid.

'Forgive me, Uncle,' she cried piteously.

Grasping her thick curls, Zeus gave vent to his temper.

'So you're discontented with your lot?' he bellowed, jerking her head this way and that. 'For a dream of mortality you would make fools of us all?'

'Forgive me, Uncle,' cried Poseidon's daughter, 'but I am young and foolish and in love.' And she sobbed and sobbed until her hot tears poured over her uncle's sandalled feet.

Somewhat mollified, Zeus slapped her lightly on the cheek. 'To live for such a brief time and float up like a dry leaf? Is this what you wanted?'

'Yes, Uncle, forgive me for my foolishness,' she sobbed.

At last Zeus picked her up and, stroking the tears from her reddened cheeks, said, 'Indeed you are young and foolish, my dear. But' – and now his lids drooped and his smile, if she had but noticed, was the smile of the panther before the pounce – 'unlike Poseidon and Amphitrite, you are at least ardent in your discontent. And this moves me to grant your wishes.'

Hearing this, Poseidon's daughter threw herself once more at Zeus's feet, but this time the tears she wept were tears of gratitude for his generosity.

'So up, my dear, and away to your Hanni,' purred Zeus. And taking his silver scissors he cut meticulously around her edges, leaving a mermaid-shaped gap in the sea for her hapless parents to mourn over.

Like an arrow Poseidon's daughter sped to the beach of Plati Yialos, where Hanni the windsurfer breakfasted moodily and alone. Up came her head from the tossing waves; her sharp eyes saw, and her sharp nose scented. On the shore the sand was smooth and yellow and stretched a mile on either side, and there was a dog-rose hedge which lilted pink in the wind and smelled of heaven.

Out of the foam came her tail, shaking off the last salty drops. Then she lay down on the sand to dry, as she had seen mortals do. Her tail, being the thinnest part of her, dried first, and the wind tickled it up and played with it. Then her belly and breasts dried and narrowed and the wind, having more purchase, blew her body straight up until she stood, as it were, on her narrow wet head, until finally, all dry and thin as paper, she floated up entirely.

Poseidon's daughter felt loose and tumbled and free, soaring in arcs as the wind willed her, and so happy was she with this fine flight that she did not hear the rumble of Zeus's laughter in the wind that tossed her. Presently, however, when she turned her will against the wind and sought to swoop low over Hanni's tent, she found that there was no weight in her, and although three seals in their half-sleep saw her flutter in the air helplessly, like a rag, later each remembered it as a dream and told nobody.

Meanwhile on the bright beach Hanni the windsurfer noticed nothing but the freshening of the air and the quickening of the wind, noticed not at all, as he ran down the shelf of the sand and sprang on to his surfboard, the sliver of celluloid which lay drying on the shore, glossy and transparent as a stranded jellyfish.

Only Athena on her rock promontory saw the trick that Zeus had played, and wrung her hands at the cruel fate of Poseidon's daughter. And turning her gaze vengefully on the belling sail of the surfboard and the mortal man who was the source of so much trouble, she sent up from the deeps in a great turmoil of waters a galleon fit for an emissary from Spain, and on the deck with her back to the mast was a grave-eyed dream of a woman with her face coolly empty and her fine straight hair adrift on the wind.

Hanni, seeing this vision erupt before him, spurred his surfboard until his sails filled and his board scudded, and with a soaring heart he set off in fleet pursuit across the blue Ionian sea. And for weeks afterwards the old men in the taverna, knowing nothing of Poseidon's daughter or the self-shaped gap she had left in the sea, speculated on the melancholy of the Nordic races and the madness the sun makes in them, and how poor Hanni with the heat in his head sped like a white stallion towards Turkey and was never seen again.

THE POWER OF LOVE

Patrick Roscoe

A Jose M. Polo Bueso

For one moment after the town was plunged into darkness there would reign shocked silence; then began a wailing as ancient as the loss of love itself. As a single being, townspeople uttered one loud protracted shriek at still another failure of power, protesting that such sudden darkness was impossible, disbelieving that it could fall without warning, unable to recall what had happened countless times in the past. For this event occurred with frequency during the rainy season, when lightning, which with thunder preceded every afternoon torrent, would strike one of the poles which suspended electrical cables above the earth; but in the dry season, too, a cow was apt to blunder disastrously into one of these tall wooden posts, and, in fact, the state electrical company was so negligent in affairs of maintenance that the poles invariably leaned this way or that, less erect than any Tower of Pisa, and the cables always drooped dispiritedly. Often all it took was one crow to rest a moment upon a wire to send the whole system crashing down to earth. Really, it was a miracle that the power did not fail more often; in times of pitch darkness, however, no one was inclined to count this or other small blessings.

How had the people of this place allowed themselves to become so quickly dependent upon a system which they did not understand and could not control? Only thirty years before electricity had been non-existent in the area, yet there had been no sense then that light was lacking or life was limited. People possessed kerosene lamps which operated upon principles simple to comprehend, and in the main room of each house, beneath a ceiling-hole to let out smoke, burned fire that was the same fire Prometheus had once stolen from heaven. Vision was adjusted for night, and daytime activities replaced by others after sunset; this would be the time to sit in a circle and tell stories, recalling the past from darkness, casting imagination into an equally obscure future; and then also there was time to read stars, to rest eyes, to romance. Night arrived at a more or less fixed hour and dawn followed a determined distance behind; this darkness was reliable in its comings and goings, unthreatening and familiar, not to be feared but only respected.

As soon as electricity reached the town, though, everyone threw away kerosene lamps and filled chimney-holes in ceilings. For many months all houses blazed with brilliant light from dusk to dawn, and during this period people bragged about the enormity of their electric bills and took pride in their gigantic consumption of watts. Very quickly it seemed that the skill required to strike a match, never mind to build a healthy fire, became irrevocably lost. 'All that time wasted in gloom,' was a common observation made beneath naked bulbs casting harsh light upon people who now seemed to see each other clearly for the very first time. (Indeed, one Señora Pérez promptly left her husband of thirty-seven years upon a first glimpse of his illumination by electricity, saying that until this moment she had never really known what he looked like, and that the sight was the farthest thing from favourable.) Even after this form of power became familiar, adults as well as children still enjoyed flicking a switch off or on, to see that miracles did in fact recur and to feel deep satisfaction that darkness could be defeated with the lightest touch of one finger. Yet there was poor understanding of how this victory was achieved: anyone could ponder the electrical cables running alongside the road in the direction of the capital city across the hills; but it was more difficult to envision their source in some massive generator constructed of concrete and wire and steel, and operated by men who at any moment might, through whimsy or carelessness or spite, cause current to cease flowing towards a town lost without it. Was this power nuclear, solar or hydro-electrical? Where exactly did it come from? What principles lay behind its production? Would it last for ever?

No one considered such questions. And it was characteristic of these people that they never had on hand candles in anticipation of an imminent electrical crisis; always after light was restored, as quickly as one hour later but sometimes not until the next morning or the morning after that, everyone firmly believed that it would never fail again – perhaps simply because it is impossible to imagine utter darkness when there is sufficient light, just as one cannot truly conceive of death during life's illumination. Inevitably the oldest child of each family would be sent out into the sudden darkness to buy candles at the store; but these always sold out in a matter of seconds and there would be left numerous households without the least spark of light. Their grown members would stand in doorways and gaze bitterly at candle flames wavering in neighbours' windows. They would flick light switches to no avail, sigh heavily, then retreat to bed no matter how early the hour, all at once unable to dream up a single occupation not dependent upon light, even that of making love.

But the children went out to play. Here could be seen in sharpest definition that the difference between younger and older beings was almost as great as that between any two distantly related species, such as the rhinoceros and the humming-bird, for the children had not yet learned how much there was to fear in darkness, or the many reasons why the unknown was necessarily dangerous, or that what was unseen must always be dreaded. The children ran screaming through familiar streets obscured into a strange landscape demanding exploration, and old games were by this same darkness transformed into new games which offered fresh challenges and operated upon distinct rules. Yet the force of darkness was liberating and disordering, like revolution, and to organized amusement the children preferred that of simply racing around a plaza no longer lit by lamps which on other evenings glowed softly upon blossoms and leaves. Why did every one of these children, without exception, feel stronger and surer, as if they had gained rather than lost the function of one sense? It is commonplace to observe that the absence of one sense prods others to come more alert; but this is cheap consolation at best, a grasping at straws of compensation similar to an abandoned lover's insistence upon the intense pleasure afforded by extra space in a bed that before was crowded. Once the mystery of night was supremely powerful, ruling without interference over lovers clinging together in the dark, background for blazing comets and emerging novae, a medium through which what was wild, come out from hiding, could prowl safely until dawn. Every step into unfathomable air was as frightening and exhilarating as a leap off the highest cliff above Christmas Bay: would you splash safely into water or would you land upon the rocks? Now stars seemed to shine more brightly, like the moon possessing greater significance, and the Milky Way was creamed thickly across the western slopes. Swooping like bats with sonar assistance, children pursued fireflies in the night, wishing to fill glass jars with specks of coloured light, decorating but not destroying darkness. Perhaps voices sounded more clear because they travelled from an unseen source and across distance unmeasured by vision. How then could you find a true friend except by pricking your ears to attention, turning your face in the right direction, following laughter that like a lighthouse beams you through dangerous dark water and safely on to shore? 'Where are you? Where are you?'cries someone suddenly lost from every companion in the world. 'Here! Here!' answers a saviour's voice; and so you journey towards this beacon, stumbling over unseen things a dozen times along the way, until a face regarded indifferently in daylight but dear in darkness emerges abruptly from obscurity, smelling of apples ripened slowly by sun and rain, only an inch away.

But no one called for Lindita Lopez to light them up the road when her mother sent her through darkness with a wand of wax clutched in one hand and the other hand curved around a flame that trembled with every step she took. Indeed, children fell silent and still during the slow passage of this girl, awed for reasons they did not fully understand. (Once, not so long ago, the simple appearance of a girl with Lindita's sixteen years who was not yet married, never mind engaged or at least in love, would have been sufficient cause for amazement.) 'Linda Lopez!' exclaimed some children, mistakenly. 'Rosario Lopez!' called out others, also inaccurately, also unsure exactly what the name signified, knowing only that when Rosario and Linda Lopez had existed there had been no failure of power.

Hearing these two names evoked outside, adults would bumble from beds to windows and look after Lindita's measured progress up the road, observing how the candle's flame threw sharply defined and shifting shadows across her face, lending its unshadowed areas a rosy hue and waxened complexion similar to that of the Virgin at whose feet you kneel and pray and beg. No matter how many times they witnessed this sight – and it occurred without fail on every occasion the power went out – townspeople would for a moment be tricked into believing that Linda or Rosario Lopez had returned to them; therefore, the darkness would go away at once and it would not come back. (During this moment the figure of Linda was interchangeable with that of Rosario, as if the two sisters had been made twins by their always being coupled together in the town's memory as the pair of girls who had disappeared with love, and had left darkness behind; in fact, Linda and Rosario had never looked the least alike, and it was Lindita's mother, Lupe, the Lopez girl who had stayed behind, who was the identical twin of Linda; but do not hope to convince anyone of this reality.) As darkness did not turn to light, the true identity of the girl stepping carefully up the road emerged upon the town's consciousness as the features of the world appear out of dawn's greying light, an unwrapped present that has been there all along; but still watchers remained fixed behind windows, driven to witness once again how the girl's head seemed disembodied, a face floating several feet above the earth, unconnected to anything, for the candlelight extended only part-way down her neck, leaving the existence even of supporting shoulders to be doubted. Sometimes the girl would stretch out her hand to hold the candle farther into the darkness, as if she heard some sound to the right or left of her and wished to illuminate its source; then her face also fell into obscurity, and only one hand and wrist remained visible. There were times, too, when a breeze would slip through the air and extinguish the candle altogether, creating a moment of suspense for its audience. Would Lindita stand still and attempt to relight her candle? Or would she walk forward into the darkness and risk becoming lost as her two aunts were lost – hopelessly, tragically, eternally? Suddenly a match flared, the candle's wick hissed, sparks subsided into steady light. Lindita's face re-emerged from darkness as she continued up the road like the single figure of a parade or a leader without followers, leaving behind adults who returned to bed more uneasy than before, and children who once again called like owls through the night. 'Who? Who?' they questioned. 'You? You?'

Yes, in the end this was Lindita Lopez, carrying a candle to her grandmother who sat on a sidewalk chair before her house, the single grown being out in the darkness, unaware of the present failure of power and unimpressed when Lindita brought her news of it. 'Is that you?' the old woman would query nearing footsteps. 'Oh, it's you,' she remarked, perhaps disappointed, when Lindita spoke her name. It was only Little Linda, forever a diminutive being, never more than a second, smaller version of an original Linda who once upon a time had run away with a carnival, her namesake's unknown aunt, her mother's always expected visitor, a presence concealed by the darkness of time and distance even when God's light shone as brilliantly as it had when the world was white; but that was long ago, everyone knew.

Or Señora Lopez waited for her other vanished daughter to return from the well into which she had descended without so much as a goodbye. Rosario would come up the road in soaked skirts and with dripping hair, the scent of fish encircling her head like a halo, a watery look in her eyes. Both prodigal daughters would arrive on one of these darkened nights, taking advantage of blackness to slip unseen towards their mother's old house kitty-corner from the school. The next day the two girls would be discovered lounging in nightgowns around those cluttered rooms, apparently not aged or otherwise altered by their long absences and various adventures, unable or unwilling to discuss whatever exotic experiences they might have undergone, already quarrelling with their mother over who would prepare the afternoon meal. At the sight of these reincarnated girls, townspeople would feel that all the hard nights of darkness they had suffered were only chapters of a single long dream: at last they had woken to find Linda and Rosario nibbling toasted bread in the plain light of morning as if they had never been away.

But Señora Lopez would not wish to touch the familiar hands and faces of Linda and Rosario, or to reclaim the shape of their bones as her own, for she was neither nostalgic nor sentimental, having cast aside such emotions long before she had woken one recent morning to find herself blind, although she had suffered no stroke or even unpleasant dream during that night of sound sleep. Her remaining daughter, Lupe, had discovered this blindness only by accident, only a number of days after it had occurred: Señora Lopez had not thought the subject worth mention, and gave the impression that since she had already seen everything in the world, it was no great loss in the end. Possibly she was relieved to be spared looking longer upon the same faces and streets she had looked upon long enough already; although this may have been quite a different matter if the world were entirely a place of beauty, such was clearly not the case. Señora Lopez might even have gone down on hands and knees to thank the Lord for rewarding her with failed vision, if she had been the kind of woman to express gratitude for what has already happened and cannot, more than likely, be reversed.

'This is just another phase,' she sometimes remarked to herself, not flinching when her fumbling fingers sent pots and pans crashing to the kitchen floor, as if she had lost the sense of hearing also. For several decades Señora Lopez had routinely knocked five years off her real age; after a certain day she began to boast of being more ancient than the oldest soul in town, all indisputable evidence to the contrary. Now, to herself if no one else, it appeared clear that her life had a history as long as the world's, and could be divided into eras and epochs each lasting millions of years. For example, ferns and evergreens first flourished in the Mesozoic era, precisely as when did Señora Lopez's maternal instincts. During the Pleistocene era she had been a slave to fashion, and her interest in science had in the Palaeozoic era emerged with the anthropod. When were rocks formed and at what point did fossils first appear? Hand in hand with the physical world Señora Lopez had evolved through romantic, nervous and cynical phases; subsequently she had turned philosophical, then mystical. Now she was blind and the world was in darkness. 'Of course it was dark last night,' she would impatiently reply when Lupe dropped by to discuss another failure of power. 'It's been dark for quite some time,' she would dryly add. Señora Lopez firmly believed that the day she had woken blind the world had lost its light, and it was true that from that time the electricity did begin to fail more frequently. She maintained an incredulous expression when Lupe tried to persuade her that a morning was brilliant with sunlight or that clouds resembling white horses chased each other across a deep blue sky. To compensate for the present lack of solar heat, she wore several layers of sweaters over her cool dry skin on those April afternoons when all her neighbours sweated, and predicted the commencement of a new ice age within the next six months.

Current events were, of course, only the beginning of the end. It would, however, have been difficult for Señora Lopez to defend herself against a charge of egoism if she were incautious enough to voice a further conviction that the end of her life, surely not too far in the distance, would coincide with that of the world. Certainly every human being believes, however irrationally and silently, that the world stops turning precisely when we draw our last breath. The most unbearable among death's many unbearable aspects is a suspicion that the planet will continue to spin after we are gone. Linda and Rosario return, finally, but only when our eyes have closed for good; again there is light, and love, from which we are excluded: no, this cannot be.

Characteristically, Señora Lopez had shrugged off Lupe's suggestion that, now blind, she might be more comfortable living with this surviving daughter's family. The old woman stayed on alone in her house across from the school, from which those relatives closest to her – mother, husband, daughters – had one by one departed in almost stately rhythm, at almost measured intervals of time, lending the emptying of this structure a kind of progressive and inevitable quality leading steadily toward the day it would be completely bare of life. Señora Lopez continued with her former occupations – she described herself as a student of the universe – with the same conviction in their great importance as before, except that now day and night became a single element and her activities could be pursued with greater flexibility and freedom. She might stroll down to the shore to sniff the sea at three a.m. or in her kitchen prepare a midnight lunch. Often she showed up at Lupe's with a bouquet of weeds before dawn, inclined to impart to her sleepy daughter the broad outlines of her latest philosophy. She wore, usually, a pair of fancy sunglasses with rhinestone rims even after dark, even when the night was moonless.

By this point in her history Señora Lopez had achieved a singular status among the townspeople; but this is not to say that she was either popular or particularly liked. Rather, through the years she had somehow slipped beyond the limits of those critical standards by which one neighbour judges another, and was finally regarded as an original phenomenon, some alternative form of life more similar, perhaps, to that which flourishes upon Venus than to any here on earth. No one, for example, would dream to consider whether this woman were good or bad: such distinctions, in this case, did not quite apply. By means of sustained energy and sheer stubbornness she seemed to have achieved some kind of final victory over neighbours who after all their cruel battering by love and loss simply lacked sufficient force to put the woman into that place where she so assuredly belonged. She was only too well aware of her historical importance to the town, a position founded chiefly upon the legendary disappearances of her two daughters, Rosario and Linda, which mythology was primarily a work of her own creation. There had occurred one deciding episode wherein Señora Lopez had triumphantly battled the schoolteacher over whether the events surrounding her daughters' vanishings should be taught in the classroom, and, if so, whether they should be given more or less weight than, say, the discovery of America. Even after she became blind Señora Lopez did not relinquish her habit of marching down the main street conscious that every eye was fixed upon her famous figure; pretending oblivion to this constant attention, she only managed, in the way of incognito movie stars, an air of showier self-awareness. There was, too, her custom of entering any house in town without so much as a cursory knock, during night as well as day, in order to issue some pronouncement which simply could not wait. More than one legally married couple, making love in what they believed to be the privacy of their bedroom, started guiltily in the midst of everything to hear, just inches from the pillow, that somewhat hoarse and decidedly unmusical voice inform them that the circumference of a circle is twice its radius.

If Señora Lopez did fancy herself the unopposed leader of the town, this was through fault of no one but the citizens themselves; for they had never got around to electing a mayor to act as even a symbolic figure of leadership, and, in addition, that loose body of civic government known as the junta had some time ago stopped meeting for reasons no one could recall but which, more than likely, had something to do with plain indolence. Also, there was no police chief in the place, though, it must be admitted, extra unruliness did not seem to result from this lack. Still, no recognized power existed within the town to take Señora Lopez in hand and instruct her that she could not out of the blue inform the priest that he had only until sunset to pack his bags and get out of town, since icon-adoring would no longer be practised in his church when the building was, at once, converted into a gymnasium.

What seemed most unbelievable about this whole business was that, at the same time she ran roughshod over private as well as public affairs, Señora Lopez made not the slightest attempt to conceal her firm opinion that these concerns were unworthy of her attention. It was no secret that she had for years held the town and its inhabitants in contempt; hardly less well known was the fact that she had, to all intents and purposes, driven Rosario and Linda from the place, and, as anyone could plainly see, held Lupe only in disdain for remaining behind. Why then had not Señora Lopez herself gone out into the wide and wonderful world about which she continually bragged, as if it were one among her many prized possessions? 'She is a big fish in our little pond,' was all anyone could reply to such a puzzle. The woman in question made it a practice to hint now and then, in a martyred tone of voice, that she had a moral, if not spiritual obligation to the town, and at the price of considerable personal sacrifice was prepared to see this unrewarding duty through to its bitter end. It may be remembered that once, at one of her lowest points of popularity (this was when she had strutted into the midst of honeymooners' pleasures with pills and prophylactics, advising the young lovers to forego the privilege of procreation until they themselves had grown out of infancy, a maturation which might not, it was implied, occur at any near date in the future), there had formed a furtive campaign to buy the woman a one-way ticket out of town on the battered blue bus that each dawn passed through on its way to the capital city. Since the fare for this journey was less than one hundred pesos, one suspects that lack of funds was not the principal reason why the scheme did not materialize into reality. Less popularly known, but also aborted in the end, was the plot to pay a certain young man, well-endowed physically if not intellectually, to make discreet thrice-weekly visits to Señora Lopez. Her husband had been dead for years, there had been no known suitors since: the fulfilment of specific desires presently not satisfied might, it was hoped, serve to lessen Señora Lopez's discontentment with the world outside her door by increasing her enjoyment of more intimate matters within it. By this point in its history, however, the town was so mistrustful of even the most mercenary manifestations of love that it did not pursue what was, potentially, this excellent idea.

So it seemed that more than any particular genius, Señora Lopez's dominance of her neighbours was due to the passivity, or lack of energy, which had befallen them like a virus without cure. At present there was a palatable heaviness in the air, not only during the rainy season but in the fresh dry months of winter too. Yet so sluggish were the townspeople's movements, so unhopeful their faces, so dull their eyes that one had to suspect these to be symptoms of more than just physical ill-being. Such, indeed, was the case. For years Señora Lopez had waged the kind of bold and persistent propaganda campaign which would have filled the most hardened politician with respect, and all her slogans hammered home the message that love was gone from this place for good. If Linda and Rosario returned things might change, the old woman intimated; but she did not seem particularly expectant, or eager, for this to transpire. Brainwashed citizens were absolutely convinced that they had ridden the ferris wheel of love once too often: there had been a vast number of expeditions up toward the white stars and moon but each of these exalted journeys on the wheel had swiftly taken a downward turn before the heights could be fully appreciated, leaving passengers of especially rapid descents to wonder afterwards if the elevated altitudes had even been achieved. Now the mere idea, never mind mention of love caused experienced beings to shudder: who would willingly choose to undergo again the inevitable disappointment, the certain heartache, the sure souring of what once was sweet? And the heavy air was simply void of romance. Poets, philosophers and scientists claim love to be the most natural and universal human emotion, in addition to being the force that turns the world; this might not be entirely true, for adolescents in this place did not stumble willy-nilly into the swamp of sexual love, nor did they pen sonnets in the thrall of more rarefied emotion. One must take into account the decided influence which the overt example of elders may play in this and other matters: here there was precious little mature hand-holding or smooching for youth to imitate, and one wonders if we are still monkeys in the end to ape the act of kissing and caressing just as if we had never left off swinging on vines through the jungle. There should also be acknowledged the importance of ambience, or suggestive scenery, in this business. Now, as everyone dully repeated, Aprils were not sweet, nor was the moon composed of honey. But didn't the same blossoms exude the same scent as in days of old, and weren't the present moon and stars in possession of the very same properties they had owned while acting as stimulating symbols of love? Señora Lopez, who might once have been relied upon to brush aside this question with a lecture concerning the undeniable drive of hormones and the unquenchable thirst for reproduction, remained curiously silent. Really, it was astounding that children continued to be born in the town, to such a dry and uninspired chore was the act of lovemaking now reduced. 'If only those two Lopez girls hadn't left us,' mechanically remarked younger citizens who had never had the opportunity to experience ecstatic love, repeating by rote what they had heard several million times before.

After the failure of her vision, several neighbours

offered to lend Señora Lopez their spectacles, feeling that her blindness might only be an extreme visitation of myopia in a woman who had always welcomed the extreme. Others presented her with walking sticks with which she might feel the unseen earth like a handy third hand, or a divining rod. But outnumbering such good samaritans by far were those who were content to mutter that in several ways Señora Lopez had been blind for years. Still others believed her to be as sharp-eyed as ever; for some particular reason she had chosen to play blind at this moment, and her motives might or might not emerge from obscurity one fine day. On several occasions suspicious citizens crept up behind the woman and suddenly waved a hand before her face in an attempt to catch her blinking; the failure of this ruse only reaffirmed to the doubtful that Señora Lopez had accumulated an impressive amount of experience as actress as well as spy. If there was any hope that disability might diminish the woman's vigilant posture in regard to her neighbours' affairs, this was quickly dashed. She strode the streets with exactly the same speed and decisiveness as always, and offered the same kind of uninvited criticism to all and sundry. 'Carmen, aren't you going to cut that mop of yours some day soon?' she might inquire, passing an extravagantly coiffured lady on the corner. 'There does exist a phenomenon known as second sight,' was Señora Lopez's explanation for her continued ability to see. In fact, and perhaps inevitably, this particular form of vision was even more selective than the woman's formerly capricious style of viewing the world. She now gave a fairly convincing sense that to see merely with one's eyes was the most vulgar, and limited, mode of vision.

Several changes did occur in Señora Lopez's behaviour after her ocular alteration. For one, on evenings when the power failed she refrained from making her usual unannounced visits to townspeople, and was conspicuously absent during those hours of darkness. Cringing within unlit rooms, people thought bitterly that this was just like the woman; now, exactly when they would have welcomed her rude rupture through their doorways, no doubt full of intricate explanations for the failure of light, and sprinkling terms such as neutron, electron and ion like dazzling stardust through the dark, she seemed resolved to leave the townspeople to their own devices. Also, in her movement around the town during illuminated hours, Señora Lopez made none of her prior constant mentions of Linda and Rosario, although people were at this point especially anxious for word of the two girls, and of their mother inquired a dozen times an hour if either had sent a written announcement regarding an overdue return, with constant light and love, to town. It seemed that, precisely when she had achieved the complete taming and entrapment of her neighbours, Señora Lopez opened the doors of cages they were too frightened to leave.

It is no wonder, then, enclosed inside on all those obscure evenings, that people automatically cast blame for this darkness directly upon the erect shoulders of Señora Lopez. Who else could be held accountable for such a failure of power, for so sudden an extinguishing of brilliant light? How much easier was it to travel straight to this conclusion than to undertake inner searches for the solution to that difficult equation which might balance love with loss, dark with light, effort with reward. It was not impossible to imagine, with some degree of clarity, one old woman situated at the base of a pole that with the aid of many others supported above the earth a cable both thicker and longer than any umbilical cord. She saws vigorously at the wooden post with one of her dead husband's rusted saws, pauses only once to wipe sweat from her forehead, stands back to watch the tall pole crash to the ground with a force that shakes the world, walks away through the resulting darkness, never once tripping on the way. What else could the woman do during all the nights she withdrew her presence from people who had, though they might be loath to admit it, become dependent upon it? Did she return home after the job was done to cower in a dark corner, more frightened and alone than anyone? Did she with calloused hands turn over silver pins encrusted with eyes of jewels, shining souvenirs from old lovers dulled by death? Perhaps she powders her face white and dances with named shadows in her kitchen. Or with a grim smile of satisfaction she raps the knuckles of one hand against the bones which enclose her heart, confident that the stage of human evolution in which love flourished has gone for good. Or she stuffs sweet cakes and candy into her mouth, after all this time still sick with hunger, more starving than her thinnest neighbours.

If so, all crumbs were carefully brushed from sight by the time Lindita set her candle just inside Señora Lopez's doorway, where a breeze could not blow it out. She settled herself on the sidewalk beside her grandmother, who immediately forgot the girl's presence, or decided to ignore it. Lindita breathed heavily from her walk up the road, as if this journey were one of miles instead of metres; it seemed, always, to exhaust her supply of energy, leaving her to wilt upon the sidewalk, her face without expression, even more silent than usual. The night was also quiet: no voices of stars floated from the Tropicana Cine, and the playing children had fallen asleep somewhere on the sand, or in nests of leaves beneath banana trees. Señora Lopez removed her rhinestone sunglasses, glanced once at her granddaughter, then peered more sharply into the darkness before her; apparently, this sight did not bring her pleasure, for a more than usually disagreeable expression creased her face. 'Tomorrow is Tuesday,' she remarked aggressively, if only because the next day was, in fact, a Thursday. 'September is always my favourite month,' she added in a similar spirit of challenge, showily inhaling what was, beyond any shadow of a doubt, April air.

Lindita tunelessly hummed a mambo number from one of the record albums she had discovered in her grandmother's house one day. Digging through the accumulation of years in those rooms was like boring into the ground and encountering variously coloured and textured layers of earth, rock and fossil: one passed through a dizzying number of distinct strata. Here were notebooks containing the data of unfinished scientific experiments, there ran a thick vein of moulded movie magazines; a little deeper lay the crushed remains of a thousand brandy bottles, and farther below rotted dried flowers, love letters and valentines. Through a process of alchemy these disparate elements could be combined to create the philosopher's gold, the priceless alloy of experience or, at the very least, some fuel like coal capable of producing a seemingly endless supply of energy. In daylight Lindita often studied her grandmother's skin like a map, viewing wrinkles of rivers, creases outlining whole continents, discoloured patches that urged the imagination to work; yet the girl gave no sign of encountering in this living atlas certain places she wished to explore and to know. Sitting beside her grandmother, Lindita could very well have felt her own self to be as unmarked and thin and light as a sheet of blank paper easily able to float upward or downward on any wisp of wind, and waiting to be written upon in ancient hieroglyphics or in language yet to be invented.

'It feels like rain,' Señora Lopez now abruptly mentioned, when the first drops of the year's moisture would not fall for at least another month, her voice a rough smelting of all the raw materials that striped her mind. When Lindita did not demur, Señora Lopez realized anew that here was another in a long line of silent Lopez girls, one with eyes as blank and mind mysterious as Rosario or Linda. It had seemed, long ago and briefly, that Lupe was also a member of this enigmatic species; but she had, upon her twin's disappearance, become astonishingly earthbound and ordinary, and more like her mother than either she or Señora Lopez would have cared to admit. Lindita never once expressed the smallest opinion or slightest volition of will. Without a word she carried candles up the road on darkened evenings, appearing to feel neither satisfied nor discontented with the job but performing it thoroughly and with a certain sense of its weight. It seemed that she accepted this to be, at least for the present, her sole function in the world, and that all the hours between the bearing of flame were only time to rest from a recent journey or to prepare for the next one. If the girl had not been especially quick and clever at school, Señora Lopez might have believed her a complete idiot; as it was, the grandmother never found the girl's silence and stillness restful, but fidgeted beside her in the dark, tapping toes and cracking knuckles, annoyed that she could not begin to fathom what, if anything, transpired in Lindita's mind. Was she secretly planning to disappear from the town, to follow in the footsteps of her equally silent aunts? Just as likely, thought Señora Lopez, she was capable of murdering in their bed everyone whose last name began with an R.

'Perhaps you should think of going home now,' Señora Lopez presently suggested in the tone of voice one uses to address a very small child or a mentally handicapped adult. Mutely, Lindita rose with one sudden, seamless motion, brushed dust off the folds of her white dress, and walked away down the dark, deserted street. She seemed to find no difficulty in making her way without illumination; now the paleness of her dress seeped into the air around her, revealing precisely where she should place her feet. When her phosphorescent form disappeared around the corner of the school, Señora Lopez turned her gaze toward the candle still flickering in the doorway. It had shrunk several inches, nearly melted into a flat pool of wax. Señora Lopez considered the physical relationship between liquids and solids, and how heat or cold could transform one into the other. As the candle burned out, she shivered. She set her rhinestone sunglasses more firmly upon her nose and strode off to take the temperature of the river that cascaded down the hills to the sea.

Within the sound of the latter's waves, Lupe stood heavily at the window of her pink house down the road, blinking blindly into the darkness beyond. 'She's been gone too long,' she stated flatly. 'What's taking her?'

'Who?' asked Pedro, the glowing end of his cigarette marking the place he occupied across the room.

'Greta Garbo,' replied Lupe sharply, her mouth twisting at its corners.

Who? Her twin sister, Linda. Her younger sister, Rosario. Her daughter, Lindita. Her grandmother, her father, her mother. Her own younger self. They had all been gone too long, and, lacking knowledge of Braille,

Lupe could not read the darkness to know if it spelled their continued absence, or their quick return.

'I was a fool to send Lindita up there,' regretted Lupe, as she always did at a certain point after pushing her daughter with a candle out the door. 'The old lady doesn't know the difference between day and night. A candle or a chandelier, it's all the same to her.'

Yet it would, Lupe knew, have been wrong to allow Señora Lopez to sit alone before her house perhaps unaware that the power had gone out, in the same way it would have been wrong to permit a human corpse to lie unprotected in the jungle and be devoured by wild animals during the night, reduced to a number of clean, widely scattered bones by morning. Whenever Lupe visited her mother, she made a point of turning on all the houselights when she arrived and leaving them on when she departed. Often she found herself walking up the road to do this very thing: illuminate the space around a woman who was seemingly indifferent to such light. Sometimes Lupe deliberately passed by her mother's house an hour or two after leaving it; invariably, she would see that the rooms had been returned to darkness, and could envision her mother – white hair pulled back into tight pony tail, dark skin stretched tautly over strong facial bones, lips pressed firmly together – moving purposefully from room to room, snapping off the lights.

This regard for whether her blind mother sat in a dark or a lighted room was not, Lupe realized, the most useful expenditure of her energy. It was also one of the things people would point to if wishing to offer proof that Lupe was as unremarkable as one more coconut tree. It was so common to speak of Lupe as the only ordinary Lopez woman that, she often suspected, her mind and body bowed obediently beneath the weight of such unanimous opinion, and assumed a degree of conventionality far beyond what might, if left alone, have been their natural inclination. To her own amazement, Lupe frequently heard herself utter the most dreary commonplace even as she was aware that it was the last thing she really wished to say. Thoughts would stray into her head which she would stare at in disbelief, as being alien and even inimical there. Even her body had thickened and blurred as it passed the age of thirty, losing its original lines and genetic uniqueness, becoming interchangeable with the form of any similarly-aged woman in town.

But sometimes she was able to view her destiny as the daughter who had stayed behind to be as thrilling and potent as those of her escaped sisters. Wasn't there, in fact, something profoundly flashy and facile in the melodramatic disappearances of Rosario and Linda, one down a wishing-well, the other with a travelling fair? Might it not require a certain strength of character to stay behind and marry undistinguished Pedro, bear and raise unfathomable Lindita, deal with the continually difficult Señora Lopez? 'I have accepted my fate,' Lupe sometimes thought, with a mixture of bemusement and pride, as she swept her living-room floor for the second time in one day. Then the ordinary shape of her life, its straight edges and tidy corners, took on an aura of grandeur, and the muted colours of her existence glowed with quiet, almost religious light. Yet there were also moments when it seemed that the inheritance promised the earth's meek was decidedly vague: when, precisely, would that famous will be read, and upon exactly whose death?

Still, it could seem that the unassuming manner in which she occupied her space upon the earth was celebrated not only by the people of the town, but by the earth itself. The song of birds, the sighs of sea, the rustle of leaves in the field across the road: this was, perhaps, universal acknowledgement of her role in the world, and natural acceptance of her manner in performing this role. There were times when, it seemed to Lupe, the town was increasingly taking on its own character: houses, streets, the entire framework of inanimate objects which supported the existence of the townspeople, seemed to grow more expressive in direct ratio to the inhabitants' deepening wanness. Whatever finally happened to the people here, the place itself would live on, and, more than that, would not, uninhabited, necessarily be a lesser entity. Whatever resonance of emotional current that still flowed through the emptied town would not have to be that of ghosts haunting humanless houses or, if it came to that, of inanimate matter simply echoing sentiments it had over a long period of time absorbed from now absent beings. To see the physical structure of the town as functioning solely to support human life was to view things strictly from the human side of the fence. It might be more intelligent to suggest that in the larger scheme of things the people of this town had a very limited, if useful role to play in its development. Yes, they constructed streets and buildings which without their labour would not be there, and even inhabited them for a space of time; but, especially during those long evenings when the power failed and all lay in darkness, it seemed more and more that the town was waiting for these people to leave, as any place occupied against its will waits for the invaders to depart. Lupe could quite easily envision the town several hundred years in the future, in more or less the same condition as at present, having perhaps been spruced up once or twice in the interval by batches of citizens who had married, given birth and died there;

that is, who had to all appearances settled in to stay but, in the end, had only been passing through.

Of course Lupe did not say any of this. She never spoke of any of the thoughts which occurred to her while she did the week's wash, prepared the evening meal, or waited for the power to be restored once again. Who could she have spoken to? Pedro? Her mother? The first would ask if she were ill, the second would by reflex contradict. Anyway, maybe everyone in town secretly harboured ideas about the nature of their existence, the composition of their lives, the reasons for their need for light and love. Perhaps the place buzzed with such thought, an audible sound in the air mistakenly believed to be produced by electrical cables strung above the streets. 'I'm in love,' thought Lupe on evenings when she walked up to her mother's and heard the humming of wires overhead, a sound more constant than the complaints of crickets, and louder than the beating of her heart in darkness.

Lupe's fingers explored the table top beside her and encountered the flashlight she knew would be there. To ensure that its batteries still contained power, she flicked it off and on several times, directing the beam of light into the darkest corner of the room, into Pedro's eyes. He sat placid and fat and unblinking as a Buddha, or the icon of some obscure religious ceremony to which she had been attentive for years without, finally, understanding its purpose. What God was Pedro meant to represent, to evoke, to summon? What was the name of the faith which he had inspired in her for seventeen years? 'I'm a fool in love,' Lupe always thought, hurrying down the road after turning on her mother's lights, seeing the lights of her own house burning before her, arriving there breathless and ecstatic, struggling to choke the prayer of love that of its own will rose through her throat at the sight of Pedro twanging his guitar beneath the avocado tree while up in the plaza the church bell tolled. At the same time, it appeared that this worship were performed in darkness or in blindness: on nights when the power failed and was then restored, Lupe would be shocked by sudden illumination into wondering how it were possible for a human being to alter drastically during what was apparently only several hours of darkness. Could, for example, an alert, handsome young man evolve so quickly into his complete opposite? Could this being before her – dreamy, docile, distant – be Pedro? Had she only shaped from empty air the figure that was the object of her love? There occurred similar instances when Lupe would glance out her window to see the figure of a young girl coming down the road, and with the speed of light flashed through her mind images of Rosario, Lindita, Linda, her mother. Then she would feel herself bound tightly by a rope of love so tangled that it was impossible to determine which end of it came from the past and which led to the future. For a moment she would feel herself hopelessly entrapped in this dark, knotted religion of love, this adoration of what she could not really see, and she would not feel released upon realizing that the girl on the road was unrelated and unknown to her.

She would miss Pedro when they were parted, when she was gone. She missed him already. 'What do I mean?' thought Lupe, moving toward the doorway, preparing to go out alone for the first time on a night when the power had failed. In search of her daughter, or someone else? She wanted to write out a list of instructions which would tell Pedro exactly how to take care of himself when she was not there to do the job. Remember to eat lots of fresh fruit. Be careful not to swallow fishbones. If it rains, put a pot beneath the hole in the kitchen ceiling. And try to look after Lindita, although I suspect that there will be no way of looking after her in the end.

Instead she said, 'I'll go up there and bring Lindita back myself.'

Lupe stepped from her doorway and began to walk up the road. There was no moon. She felt the world welcome her presence; she could almost hear it murmur invitingly, like a host finally faced with a long and pleasurably anticipated guest. Lupe trained her flashlight sometimes a little distance upon the dark road before her, sometimes directly down toward her feet. Once she paused to point the light straight up into the sky; the beam travelled only a short distance before it was blotted out by inky air. 'I've walked this road a million times,' she thought, just as the road seemed to take on a new curve and she found herself in the middle of a patch of thorny bushes. Swinging the flashlight to bat away a branch that touched her face, the instrument flew from her hand, twirled like a baton through the air, and fell with a thud some distance away, its power extinguished by rough impact with the ground.

Lupe stood still and thought clearly. She hadn't walked far. She couldn't be more than several steps from the road. The plaza was probably just on the other side of these bushes; if she walked in a straight line, she must find it. Or could the world change its features in the blink of an eye, alter itself into only a stranger of the moment before? Was it only yesterday that she had been a slender girl swimming naked through the moonlit sea, parting the dark water surely, diving through the salt, able to see even in the dark?

Lupe did not consider calling for help at this moment, in part because she did not feel in need of assistance and in part because, even if she were, frightened townspeople would not leave safe houses to venture into unlit streets and become, possibly, more lost than the person they hoped to find. Could her voice travel through these bushes, across the plaza, up the main street, around the corner of the school, to the doorway where her mother and daughter gazed into this same darkness but in it saw distinct things?

She could stay where she was and wait for the electricity to be restored or for dawn to arrive, and the power of light would guide her safely back to the ordinary road she was familiar with and from which she had not once dreamed of straying, except in a past so distant it might have been a separate lifetime. Or the power of love might be strong enough to draw her like a magnet to its source, that unlike pole re-aligning her atoms, attracting her. Before Lupe could consider the merits of either patience or paramagnetics, she felt herself move through the bushes, journey deeper into their thickness and their darkness. When sharp thorns pierced her skin there resulted immediate satisfaction, almost painful pleasure, in having obscure, inner discomfort concentrated, and relieved, in a specific, physical way. What was the name for this pleasure mixed with pain? Two sensations inextricably entwined, utterly interdependent, unable to exist without their opposite. There were Rosario and Linda walking before her, not looking backward, perhaps unaware that she followed a short distance behind, soon to catch up. Their white dresses gleamed in the growth, which seemed now an ancient forest untouched by man, old trees the trunks of which, if viewed in cross section, would be seen to contain rings like the ripples which expand around the place where a stone is tossed into water, each circle of wood representing decades, together adding up to centuries. This forest was the growth of the distant past or of an equally distant future. Where had she come from and where was she going? Lupe resisted the urge to glance behind her, and felt a sharp stab of regret mixed with curiosity: what would happen to the town, and to all its inhabitants who believed themselves lost without light and love? Lupe shook her head once, as if negating doubt or disagreeing with fear. Then she fixed her eyes more firmly upon her two sisters, and walked farther toward the light beyond the dark.

It was an indication of exactly how deeply the town had sunk into apathy, descending far lower, obviously, than any of its frequent descents of the past, that the disappearance of Lupe went nearly unremarked, causing scarcely more comment than the straying from sight of a favourite pet mouse. Was this event only what everyone had anticipated for years, come to pass anticlimactically late? Was it merely the sober completion of unfinished business, the tidy closing of a circle, the neat end to a chapter that had dragged on far too long? There was, in fact, absolutely no sense of recognition that this was the kind of cathartic occurrence which can release pent up emotion of the deepest power and significance, thereby clearing the way for new calm, or further tragedy.

In the pale light of morning townspeople seemed, as after every night of failed power, relieved that light had been restored (the electricity had recommenced to function just before dawn, almost exactly when its lack became a less crucial concern), but too drained by the ordeal of surviving darkness to celebrate such relief, and overly fearful of returning night to enjoy what was, undoubtedly, only its temporary defeat. There arose, in any case, no excited speculation that Lupe had gone in search of her two sisters and would, on the day after tomorrow at the very latest, return with them to town, each astride a gleaming white horse, together forming a triumphant trinity. No prophets proudly proclaimed that they had seen the disappearance of Lupe from a distant point in the past, and few fabulists imagined that now the town might be free to reinvent itself by trading in its old symbols for fresh ones of entirely different size and shape and import.

True, several women did at noon visit Pedro in the small pink house, bearing prepared meals which might compensate in part for the loss of Lupe's culinary skills. They spoke with the husband as if there had befallen him an inconvenience that presented only practical problems, something more akin to irritation than to tragedy. Neither Pedro nor Lindita seemed terribly affected by Lupe's absence; certainly, there was no public crying or keening. It was as if Lupe had departed on the most mundane of journeys, one taken strictly out of necessity and without delight, something more similar to a trip to the dentist in the capital city than to any glamorous, pleasure-seeking jaunt to Acapulco. It might have been considerate of Lupe to have left a note informing her husband and daughter of her destination, and the probable length of her sojourn there, but the absence of such information was most likely due to a hasty, spontaneous departure; really, there was no harm done in the end. By and by Pedro remembered that once Lupe had voiced a vague desire to visit a girlhood friend, Anita, who some years before had moved to another town several hundred kilometres away. Lindita remarked that her mother had forgotten to take along a favourite silver bracelet. Mention of a return, either sooner or later, was not made by husband or daughter; nor, indeed, by anyone else in town.

No, there was no anguished protest that here was the

final straw, the last unbearable loss, the real end of hope for returned light and love. Perhaps this was because townspeople had more pressing, immediate concerns on hand: after Lupe's disappearance, it seemed that the electrical situation grew more serious, although no one made a connection between these two things. Surely now the power failed more often, and was on each occasion restored less quickly? 'We've paid our bills,' people puzzled, studying official stamped receipts from the state electrical company. Soon one night out of every three was dark, and on the other two nights bulbs burned weakly, emitting light that was tinted grey or brown, and never brilliant, never white. Such electrical inconvenience was augmented by the fact that with time dusk came to fall earlier in evening and dawn to rise at a later hour of morning, when there was no reason involving equinox or solstice for this. Astronomy aside, only the blindest of faith can hope that the world will keep turning for no other reason than because it has already spun for so long. If there is solar eclipse, why should it last only briefly? And why should there be daylight simply because yesterday a sun was in the sky? Repetition lulls in science as well as in love, and is often confused with constancy: when a lover expresses devotion for the thousandth time, we are unable to entertain the possibility that this may be the final time, although the light of love burns with unmistakable weakness in those fickle, starry eyes.

During the years it had enjoyed uninterrupted electricity the town's powers of imagination and memory had atrophied, for these gifts are strengthened by darkness. When a room descends into obscurity, you must call upon memory to know that the chair is by the window and the table in the corner; and for love to be sustained without light, imagination is required to conjure up the expression of concern on an unseen lover's face. In darkness the townspeople strained to exercise these two flabby muscles; but they seemed hopelessly weakened, and left pairs of lovers to feel alone and unadored even when they shared the same dark room. Whose body is in my arms? What is the shape of the mouth pressed upon mine? These kinds of questions evolved into doubt in the very existence of present love, and during all its unilluminated nights the town attempted in vain to retrieve old flames from the past, seeking the consolation to be found in clasping a known shape to your breast, even if this body is only recollection. What had happened to the stories of the white horse, and to stories of all the other beings which once had soothed the town while it drifted in oceans of darkness, far from any shore that gleamed a white promise of solid ground? The town disremembered the part it had played in the departure of its former lovers, and ignored also that it had not wished for their return until these absent beings had lost their sharp outlines and visible forms. It seemed that each charged wave of power that had flowed through the town had been a part of electroconvulsive therapy, whereby alternating currents of eighty or ninety volts are passed between electrodes attached to the right and left temples of the patient until unconsciousness is achieved, leaving him or her to wake up groggy and confused, and with large portions of memory irredeemably lost. Now the town was unable to recall the true significance of Linda, Rosario and Lupe Lopez; these became three names which could suggest a number of details unconnected to each other, emotionally flat and without power. Might the quick destruction of painful memory be a mercy in the end? Should we thank the cold-eyed doctor in his clean white coat? Was it finally for the best to forget light and love when they had even during their shining hour been unfaithful and untrue, and always the cause for more suffering than joy? 'No and no and no,' insisted Señora Lopez before her unlit house, pounding her leg with one hard, clenched fist to emphasize her denial of compromise and defeat. She gazed wildly into the surrounding darkness, she trembled in her sidewalk chair. The dark houses beyond pulsed weakly with hidden life; there was no witness to the moments when Señora Lopez arched her back, stretched her neck and pushed into the darkness a face upon which waves of wild emotion washed one after the other. Was that a tear in her eye, or only irritation caused by dust suddenly risen by wind from the road? Night after night Señora Lopez would at a certain moment place her rhinestone sunglasses upon her nose, as if in the deep darkness before her appeared a light, too blinding and too bright, from which she needed protection. She was always composed, if also sometimes cranky, by the time Lindita drew near, shimmering up the street.

The girl carried a candle up the road on the very first night of failed power after her mother went missing, although of course Lupe was no longer there to urge her to perform this task. The expedition was regarded by townspeople as a shocking lapse of taste, a rude refusal to undergo even the briefest period of mourning for the missing mother; Lindita's failure to eschew her white dress, or else to sew a black band on one white sleeve, was unpardonable. 'A Lopez is a Lopez is a Lopez,' judged jaundiced citizens. The girl walked as slowly and steadily as before, but it appeared that the central purpose of her walk was no longer to take light to her grandmother; it seemed, instead, that the journey and not the destination was what counted now. Lindita circled through the town, passing up and down every street, even the least populated and poorest ones, extending her passage so far and long that by the time she reached Señora Lopez the candle would have very nearly burned out. Although her face was as uninterpretable as always, there was something stubborn or determined in Lindita's very insistence in making this journey in the face of what became the complete indifference of the townspeople. They began to close shutters against the sight of her passing: the flickering candle set off disturbing sparks in their minds, annoying them for reasons they could not understand, bothering them with suspicion that there was something important, perhaps a matter of life and death, that they had forgotten. What was it? To endure pitch darkness behind covered windows seemed preferable to viewing this girl in white slip past the corners of their eyes.

Yes, it was a silent and solitary voyage that Lindita made now, for since her mother had abandoned the town no children darted through the darkness, or hooted like owls across the vacant plaza: 'Who? You?' At present the town's youngest beings also remained inside when the power failed, as frightened as their parents of darkness which soon seemed to possess a density greater than atmosphere can possibly possess, resembling a nearly liquescent medium in which one could wade or swim or drown. The quality of darkness became such that the candle did not illuminate even isolated portions of the girl who bore it, but appeared to travel the streets of its own power, independent of human or inhuman assistance.

On these nights when Lindita arrived at her grandmother's she would appear more tired than before, and was more silent, too. Communication between her and Señora Lopez, never extensive, became severely reduced. Often when the old woman did strike up conversation, sailing into one of her old monologues upon the implications of thermal power, it was only to discover that her granddaughter was sleeping. Señora Lopez would remove her sunglasses and study the unconscious girl for several moments, apparently seeking to reach some sort of conclusion about her; then she showily cleared her throat, or lightly kicked the girl to wake her up and send her home. On days following dark nights Lindita would enjoy a sleep so deep it resembled coma, as still as stone upon her bed in the front room of the small pink house, always clad in her inevitable white dress, which by and by became rather worse for wear, with frayed hems and missing buttons and unvanquishable stains. Pedro tiptoed about his dreaming daughter, housekeeping with an efficiency that would have surprised no one familiar with his work in the plantations above the town. With a mixture of puzzlement and pain he watched his daughter sink more deeply into silence, move nearly beyond language, go without a word to the cupboard where she stored her candles, ordered by bulk from a capital city wholesaler, the moment the power failed. Often on those afternoons which were each a little dimmer than the one before Señora Lopez would penetrate the door with a scientific magazine or the text of an eastern religion beneath one arm. Nodding once to Pedro, she would sit by Lindita's bed, draw back the sleeping girl's closed eyelids for quick inspection of the pupil, then become absorbed in her reading material; although her eyes did not appear to travel along the lines of words, the old woman's lips moved continually.

'Don't worry,' she said to Pedro once. 'I've seen this before. She'll be all right in the end.'

Señora Lopez's response to her loss of Lupe may only be guessed at: this was something to which she made not the slightest allusion, and from all anyone could tell, she was not even aware that her last daughter had vanished. At this time, however, she did come to appreciate her son-in-law for the very first time. Previously, Señora Lopez had disregarded Pedro past the point of rudeness, as if the politest thing one could do was to pretend he did not exist. 'Who?' she had always asked when Lupe mentioned her husband. Now she let it be known around town that she had discovered several excellent qualities in the man, citing his ability to grasp certain principles of trigonometry, and his contribution to a heated discussion concerning test-tube babies. Her implication was that Pedro's good points had been overlooked by everyone, including Lupe, until this time; only her own keen powers of perception were strong enough to present these to the light of day.

Yet as far as anyone could tell, the old woman's blindness persisted, and even deepened. This did not stop neighbours from dropping by, on those afternoons when the light was so murky that it was difficult to employ effectively even the fittest eyes, to ask Señora Lopez to read, for example, their watches. Unfortunately, by this point she no longer believed in a linear conception of time, and did not care to discuss seconds or minutes. 'It's all relative,' she would comment, impatiently tapping her toes. Upon the worsening electrical situation, at present the only topic of conversation in town, she made no comment. (By now current had not flowed from plugs or sockets for weeks, and people stared at electric irons and toasters as if they had forgotten what these appliances had ever been used for.) Also, she would not explain why there were no longer stars shining in the sky and why there was never any moon.

Indeed, watches and clocks quickly lost their usefulness as darkness became continuous and unrelenting. Was it four in the morning or four in the afternoon? Was time moving forward at all, or only at a much slower rate crawling through a single night that seemed as long as several years? Was each of Lindita's candlelit journeys through town the continuation of one journey that had commenced before the dawn of history and would not end until the earth's last record had been kept? Was life just a dream from which the town would waken only once it was over?

The confusion that reigned in this place during its brightest hours deepened. There were instances when children stumbled into wrong houses and were claimed by adults who were not their parents but were incognizant of the fact. Once Conchita Velázquez and Vera Aquino went to visit one another, crossed paths in the darkness, and took up with each other's husband unaware of anything, despite the circumstance that the two men involved were as different as night from day, Paco Velázquez being the fattest fellow in town and Joaquin Aquino a thin reed of a man. Eventually, as darkness became unremitting, all but the most necessary sallies from home were renounced. While it might have been hoped that isolation from the outside world would draw families together, and strengthen bonds of blood, this was sadly not the case. Everyone felt gnawing discontent with those companions right at hand, even as they desperately feared losing their presence. It was believed, moreover, that currently the darkness teemed with scores of unseen ideal lovers, flocks of certain saviours, and the answers to every prayer.

The school, shut down on numerous occasions of crisis in the past, now closed with apparent finality, becoming like the church and movie-house a dark, empty tomb uninhabited even by ghosts. Beached fishing boats were covered with sand until they resembled dunes. Fields turned wild and weedy. Fires, constructed clumsily by unpractised hands, burned before each house, and families with faces blackened by smoke huddled around the flames, eating their last reserves of rice and beans, not glancing up as Lindita walked right by them, the hem of her white dress nearly brushing their faces, a drop of molten wax falling like a bead of holy water on their heads.

One day (or was it night?) Lindita carried one end of a long length of rope in the hand which did not hold her candle. Behind, also grasping this rope, followed Pedro. Father and daughter went from house to house and formally invited everyone to take hold of the rope and accompany them through the dark. 'If we do get lost, at least we'll be lost together,' said Lindita, for the first time in her life speaking with some of her grandmother's convincing authority. The file of townspeople grew longer, until the entire populace was shuffling through the dark, only partly in step with Lindita's brisk cries of 'Right' and 'Left'. This would be the first and last time that the town was completely unified, taking the same direction at the same moment, agreeing unanimously upon a common course of action, for once free of grumbles of dissent and doubt. They marched toward the house of Señora Lopez, who was, as always, sitting on a sidewalk chair before it. Still clutching the rope, the townspeople gathered in a large half-circle around the old woman. She did not appear pleased to have all this unexpected and uninvited company, and made no move to offer the most rudimentary refreshment or conversation. Later, some people would say that she was specially dressed in one of the ancient, lace-frilled affairs from her long ago fashionable phase, indicating that she had expected this occasion and prepared for its significance. At the time, however, she only sat motionless in her chair, and gazed fixedly at her feet, or at Lindita's candle there. People would also say, afterward, that her lips appeared to move during this moment, as if she were mumbling a silent prayer or spell, or at least going over tomorrow's shopping list; such observation would, of course, be denied instantly by an equal number of eye witnesses. While all the townspeople peered at her expectantly, Señora Lopez leaned forward and downward with the most deliberate motion, having perhaps rehearsed such a movement for so long, and anticipated its realization so often, that now it took no conscious effort to enact, but could be made in the soundest sleep or the deepest grief, and blew the candle out.

It would be pleasing to report that this was a moment as decisive as the striking of lightning or love at first glance: the town's electricity suddenly functions again, and does not fail in the future; day and night re-assume their correct qualities and proportions; again the townspeople live sometimes in darkness and sometimes in light, but unmistakably improved by their intense experience with the failure of power, and henceforward able to love with the constant threat of loss, and to speak now and then of Rosario, Linda and Lupe Lopez as three beings who had left the town for reasons which might or might not be of greater interest than any other event in the history of the world. One longs to say that at this instant the town became a better place, no more distinguished than any other town in the immediate vicinity or the far-flung reaches, perhaps, but certainly no worse either. There remains the urge to state, in Señora Lopez's tone of absolute certainty, that all the catastrophes of love which one after the other had befallen the town during the past fifty years, and in the years before too, had been the essential, specific components of a mathematical formula which was now perfectly resolved, balanced, complete. *This* is why we suffered and *this* is why we were lost, and now we see precisely why those times of confusion and pain were so very necessary, for they have led us directly to this state of clarity and knowledge and grace.

Well.

One can only say, finally, that on a certain dark night an old woman blew out a candle. An ordinary candle of white wax, neither coloured nor scented, and not sculpted into a strange or beautiful shape. Anyway, one reluctantly admits, the candle was so near its end of life that it would have gone out on its own, without that lungful of air that Señora Lopez directed toward it like the honoured child at a birthday party. The world's deepest and darkest secrets do not rise through cracks and crannies to present themselves for easy inspection upon the surface where we struggle to learn to love; nor do the mysteries of the heavens, hovering high up in space, far above the most ascendant stars, drift down like white snow to melt into shallow puddles at our feet. 'Nothing is simple,' Señora Lopez would tell you, if you asked if she had plotted as silently and patiently as a master chess-player to save the town from losing its way forever in the dark. 'Everything is hard,' she would say in response to your wondering how she managed to persist in pursuing her own form of sentimental education, finally, in the last year of her life, when by her own count she had long passed two hundred years, falling in love with a boy aged seventeen who was as graceful as a deer and as strong as a horse, and who shared with Señora Lopez a love that was so powerful it caused static to scramble radio signals and sparks to fly from trees.

Anything would be easier than to leave the town behind for good, to walk away with no backward glance, like Lupe, unlike Lot's wife, free of curiosity as to what happens after Señora Lopez blows out the candle: a grey dawn breaks, ordinary daylight follows, current hums once more within wires strung like arteries above the earth? One sees, at this moment, how Señora Lopez suddenly presses a hand against her heart, as if the effort required to blow out the candle were more than she could survive, as if it were her last breath she generously sacrifices to her neighbours, ushering them into a state of darkness so pure and total that when light returns they are able to appreciate it fully, and not scorn it for failing to reveal Linda or Rosario or Lupe, wherever they might be, and not curse it for shining less brilliantly than white horses which gallop between the stars.

It is tempting to say, simply, that in the days to come Señora Lopez admitted to a blindness that allowed her to see less than her neighbours, and learned to accept the aid of a walking-stick, or the shoulder of a friend. One imagines her taking motherless Lindita in hand, encouraging the girl to exchange her white dress for brighter garments, seeing her off to the Honeymoon Hotel as a radiant bride. Let us suppose that one day there arrives a letter from Lupe, who is taking a secretarial course in the capital city, and planning to ascend an office ladder to reach heights which will satisfy ambitions hidden for years. In the lazy afternoons Pedro plays chess with his mother-in-law, both manoeuvring their pieces with such deadly concentration and skill that the game never ends, and the two opponents remain suspended in a respectful tie forever. The church bell tolls on Sunday. The plaza fills at evening. The school reopens and fishing boats set out to sea and fields are robbed of weeds. A length of rope lies forgotten in the dust before Señora Lopez's house, resembling sometimes a twisted snake and sometimes a coil of electrical wire.

Is that all? Is that enough?

Of course not.

I had been only the instrument here, the conductor through which power flows and light is produced, without power of my own. Now I am somewhat worn; my usefulness has come to an end, though my heart beats strongly still. Lindita would tell you that there will always be another bearer of the torch, another candle in the dark. You might say that I have only been a child darting through this darkness, unafraid because ignorant. You might also say that love is blind; I must politely disagree, for as my eyes close for good upon this town, and all the people in it that I love, I see more than I have ever seen. It is perhaps a pity that I am no longer capable of transmitting this vision; but in the end I can only say that I too, like Linda and Rosario and Lupe, and like all the people they left behind, have learned to accept what is lost as part of what is loved, and to understand that in this acceptance of constant longing lies the secret of power, and of love.

I'LL NEVER KNOW

A. L. Barker

Recently I heard myself referred to as a 'sensible' woman. I wasn't altogether pleased. The word has tweedy associations. I have never worn coarse-weave and don't intend to start at my time of life, well past what is known as the first flush of youth. And the second and third, come to that. I accept the sentient and rational interpretations of the word; I believe I'm commonsensical enough for most practical purposes. But where does practice end and theory begin? The question has been bothering me since that visit to Araby.

I love all things beautiful; we both do, though Adrian, my husband, hasn't made a study of the beautiful *per se*. I'm known for what could be called a non-oppressive knowledge of antiques. That's to say I don't labour it; I leave people to pick out what they like and can take in from my articles and lectures.

Araby is a mid-eighteenth-century country house in deepest Sussex. It's under threat from a proposed new A-road. I had a commission to do a piece about it for the only surviving ladies' weekly which isn't wholly consecrated to Royals, eat-and-grow-thin diets, fashion, hormone therapy and sex.

Adrian drove me down to Araby. He was planning to go and look at a promising stone quarry some twenty miles farther on. He's managing director of a thriving construction business which builds environmentally friendly houses in golfing and pony club country.

Thinking back, as I do constantly, I can't help putting two and two together and adding it up to an unpleasant and quite unacceptable total. I shall never know if I've got the sum right. He definitely tried to put me off going to Araby. There wasn't a lot to see, he said, Pevsner hadn't mentioned it. I said Pevsner couldn't mention everything and I was actually going to look at the panels.

Adrian said there hadn't been any panels when he was there and I said when was that and he said years ago. So I told him these were genuine Rodrigo Clemency carvings which had been boarded over by some philistine who preferred wallpaper and they had only recently been discovered.

'Come and look,' I said when we stopped at the gates. But he said he'd go to the quarry and be back in time to pick me up about four o'clock.

A woman came out of the lodge house and unlocked the gates. She was big and floppy, held together by something which creaked under the strain. Stays, probably. She told me her name was Woolgar and not to smoke in the house. As she didn't bother to say 'please', I didn't bother to say I don't smoke. We started up the drive which is at least half a mile long and overgrown with thistles and golden rod. I said it reminded me of *Rebecca*. She said her name was Iris.

The house is the usual Georgian: a portico of three columns with Ionic volutes, sashed windows and the original roof – though there are some ominous holes in it. The front door was a disappointment; it's a Gothic sham with iron studs and gargoyle knocker. Mrs Woolgar selected an incongruous Yale from a bunch of keys and opened the door.

The first thing that struck me was the smell of dust. It was really bitter, bit my olfactory nerves. Mrs Woolgar obviously hadn't been doing her job, but she probably reasoned that care taken at this point in Araby's history would be a waste of time. I was seized with violent fits of sneezing and she said 'Don't you bring that cold near me,' as if it was a mucky pup I had on a lead.

I said 'Can you tell me anything about the house?'

'It's coming down,' she said.

I said I'd heard it had been a school for girls during the war.

She was coming to that, she said, and her stays creaked. I got the impression it was the only sign that her interest was aroused.

It had happened years ago – donkey's years, she said – and I thought I was going to hear some old tattle about girls being girls. But as it turned out it was quite a little drama which I would be able to slot into my piece; the ladies' weekly readers would just love it.

She said the school had been a 'posh' one, for the daughters of rich people. Discipline was strict, the girls weren't allowed to look sideways even at the gardener who was sixty or his boy who was, as she put it, 'mental'. So when workmen came to repair the chimneys there was quite a flutter in the dovecote. One of the girls fell in love with a young brickie. As Mrs Woolgar put it, a bit of hanky-panky went on. The workmen left, the girl was marked down for expulsion.

'Oh dear,' I said. 'Of course it was a disgrace in those days. Now it's a feather in your cap.'

'Hung herself, didn't she,' said Mrs W. 'In the bicycle shed.'

I said, thinking I'd definitely make it an apple tree, so much more romantic, 'What does Pevsner say? A bicycle shed is a building; a cathedral is a piece of architecture.'

Mrs Woolgar glared. 'You can't see it now, they pulled it down.'

'Goodness, how sad,' I said. 'Was the girl pretty?'

The corsets crackled. 'Men always think they are at that age.'

I said I needn't keep her, I'd find my own way about. 'Bring the keys to the lodge when you're done,' she said.

I watched her lumber away through the couch grass and past some mossy statuary.

The house was in a bad state. Winter rains – of many winters – had leaked through to the ceilings: such a pity, lovely old Adamy garlands stained and bloated and some walls actually growing fungus.

Thank heaven the panels, which were downstairs in the dining-hall, hadn't been affected. They were in desperate need of attention; I saw I should have to approach the National Trust, English Heritage, Sotheby's, Christie's and the Antiques Road Show to organize a rescue. Meantime, there they were, those exquisite Clemency carvings, for my delectation and mine alone. I could touch them – I did – was stroking with my fingertips the weird aerial shapes of men and beasts, exploring the exotic flowers, whirling suns and rampant dragons, birds, butterflies, beetles – God, how that man could use a knife! – when a voice said, 'Dirty old things, aren't they?'

I turned round. There was this girl, could have been fourteen, fifteen, sixteen years old, wearing one of those awful gym-slips of shiny blue serge, her hair in pigtails, and pebble glasses.

'Hi,' I said. It's what you have to say to youngsters nowadays.

'Have you really looked?' she said.

I took out a tissue and wiped my fingers. Of course they were grimy: the panelling hadn't been touched for years.

'At that, I mean.' She pointed to the panels.

I looked at her. She was fattish, pale, and had a liberal crop of acne, and more than a hint of Mrs Woolgar in her. A few years from now, I thought, she'll need those corsets.

'It's porn,' she said. 'Know what I mean?'

I said I was afraid I didn't.

'You can't be that green', she said, 'at your age. Look.' She moved close to the panels, almost touching them with her nose, she was painfully short-sighted. Where I had been feeling and delighting in sheer beauty, she pressed her thumbs on the wood and squeezed out something quite other. Delicate, yes; fantastical, yes; superbly executed, yes. Beautiful, no. I'm no prude, I just happen to think some things don't belong in public. They should be kept strictly private, part of the rich tapestry of the imagination. Personally I find it too rich.

So there I was, looking at a complex bacchanal of nymphs and satyrs, gods and beasts, and sure as I could be that it had all been innocent and lovely until that girl put her thumb on it.

I got out my little pocket magnifier and took a closer look and frankly I wished I hadn't; it brings out every detail.

'I don't believe it!' I cried.

'Suit yourself,' she said, and she bounced out of the room with a toss of her pigtails.

I was glad to see the back of her, but I was in a quandary about the panels. Should they, *ought* they to be preserved? What for? To deck the walls of some City men's club, or be packed away in the vaults of a museum?

To concentrate my mind I went upstairs, opened doors, looked into room after room. Everywhere was that same bitter dust, undisturbed except in the biggest room of all where soot and old birds' nests had fallen down the chimney.

'This used to be the dormitory.' The girl had got there before me and was looking out of the window.

I was none too pleased. I asked her her name, preparatory to requesting, as nicely as possible, that she leave me to get on with my investigation.

Her name was Marilyn, she said.

'Woolgar?' I said.

'No, Monroe,' she said, and giggled.

I was rapidly losing my cool. I started to say I needed to concentrate on what I was doing here.

She said, 'I'm waiting for my boy-friend. He comes every day, can't keep away from me. He's really passionate.' Grinning, she fingered her cheek. 'I gave him a love-bite yesterday.'

I said, 'Does your mother know?' Of course it was stuffy, but I could see that the stage was set for goings-on which I shouldn't care for a daughter of mine, if I'd had one – which thank goodness I haven't – to get involved in.

It seemed to subdue her. She turned back to the window. 'Nothing to see but boring old country!'

I didn't say anything, recognizing the young creature's eternal cry of disappointment with life.

I went to examine a graffito on one of the walls. It was of the 'Buddy woz here' type, and when I turned round she had gone again. She had traced something in the dust of the window-pane: a circle with dots and a dash for eyes and mouth. A crude face of the sort not very bright children draw. It was slightly mocking. But what really annoyed me was the fact that her feet, which were a lot bigger than mine, hadn't disturbed the dust, whereas I was leaving size three prints everywhere.

I went back to the dining-hall, determined to be

open-minded about the panels. And would you believe it – I didn't – they weren't naughty at all. If evil is in the eyes of the beholder it had certainly gone from mine. I examined every panel, every figure, every bird, beast and flower, took measurements, checked for cracks. Those carvings were quite simply beautiful and fantastical and utterly charming. Nothing more.

I stood and gazed until my eyes misted and the figures seemed to move and I knew it was time to go. Anyway, it was getting on for four o'clock. I locked up and walked down the drive, no backward looks. I hoped I wouldn't see the girl again. Birds were singing, the sun was shining, the boring old country was glowing.

Mrs W. was waiting for me at the door of the lodge. 'Finished?' she said with her direct charm.

'Thank you, yes,' I said. 'I'll be in touch. By the way, I met your daughter up at the house.'

'I haven't got a daughter,' she said.

'Your niece then. Such a sweet girl; I could see the family likeness.'

'There's no girl.'

'But there is,' I said. 'I saw her, we talked about the school. And other things.'

'Don't you go spreading no nonsense!' She backed into the lodge like a sea-creature retreating into its shell. 'I've got enough trouble as it is.'

The door slammed in my face. I still had the keys of the house in my hand. I pushed them through the letter-box.

As we drove away Adrian asked how I'd got on. Well enough, I said, though there was a girl hanging about – I swear I didn't use the words advisedly, they just happened – she had been a bit of a pest.

Adrian was concentrating on overtaking a petrol tanker. I said, 'What were *you* doing at Araby?'

'Doing?' He frowned. 'It must be getting on for fifty years ago when I was there. In those days I was starting out and had to take any sort of job. I went as a builder's labourer.'

I didn't say anything. I put two and two together and snatched them apart again.

When we were speeding along the fast lane he said, still frowning, 'Do you know I believe I've got another of those brown blotches on my face. The wretched things seem to come up overnight.'

I didn't say they're called grave-marks. He still values his looks, so I didn't say anything.

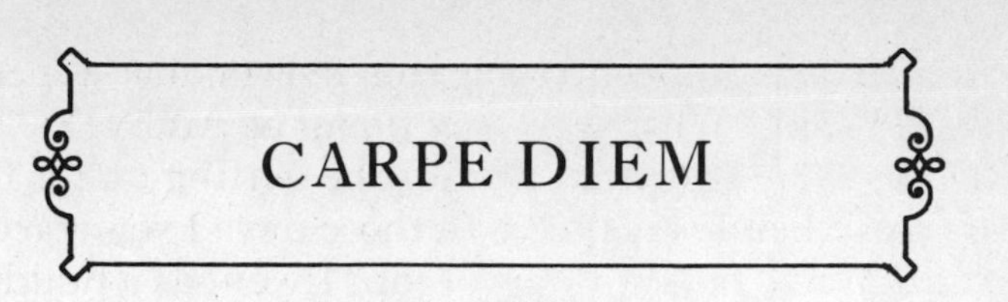

CARPE DIEM

Isidoro Blaisten

Translated from the Spanish
by Norman Thomas di Giovanni and
Susan Ashe

'"As I'm in a hurry, dress me slowly,"' he said.

Napoleon, I thought to myself – fairly obvious – and I trumped him with, '"What if the child inherits my body and your brains?"'

'I know that one,' he said. 'Einstein.'

'No, it isn't,' I said. 'It's Bernard Shaw.'

My wife said it wasn't Einstein or Bernard Shaw – it was Rubinstein, and why did I always get it wrong?

His wife poked me under the table with her foot. I thought she was going to say, 'Sorry,' or 'I didn't mean to,' but she didn't, and I took hold of her hand and under the overhang of the tablecloth began tickling her palm. She tried to pull away, but I wouldn't let her. Meanwhile, he was saying that people got the governments they deserved.

'Lincoln!' I said.

'Napoleon!' he said.

I said, 'No, what Napoleon said was "Donkeys and Savants to the middle of the square."' Even my wife gaped. This was a new one. I'd heard it that morning from a customer. To explain what a square was I had to let go of his wife's hand. But she kept it there on my knee. With the sugar-tongs and three teaspoons I showed them what a square was.

'This, in military terms, is a square,' I said. 'As its name suggests, it's square. It's in the middle of the camp ground, in the middle of the bivouac. This is where the general staff sets itself up. It's straight out of the Egyptian campaign,' I told them, 'when Napoleon invaded Egypt.'

'What year?' he said.

'Early 1800s.' I looked him straight in the face and, out of the corner of my eye, saw my wife grin. I went on. 'In the square were the powder magazine, supply depot, the quartermaster, the ordnance stores, the bivouac tents, and – most important of all – the donkeys.'

'Donkeys?' his wife asked, and she ran her hand over my thigh. You could almost hear the scrape of her nails on the cloth of my trousers.

'Donkeys,' I said. 'Napoleon was a genius, a statesman, and he was well aware there was no way you could invade Egypt without donkeys. The donkey in those days was like today's armoured car or jeep. But that's Napoleon all over – that's a statesman for you! As well as donkeys, Napoleon took along his Savants. Napoleon took the Savants to decipher the hieroglyphics on the pyramids – Savants, no less.'

'What were their names?' he asked.

'They were French – they had French names.' And his wife ran her fingers over my trousers as though she were stroking a cat. 'That's where Savants and donkeys to the middle of the square comes from. That's the importance Napoleon put on his Savants. Same as we do in Argentina.'

'The interesting part', said his wife, 'is the double meaning – donkeys and Savants,' and with her free hand she twirled the lid of the sugar bowl as if she were pondering.

'Lots of words have double meanings,' he said. 'How about this one – night rate, nitrate?'

I felt sorry for him. I think even my wife felt sorry for him. Out of pity and a sort of embarrassment, I said, 'Interesting – night rate, nitrate,' and grabbed his wife's hand and slipped my fingers into hers, and although we had to lean a bit towards each other, our hands rested on the surface of my trousers.

'Want another one about Napoleon?'

'Yes,' said his wife.

And I told the one that goes, 'Taller, you mean.' I said, 'One night Napoleon had to attend a ball, and his cravat was hanging on a very high coat-hanger. As you know, Napoleon had a height problem. He wasn't what you'd call tall.'

'A shortie,' she said. And she laughed and tried to roll my hand over. Just as I let her, I realized that the movement of my shoulder would give us away.

'Exactly,' I said. Smiling, I caught her eye and gave her hand a hard squeeze.

'Napoleon tried to reach his cravat but he didn't want his servant to see him stretching. He was almost on tiptoe when the servant offered his help. "Your Majesty, allow me, I'm bigger." "Taller, you mean," Napoleon replied.'

'Which goes to show that in a servant's eyes his master is never a big man,' he said. And he glanced at my wife.

I studied him. The man was no fool.

'More to the point, I'd agree with Lincoln that "You can fool some of the people all of the time but you can't fool all the people all of the time."' For some reason, the moment I said it I felt I'd hit him below the belt.

'That's not how it goes,' my wife said, collecting up the spoons I'd used to make the square. She placed them on a tray and said in a voice close to tears, 'It's "You can fool some of the people all of the time, you can fool all of the people some of the time, but you can't fool all of the people all of the time."'

'All right, but the order of the terms doesn't change the meaning,' his wife said, and I thought she was going to squeeze my hand but she didn't.

'It's not a question of terms or meanings,' my wife said, now laying the three spoons one on top of the other on the tray. I wondered why she left the sugar-tongs.

He offered me a cigarette. I said, 'Not now, thanks.' I didn't see how I could manage it with my left hand.

'Well,' he said. 'You know what Horace said?'

My wife gave him a strange look. She passed him an ashtray.

'He said a lot of things,' I said.

'"*Carpe diem*",' he said. '*Carpe diem*. Do you know what *carpe diem* means?'

The question was rhetorical. He stubbed out his cigarette.

'*Carpe diem*', he said, 'means seize the moment.'

His wife laughed again – softly at first, then louder and louder until it was impossible to stop her. She let go of my hand, threw her head back, and just laughed and laughed.

'The thing is', my wife said, gathering the coffee cups with that ease in an uncomfortable situation that she got from her mother, 'not everyone reacts to serious things in the same way. Some people react one way, some another. One person uses his body – '

'Body language,' he said.

'Exactly,' my wife said. And his wife, who had calmed down, began to laugh again. She lowered her hand and felt for mine under the overhang of the table-cloth. My wife went on about the mind and the body making up a single whole, about this being the age of Aquarius, about how we each have a divine particle of the universe dwelling deep down inside us, about how we think we're so clever but all we do is fill our lungs with tar – here her eye darted to the ashtray – and about how we men wear ties that strangle our jugulars, thereby impeding the path of positive thinking and the irrigation of the brain, and about how we eat corpses. 'So much for intelligence,' she said.

His wife became serious. She tickled my palm. I said that intuition is one form of knowledge. My wife stared at me. He said what I said was true, that we human beings had lost one of our senses – the sense of perception – and that country people detected smells, sounds and the distant hoofbeats of a horse better than city people. I said that cities should be moved out into the country, but no one laughed. The conversation seemed to be running down. I told the one about Michelangelo hammering away at the statue of Moses and shouting, 'Speak, Moses!' They didn't seem to get it. But as it was a matter of pride, I kept on.

'Did you know that when Michelangelo was commissioned to paint the Sistine Chapel he kept putting it off and putting it off, unable to make up his mind, unable to begin. So the pope – '

'Which pope?' he asked.

'Julius the Second.' And his wife giggled hysterically.

'Michelangelo', I went on, 'was driving Julius crazy. "Well, Michelangelo?" the pope said. "When are you going to get on with it?" But Michelangelo – not a word. He was the all-time introvert. He paced up and down the Vatican, stopping for a minute, staring at the ceiling, just standing and staring. Then one day the pope put his foot down. "When are you going to get your finger out?" he said. "When are you going to pick up the tools?" And do you know what Michelangelo told him? "I *am* working." That goes to show', I went on, squeezing her hand, 'that the human mind works in mental pictures. Michelangelo was already seeing in his mind what the Sistine Chapel ceiling would be like.'

'Vision comes from viewing,' he said.

'And volume from vellum,' I answered. 'A long time ago in the distant past what today are books were scrolls. Scrolls of stretched hide. Pigskin, goatskin – any soft skin, in fact. Hence the Dead Sea scrolls. They were sewn together and, to read them, you unrolled and rolled them from one stick to another. That's why today the word volume, which comes from vellum, means a book.'

He said that he'd have to look the word up, because this vellum I was talking about might turn out to be the bark of papyrus, because it enveloped the stem.

In the look everyone gave him, I could feel that he'd failed. Asking if anyone wanted more coffee, my wife got up and took away the tray and cups. His wife looked at my wife. She kept looking at her until my wife went into the kitchen.

A silence fell. It was the first time silence had fallen. Her hand was still; so was mine.

'We'll have our coffee and then we'll be off, love,' he said.

'What's your hurry?' I said.

'We have to rise early tomorrow,' he said.

'"However early you rise it doesn't hasten the dawn,"' I said. I thought she was going to burst out laughing but she didn't.

He said that punctuality was the courtesy of kings.

'The right word at the right time,' I conceded.

My wife had just appeared in the kitchen doorway. She asked if I was having coffee too. I shook my head and tried to remember another one about kings. I decided against the one about King Solomon and the two mothers with the child to be cut in half. The three of us sat there thinking until my wife came in with the tray.

Suddenly I wondered what would happen if his wife got up – if, for example, she were to say, 'Excuse me, dear, where's the bathroom?' I tickled her palm with my middle finger and talked about the labyrinths of the mind.

He said that man was the only animal in all creation who knew he was going to die and it was that which conditioned him.

'Whereas', he went on, 'dogs and cows don't know.'

My wife said what did we humans know about what goes on in a cow's soul.

'Have you ever seen a cow with a soul?' I said.

My wife didn't answer. Glaring at me, she took the lid off the sugar bowl.

He tried to talk about the transmigration of souls but he might just as well have been yawning. My wife asked how many lumps.

Then it all became predictable. Everything I said he could have said, and vice versa. Turn and turn about, he or I said: 'Van Gogh painted with coffee'; 'The Gioconda was a man'; 'It's common knowledge that Leonardo was an extraterrestrial being'; 'Quevedo and Góngora hated each other to the death'; 'So did Raphael and Leonardo but at heart they admired each other'; 'It was Chesterton and Bernard Shaw who couldn't stand each other'; 'The Incas knew about trepanning skulls'. Then, without quibbling about who said it, we rattled off: 'I don't believe in ghosts but still they exist'; 'Paint your village and you paint the world'; 'Ten per cent inspiration, ninety per cent perspiration'.

After that they got to their feet to leave.

'Well, we're off,' he said. 'Let's go, dear, we're up at the crack of dawn.'

I said what a pity, we'd had great fun, and for one last moment I pressed her hand. That was when they got to their feet. I did too – but only after I'd squeezed her hand really hard. She looked at me. Then she asked my wife the way to the bathroom. She mouthed the words, moving her lips and smiling at the same time. My wife showed her while I helped him on with his coat.

My wife came back. Then his. Then he said it had been a pleasure, that they'd had a wonderful evening.

I said, 'Same here, we must do it again one night.'

Then we all went down in the lift and my wife and I walked with them to their car. As the car started, we waved goodbye. After that my wife and I got back into the lift. We rode up without a word.

educated in England and Canada, and has lived in Central America and Mexico. A first collection of stories, *Beneath the Western Slopes*, was published to critical acclaim in 1987 in Canada. A second collection, *Birthmarks*, as well as a novel, *God's Peculiar Care*, appeared in Canada and the UK in 1991. Patrick Roscoe currently lives in Malaga, Spain. He is seeking a British publisher for his recently completed manuscript, *Love is Starving for Itself*, from which *The [illegible] of Love* is taken.

A. L. BARKER left school when she was sixteen and, after the war, joined the BBC. Her debut collection of stories, *Innocents*, won the Somerset Maugham Prize, and her novel *John Brown's Body*, was shortlisted for the Booker Prize in 1969. She is the author of nine novels, including most recently *The Woman who Talked to Herself* and eight short story collections, including, most recently, her selected stories, *Any Excuse for a Party*.

ISIDORO BLAISTEN has worked in advertising, both as a photographer and writer, in journalism, and as a bookseller. Now a full-time author, he also holds writing workshops. His first book *Sucesos [illegible]* (1965) was poetry, which he still writes but does not publish. His story collections include *La felicidad* (1969), *La salvación* (1972), *El mago* (1974), *Cerrado por melancolía* (1982), and *Carroza y reina* (1986). He is also the author of a volume of essays and reviews, *Anticonferencias* (1983). Among other awards, Blaisten received a Municipal Prize in 1974, the Third National Prize for Fiction in 1983, and the Second National Prize for Essay and Criticism in 1985. Born in 1933, Blaisten lives in Buenos Aires.